HeartQuest brings you romantic fiction with a foundation of biblical truth. Adventure, mystery, intrigue, and suspense mingle in these heartwarming stories of men and women of faith striving to build a love that will last a lifetime.

May HeartQuest books sweep you into the arms of God, who longs for you and pursues you always.

Dream Vacation

Ginny Aiken
Jeri Odell
Elizabeth White

HEART QUEST™

Romance fiction from
Tyndale House Publishers, Inc.
WHEATON, ILLINOIS

Visit Tyndale's exciting Web site at www.tyndale.com

Check out the latest about HeartQuest Books at www.heartquest-romances.com

Designed by Jenny Destree

Library of Congress Cataloging-in-Publication Data

Aiken, Ginny.
Dream vacation / Ginny Aiken, Jeri Odell, Elizabeth White.
p. cm.
ISBN 0-8423-1899-2
1. Love stories, American. 2. Christian fiction, American. 3. Vacations—United States—Fiction. I. Odell, Jeri, date II. White, Elizabeth, date III. Title.
PS648.L6 A54 1999
813′.08508054—dc21 99-051362

Printed in the United States of America

06 05 04 03 02 01 00
9 8 7 6 5 4 3 2 1

CONTENTS

A SINGLE'S HONEYMOON

by
Ginny Aiken

CHAPTER ONE

FOR SALE: Exotic ten-day honeymoon. Unused. Cheap.

In the kitchen of her small house in east York, Pennsylvania, Shiloh Morris ping-ponged a glare between the brief ad in that evening's *York Dispatch* and her nonflashing answering machine. Why hadn't anybody called? Why wouldn't anyone put her out of her misery?

She'd listed her honeymoon the day after Reginald Rodger jilted her. Although he'd paid for the trip up front, during his breakup phone call he'd "generously" offered her the proceeds of the sale to make up for the trouble and expense his defection would cause. And there had been expenses—for her parents. The hall, the florists, and the caterers had insisted on nonrefundable partial payments. She'd thought she could unload the painful reminder of their failed engagement easily. But here she was, three weeks later, and she'd yet to receive a single call about the dumb thing.

The phone didn't ring, but the doorbell did.

Shiloh sighed. She flirted with the thought of sneaking out her back door, but that would only add to her nightly visitors' worries. "Hi, Aunt Tibby, Mrs. Appelt."

A pair of white-haired ladies, one tall and heavy, the other short and spry, stepped inside and made a beeline for the kitchen, triumphantly bearing their offerings for the day. "How *are* you doing, honey?" asked Shiloh's great-aunt, the shorter of the two.

You don't really want to know, Shiloh thought, so she answered, "Fine. It's been a lovely spring day, after all."

Her guests exchanged knowing looks. "No calls on the honeymoon, then."

Aggravated, Shiloh forced a smile. "No . . . not yet. But it hasn't been that long. Someone will call soon."

She remembered when she and Reg had agreed on the trip six months earlier. They'd been so sure nothing would go wrong. Hah! How sure could Reg have been if he'd called the whole thing off a couple of months later?

Once the startling news spread, everyone had tried to comfort Shiloh. They were still at it.

"And it was such an *interesting* trip you children booked," lamented Aunt Tibby's friend, removing her lime green hat, matching chiffon scarf, and spring coat. "To such an . . . unusual place. So earthy, so lush, so primitive."

Shiloh nodded absently. Why *had* Reg called the whole thing off anyway? She still didn't know what had gone wrong. A tear prickled her eyelid, and she blinked.

"Oh, dear!" exclaimed Aunt Tibby. "Look what you did, Cora. You made her cry again."

"Did not. I just tried to comfort her," Cora fired back.

"Did not. I just tried to comfort her," Cora fired back.

Shiloh waved. "It's OK. *I'm* OK."

But she was not. She couldn't forget the bubble of joy that had buoyed her up when Reg had asked her to marry him and she'd said yes. Knowing someone wanted you for the rest of your life was such a treasure, a blessing.

Then Reg had taken the blessing away—without an explanation.

"Here you go, sweetheart," Aunt Tibby said, interrupting Shiloh's thoughts. A serving of meat loaf, scalloped potatoes, and green beans with ham, plus a box of tissues, appeared before her.

Cora dropped silverware by the plate. "Food *always* makes you feel better."

Shiloh looked at the two dears, knowing they meant well, but their efforts only made her more miserable. "Ah . . . doesn't your reading group meet tonight?"

Cora gasped. "You can't expect us to abandon you."

"I don't want you to give up something that means so much to you, not on my account. Besides, I signed up for that Potters for Charity class."

Her visitors glanced at each other, hope in their eyes. "Terrific idea," said Aunt Tibby. "Artists are *so* fascinating."

"Mm-hmm," added Cora. "And it's a good place for a nice twenty-six-year-old young lady to meet a new man."

"I have no interest in meeting a new man," Shiloh said quickly. "I want to learn to throw pots and raise money for the women's and children's shelter downtown."

The two exchanged yet another look. "Fine, dear, you do that," Aunt Tibby said. "We'll go to our group." Suddenly they couldn't put their pastel coats on fast enough.

"And tell us all about your potter—," Cora began.

"Hush," Aunt Tibby hissed, shoving her friend toward the front door. "What Cora means is for you to call us if you need anything.

Anything at all. And we'll have tomorrow's chicken potpie for you at the usual time."

"Thanks, but I'm not an invalid. I *can* cook!"

Aunt Tibby shook her head mournfully. "You *are* an invalid. You're recovering from unwanted heart surgery. You have to concentrate on mending that broken heart." She offered her soft, powdered cheek for a kiss, and Shiloh obliged.

"But you don't have to cook," Shiloh protested.

"We'll be here with supper. You be here with an appetite. For a change."

They breezed out, leaving Shiloh winded and dizzy. Not only did she have a supper she didn't want—again—but she was late for her pottery lesson. And to make things worse, she was haunted again by the thoughts that had troubled her since *that day*. Thoughts that brought back the crushing disappointment and confusion of the breakup. Thoughts that led to questions with no answers, that roared to life with every person's attempt to comfort her.

It was that sympathy Shiloh wanted to avoid, so she'd crammed more activities into her already packed schedule. Stuff like extra shifts at the hospital and the pottery class she was late for. A pottery class for *women* only.

A week later, when the phone rang after she'd tired of playing with her lovingly catered dinner, Shiloh leaped for it. "Yes?"

"Where are you?" her best friend, Carrie Kenner, asked. "I have lots of babies and only two arms. I thought you'd signed up to work the nursery with me tonight."

That's when Shiloh knew she really *was* losing her mind. "I did, and I will. I just got home and . . . forgot. Sorry. Be right there."

Wednesday nights, their church offered various programs after the regular prayer service. Shiloh and Carrie had met in the nursery three years ago and had become the closest of friends since then. She'd even been in Carrie's wedding last summer. Usually Shiloh loved the nursery, but since the debacle with Reg, she'd avoided the babies. They brought to mind the ones she might have had.

"Oh, honestly," she muttered to herself as she grabbed her umbrella. "Get a grip!"

With the strict order fresh in her mind, she drove to the church, hoping that since she was so late, she'd avoid the pitying looks, the cotton-ball treatment. She couldn't handle much more of that.

Running into the room full of toys and kids, Shiloh said, "Sorry, sorry! I don't know what's wrong with my head these days. How could I forget? I'm the one who offered to take over the nursery when the Mannings were transferred to Oregon last September."

Grinning, flame-haired Carrie offered, "You know what's wrong. Reg's little announcement has made you nuts. Even more than usual."

Picking up the whimpering Kern baby, Shiloh collapsed into one of the cushioned rockers. "Yeah, well, I have to get over that. And soon. I just wish I knew what went wrong."

Carrie looked down at a Lego skyscraper on the floor. "I tried to warn you months ago that something wasn't right. I suggested you seek the Father's will for your marriage. You assured me that you had before you guys bought the ring last July, and that you believed Reg was the man God meant for you. But I had my doubts."

"I guess your doubts were right," Shiloh conceded. "I wish I would have listened. Just what kind of doubts *did* you have?"

Carrie said slowly, "Let me answer with some questions. How much time did you spend together? You know, to share feelings, thoughts, beliefs, dreams?"

"When we first met two years ago, a lot. Then, the Harrisburg Police Department promoted Reg to detective, and I was offered more shifts at the hospital. We got busy, so we didn't spend as much time together. But we talked a lot on the phone!"

Carrie rolled her eyes. "Could that work insanity have been the main attraction? Could that busyness be what eventually pulled you two apart?"

Unsure of what to answer, Shiloh shrugged and put her sleeping armful in one of the nursery cribs. Then she sat down next to Stephanie Mimms, a dainty two year old who was working on a puzzle.

Without waiting for Shiloh to answer, Carrie continued, "I think it's time for you to rethink your career. You've been so consumed by your work that you were probably too exhausted to notice that your engagement was going nowhere. Maybe Reg's breakup call was actually a wake-up call—from God."

"But—"

"Listen. You have to get away," Carrie said earnestly. "To think. And pray. Go where you won't have any distractions. Just you, your Bible, and God."

"You're right," Shiloh said, as her friend's words struck a chord in her heart. "I *do* need to spend extra time in the Word. To check out what God has to say about commitments . . . love . . . marriage."

"Sounds like a plan to me. But do yourself a favor. Take time off from the hospital. I know what you do saves lives, but you're running on empty."

A wail from Stephanie—and the subsequent tossing of a puzzle piece across the room—momentarily ended their conversation. Gathering the tired child into her lap, Shiloh rocked her, crooning a lullaby.

When the child quieted, Shiloh told Carrie, "You do have a point. I feel I have to help whenever I can." She shrugged. "So, yeah, I take other nurses' shifts when they can't come in."

Just then Maggie Mimms opened the nursery door. "How'd she do?"

Stephanie leaped out of Shiloh's arms and lunged for her mom. Shiloh smiled. "Great. She's a sweetie, and tired. She'll be asleep before you're out of the parking lot."

As she grabbed her daughter's diaper bag, Maggie gave Shiloh that pitying look Shiloh hated. "It's too bad things didn't work out. You're going to be a wonderful mother some day. You just have to find the right guy."

With the ease of routine, Maggie settled Stephanie onto one hip, the bag on the opposite shoulder, then opened the door again. "You know," she said slowly, "my Artie has a second cousin who'd be just right for you."

Carrie flew out of her rocker and hurried the woman out. "Thanks, Maggie. We'll keep that in mind. See ya."

Shiloh dropped her head into her hands. "It's like my dog died, and everyone wants to give me a brand-new puppy!"

"You're nuts, you know?" Carrie said, with a sparkle in her chocolate-colored eyes.

"I'm serious. This is ridiculous. How can I sort out my feelings when everyone tells me I'm heartbroken and then pushes me to find another man? I don't want to *think* about another man, much less find one."

"Hey, you're right. You have more important things to think about right now than another guy. Things you need to pray about."

Shiloh stood and began putting away the toys. "I hear you. I just don't know when I'm going to find the time."

"You can't put God on hold," Carrie insisted. "And you can't expect to stay in York and have time to think. Not with *your* family—"

"Tell me about it! Did I tell you Aunt Tibby's latest?"

Knowing Shiloh's great-aunt, Carrie shook her head warily.

"I told you I was going to wear a disguise when I returned my wedding dress. And boy, am I glad Renaissance Bridals was willing to take it back since I hadn't needed it altered. Anyway, I didn't want anyone to see me hauling the dress back."

Carrie nodded.

"Well, guess who was strolling down Market Street after leaving the York Historical Society just as I got to Renaissance?"

Carrie chuckled.

"Yeah," Shiloh muttered. "And she even saw through my disguise!"

Now Carrie laughed. Hard. "Hey, I warned you that the dark gray trench coat, the 1950s chiffon scarf, and the reclusive-film-star sunglasses—in 88 degree weather—weren't going to work."

The door to the nursery opened, and Shiloh handed the sleeping Kern baby to his dad. "So?" she asked when they were gone, "what am I supposed to do? It's easier to lose a fiancé than a family."

"That's what I've been saying," Carrie said, growing serious.

"You have to get out of town. Give yourself time with the Lord. Seek his guidance. If for no other reason than to make sure you don't make the same mistake—whatever it was—in the future."

"But where would I go?"

"You figure that out. All I'm saying is that even tough ol' Gary Cooper had the sense to leave town in *High Noon* when things got hot. Things are hot for you, and you can't think around here."

Shiloh snorted. "Figures you'd drag up one of your old movies sooner or later. But guess what? You're wrong. Coop came back to face the music. That's what I'm trying to do."

"You want music? Try Professor Harold Hill, the Music Man himself. He got in trouble, and his first thought was flight. Go for it. Why not get out of town? Maybe like Leslie Caron in *Father Goose,* you'll find the perfect man in the most unlikely home-away-from-home."

"Thanks a lot. You want me marooned on a desert island during an upcoming World War III? World War II happened to Leslie, if you'll remember. Here I thought you were my friend."

"Go home," Carrie said, laughing. "Trust God; he's always faithful. He'll show you what's best *and* at the right time."

From within the confusion and jumbled feelings, Shiloh felt a spurt of thanksgiving for her friend. "Thanks for listening."

"And telling it like it is," Carrie added. "Now go to bed."

"Yes, Mother."

Later, at home, Shiloh thought about their conversation as she brushed her teeth. Was Carrie right? Had Shiloh—and Reg—been too busy with and exhausted by their careers to see what was happening to their relationship?

There's only one way to know, she concluded. *God will show me. In his time.* As she snuggled under crisp linens, a tear rolled down her cheek and dropped onto the pillow.

"Shiloh Morris to room 12. Stat!"

It had been a crazy day in York Hospital's Emergency Room. What else was new? Shiloh ran to answer her page.

As she dashed into the room, two orderlies wheeled in a teenage girl on a stretcher. As Shiloh scrubbed, she listened to the doctor's evaluation of the X ray. A broken femur.

"Hi, Shiloh," said Marcy, another nurse, as she took Shiloh's place at the sink.

"Haven't seen you for a while."

"I went to my sister's wedding in New Hampshire. Just got back."

Wincing inwardly even though it was now almost two months since Reg had jilted her, Shiloh went to the patient's right side, next to Dr. Andrea Howard. Marcy took the left.

"How was your sister's wedding?" Andrea asked Marcy as she measured a length of fiberglass for the cast.

"Beautiful."

Shiloh bit her bottom lip.

Then Marcy glanced at her. "How are you doing, Shiloh, now that you and Reg have broken up?"

"I'm fine," Shiloh answered through gritted teeth, then tuned out the rest of their conversation about weddings and marriage. She'd go crazy if she didn't. And to make things worse, she still hadn't received a single call on that stupid honeymoon. The tickets were like an albatross hanging around her neck—especially since her wedding would have been this coming Saturday, and she and Reg would have flown to Venezuela Sunday morning. What was she going to do?

"What about your honeymoon?" asked Marcy, breaking into Shiloh's thoughts. "It sounded perfect and romantic and peaceful. Boy, I'd be mad if I had to give it up because a guy dumped me."

"That's it!" Shiloh exclaimed, drawing every eye in the room with her unexpected outburst. "I'm taking my honeymoon. But it's going to be a *single's* honeymoon. No men. Just me, the monkeys, and the macaws."

She and Reg had chosen this place, a former explorer's-base-camp-cum-hotel near the base of Angel Fall in the Venezuelan rain forest, for its privacy, exotic beauty, and lack of people. The place, according to the black-and-white mimeographed brochure she'd received in response to her inquiry, boasted of only ten small *casitas,* or thatched-roofed stucco cabins, and was located some distance from the nearest village—through jungle.

The brochure also proclaimed the accommodations to be a haven of rest, proudly announcing its lack of glitz and frantic activity found at many honeymoon and vacation destinations. She and Reg hadn't wanted a resort. They'd decided to start their marriage in the simplicity offered by the plain *casitas* and the slower pace of the tropical rain forest.

Shiloh was sure the hotel would provide exactly the retreat she needed to ponder what had gone wrong in her personal life and her relationship with Reg, to seek God, and to discern how he wanted her to pursue her calling to the nursing profession.

She smiled. "What better place than a jungle for solitude, nature's bounty, and the absence of men?"

As Shiloh settled into her coach-class airline seat Sunday morning, she questioned her sanity. Again.

After all, honeymoons were supposed to be for *couples* seeking privacy and serenity, but she was still single. And this flight to Caracas certainly wasn't peaceful. Not only was it chock-full of infants, but also, to her dismay, a band of teens was in the process of trooping in. They laughed, they bickered, and the earphones uniformly attached to their heads blared music loud enough for everyone on the plane to share—even if they didn't want to.

She held her breath, hoping none of them had been assigned the empty seat beside her.

With a whoosh, she released her breath as a man about her age, maybe in his late twenties, popped open the overhead luggage bin that contained her own suitcase and a large case of medicines she was taking to missionaries. He crammed in a jacket, an oversized camera bag, and a big plastic case that looked like a first-aid kit. Placing a briefcase under his seat, he then sat next to her.

Shiloh watched him fiddle with his seat belt, noting his large, well-kept hands. They looked strong and capable—as did he.

With broad shoulders and a six-feet-plus height, her traveling companion exuded a strength and competence that surprised her. Few people she'd met came across with such . . . presence.

"Hi," he said, green eyes crinkling with his smile.

Shiloh blushed. Good grief! He'd caught her staring. "Uh . . . hi."

"I'm Mark Walker." He stuck a hand out.

Curious to see what kind of shake that sturdy hand would give,

Shiloh clasped Mark's fingers . . . and felt a warm current run up her arm. He even shook hands with confidence.

"I'm Shiloh Morris," she squeaked out, her voice ridiculously breathless.

"Is Caracas your destination? Or are you continuing to Bolivia?" Mark asked.

She nodded, then shook her head. What was wrong with her? Had Reg's jilting stolen her ability to talk with an attractive man? "Yes. I'm going to Caracas," she finally got out.

"Business or pleasure?"

"Hmm," she said, not sure whether her single's honeymoon qualified as a purely pleasurable vacation. She did have business with her heavenly Father. "Both."

"Well, make sure you take time to visit the interior. The *Llano,* Venezuela's prairie, is stunning. The Andes's peaks are spectacular—and so is Angel Fall."

Not knowing how much she should share with a stranger, Shiloh murmured a noncommittal "So I've heard."

As she picked up the novel she'd brought along for the flight, she could feel Mark's gaze on her for a minute. Then he dove for the briefcase under his seat and surfaced with a folder stuffed with varicolored papers. "Hope we have a good flight," he said. "Tons to catch up on."

The plane glided off with unexpected smoothness, and before long, the captain turned off the mandatory seat-belt lights. Then, almost as if invited, the noisy teens swarmed to Mark's side.

Shiloh groaned. With feeling.

She'd never had a problem with children, teens, or anyone of any age. But right now she craved relaxation—a chance to release all the tension that had built inside her since the breakup.

Today didn't promise any hope of serenity.

"Hey, man!" a boy with bleached white hair and jet black brows said to Mark. "Has anybody, like . . . done any work on the building yet?"

"Who cares?" asked a petite brunette. "What matters is that we get to go shopping."

The statuesque Nordic blonde beside her frowned. "Do you think a case of mosquito repellent will be enough?"

A handsome African-American male with intricate braids shot back, "For the whole Marine Corps."

That was just the beginning.

During the long hours that followed, a torrent of kids flooded past Mark's seat. Shiloh heard chatter ranging from the subject of life at school to the joy of doing what's truly right for those who need the help—this from a plump partridge of a girl—to a red-corkscrew-tressed string bean's comments about Venezuela. "This is *waaay* cool, man," he said, fiery coils bouncing. "It's a whole different world. And I'm gonna *be* there."

Shiloh heartily agreed with that statement. From what she'd read, the Venezuelan rain forest *was* a different world. One where the strident confusion of modern society hadn't yet reached. At least that's what she hoped.

As the conflicting rock recordings and the wails of infants escalated around her, Shiloh tried to shut out the commotion. The jungle would be even more appealing after this flight. She really needed this vacation. She had some serious praying to do, and she wanted no distractions.

Especially none like the intriguing, attractive teen-shepherd, Mark Walker.

CHAPTER TWO

IN THE hush of the jungle evening, Shiloh tried to make out the sights around her, but because of her exhaustion and the dark, she saw very little. Her other senses, though, rejoiced. The air bore an exotic aroma—lush, ripe, and earthy, with a moist floral sweetness. Over the thrum of the jeep's engine, the occasional birdcall sparked her imagination, sending fiery-plumed creatures soaring through her mind.

She couldn't wait to explore her peaceful surroundings the next morning. From the pictures she'd seen and the scents that now surrounded her, she expected the rain forest to look like a never-ending Georgia O'Keeffe flower painting, complete with the artist's trademark of full, curving lines and brilliant colors.

As she welcomed sleep in her unpretentious white-washed-stucco *casita* moments after receiving her key, Shiloh savored the deep, comforting silence. She thanked God she was finally off that cruel-and-unusual-punishment flight. The level of energy those kids expended and the decibels they'd emitted made her feel more tired.

Shiloh shuddered. She'd sighed with relief when she'd boarded the small, twin-engine plane that brought her to the rain forest and saw no sign of Mark Walker and his traveling circus.

Thinking of Mark made her grimace. She could just imagine the impression she'd made on him with her overattention to her book and the lousy way she looked. Since Reg had called off the wedding, Shiloh had lost weight and gained raccoon eyes. Her hair sagged, and the slightest noise made her jump. Mark's rambunctious crew was no slight thing.

She wondered why those teens had come to Venezuela in the first place. She'd been too wiped out, physically and emotionally, and too overwhelmed by the group's energy to bother asking. Not that they'd given her a moment in which to shoehorn a question.

"Thank you, Father, for sending them elsewhere," she whispered in the serene calm. "I couldn't have stood another moment around them. Not as out of whack as I feel."

Brrrrriinnnng!

Shiloh jerked out of her comfortable bed at the piercing shriek of a whistle. Her heart pounded, then skipped a beat as she tried to place where she was.

"What was *that?"* she said, struggling to focus her blurry eyes on her surroundings. "Did I dream the trip?"

Then her eyes cleared, and, with a glance around, she verified she was where she should be. The thatched roof covered her, the circle of white stucco walls surrounded her, and the solid blackwood door kept the world out. The only thing missing was the tranquillity she'd come seeking.

Beside the piercing screeches she'd heard, she now made out the tromping of heavy footwear, agitated but muffled voices, and the thuds and clanks that might accompany an invading army.

What was going on?

Still shaky from her rude awakening, Shiloh stood and quickly changed from her nightgown into khaki shorts and a yellow polo shirt, completing her outfit with matching yellow cotton socks and sturdy hiking boots. After yanking a brush through her hair, she was ready to question the powers that be on their much-vaunted and no-longer-evident restful refuge.

She opened the door, squinted against the searing sunlight, and stepped outside. As she'd suspected, a group of guests dashed in and out of various *casitas,* escalating the intensity of the racket.

"Hey! I know you." The male voice sounded familiar. But it couldn't be, could it? She was in the middle of nowhere—literally.

"You were on our flight yesterday!"

As Shiloh's eyes adjusted to the light, she identified the red-headed string bean who'd hovered over Mark Walker's shoulder through most of yesterday's flight. "What are *you* doing here?" she asked, unable to keep the irritation from her voice.

"We're here on a special summer missions trip."

Please, God, tell me this is just a bad dream.

No answer came from above.

"A missions trip. To the jungle?" Shiloh asked, disbelieving.

"That's right," answered the chubby girl who'd just joined the redhead. "Hi, I'm Sandy," she said, extending her hand. "We're here to help a small community of believers build a church. I'm so thankful God's given me the opportunity to serve my brothers and sisters in Christ in such a meaningful way."

This is a joke, right? Shiloh asked God. *They're noisy and busy, but here to do your will. Something very worthwhile. But in my "honeymoon" spot—and right when I need quiet time with you to figure out how my life got so screwed up?*

I'm with you always, my child. The words resonated in Shiloh's heart with such power that they took her breath away.

I know, Lord, but—

"Well, hello there!" At the sound of Mark Walker's rich voice, Shiloh turned with a start.

The man was impressive—powerful and confident, the epitome of masculinity. Dressed much like her in khaki shorts and a pale green T-shirt, his legs looked as solid as the tree trunks that rose a hundred feet behind him to touch the sky with their branches. And the arms crossed over his chest were muscular.

But his wide, intelligent eyes were what really stole her attention. A clear vibrant emerald, they matched the surrounding foliage.

"H-hello," she stammered, realizing he was watching her and, once again, she wasn't making a good impression.

"Wha—?" he began.

"Wha—?" she said simultaneously.

Both stopped and looked at each other.

"You go first," Mark offered.

Shiloh shook her head. "Silly of me to ask. Sandy," she said, gesturing toward the friendly student, "already said your group has come to build a church. In the jungle?"

"That's what we're here for. A summer vacation with meaning. A break from our regular lives and a chance to help needy Christians. The congregation's in a village a short distance away. It's small but faithful and rich in spirit. I feel blessed to be part of this project," Mark said, his words ringing sincere and solid.

"I've been coming here for three years to minister to the congregation of the soon-to-be Church of the Falls. I work for a Christian college that sponsors a summer trip for committed, college-bound high schoolers from across the state who want to serve their less fortunate brothers and sisters in Christ. This hotel gives us a good deal early in the summer, and they're willing to put up with the kids since it's small enough that we usually have the run of the place. This year a smaller group than usual qualified, and you lucked out!"

Shiloh rolled her eyes at his grin.

"Anyway," he added, "it's the only place to stay out here in this part of the jungle while we answer our Lord's call."

At that moment Shiloh's admiration for Mark took a giant leap forward toward respect; her irritation at their presence dropped her into shame.

"That's admirable," she mumbled, knowing it was time to hit the ground with her knees. "I guess I'll see you all later."

Mark grinned. "Can't see how you'll avoid us. Twelve kids take up a lot of room. Even in the jungle."

"No kidding," she responded, waving weakly. As she closed the door to her *casita* behind her, one of the young men called out.

"Hey, Pastor Mark . . ."

She moaned. She couldn't help it. "OK, Lord. What exactly are you trying to tell me?"

Utter silence—of the heavenly kind if not the human-teen kind—turned deafening.

So with no clear direction, Shiloh picked up her Bible and said, "Help me, Father. I'm really lost." She began to read his Word.

A good while later, Shiloh knelt beside her bed and bowed her head in prayer. "Father, I think Carrie might have been right about at least one thing. I can't remember when I last spent this much time in your presence, just delighting in you and your Word. Although I've been taking Bible vitamins—those quickie verse-in-the-daily-planner moments—I haven't followed them up with a real meal except on Sundays. And in church there's not much opportunity for listening to your still, silent voice."

A terrible thought occurred to her. "I—I hurt you, didn't I?" Tears formed in her eyes. "And you loved me anyway. Lord, when I think of your sacrifice . . . and my behavior . . . I'm so ashamed." A sob broke in her throat. "Forgive me, Father, for putting you on hold, for being so careless with our time together."

Then it struck her. Had she put her relationship with Reg on hold, too?

As she used a tissue to mop her wet face, someone knocked on her door. Great. She had to either ignore it or answer sporting puffy, red-rimmed eyes and a drippy nose.

She opened the door and stood, dismayed, as she faced Mark Walker—*Pastor* Mark—again.

"Are you OK?" he asked, concern in his voice and green eyes.

The heat of her blush singed Shiloh all the way to her bangs. "I'm . . . fine. I just have some things to work out and, well, they hit me all of a sudden."

"I'm not sure I mentioned it, but I'm a minister. I'm good for prayer, and I'd be more than happy to help any way I can. If nothing else," Mark said, cupping his hands behind his ears, "my radar dishes work great in time of trouble."

Shiloh smiled. "Stock-in-trade, right?"

"Something like that," Mark said, his gaze friendly but penetrating.

Taking a deep breath, Shiloh sought to change the subject. "What did you want me for?"

A frown creased Mark's broad forehead. "If I'd known something was troubling you, I wouldn't have bothered you."

"Tell me what you need. I'll tell you if it's a bother."

"I don't know," he said, his voice fading. Then he squared his shoulders. "Hey, you can only say yes or no, so it's worth a try. It seems the cook is under the weather this morning—something about her eyes—and the local doctor, our female chaperone here on location, was called to Caracas unexpectedly. The hotel manager said you were a nurse, and since I have twelve ravenous beasts to deal with, I wondered if you'd be willing to take a look at the sick woman."

"Hang on," Shiloh said, reaching for the case of overstocks and damaged-package medicine, bandages, syringes, and other essentials the ER nursing staff had prepared for her to take to missionaries during her trip. When Shiloh had told them how critical medical supplies could be on the mission field, they had decided to send the perfectly good but-no-longer-usable hospital surplus. "I have all kinds of stuff in here. Maybe something will help."

As she stepped out of the *casita,* Shiloh donned a straw hat for protection from the sun. "You said the cook has a problem with her eyes? What kind of problem? Are they crusted? Does she complain of sharp pains? Or did she experience sudden blindness? Because some of these I can't handle."

Mark raised his hands in a gesture of surrender. "I'm only the messenger. A nonmedical one. I haven't even seen your patient."

Shiloh laughed. "I guess I can leave the hospital, but the hospital never leaves me."

"I'll say. You're an awfully good sport to agree to pitch in while on vacation."

"Health care is what I do. And as one of your students said, I'm thankful the Lord has called me to serve my brothers and sisters in a meaningful way."

He raised a brow. "You're a Christian, then."

"Since I was a teen."

"What a blessing to have you here."

Although something inside Shiloh pushed her to say the same about him, she didn't think the words would be appropriate this soon after they'd met. So instead she continued to push ahead on her first trip into the jungle. In awe of God's workmanship, she noticed the rows of towering trees that banked the path, their canopies providing relief from the tropical heat and a place for delicate, rare flowers to blossom.

As she breathed in the scent of the jungle, she gave thanks to God, the Master Craftsman, who had led her here. She admired the rich green she saw everywhere, realizing she'd never seen green like this until now. Well, until yesterday's flight when she had looked into Mark's eyes.

She shook her head to dislodge the stray thought and turned to share with Mark her initial reaction to the jungle. The presence of three of his minions gathered outside a worn *casita* up ahead, however, reminded her of the disruption they represented—Mark included.

"Pastor Mark," cried Sandy, "the cook's crying, her eyes hurt so much. Can you help?"

"I can't, but Nurse Morris—"

"Call me Shiloh."

He gave her a questioning look. "Even the kids?"

"I'm more comfortable with my name than a title."

"OK," he said, then faced his pupil again. "Shiloh is a nurse. She'll take a look at the cook."

"Praise God," murmured the girl, stepping away from the doorway.

Shiloh disappeared into the darkened hut.

Twenty minutes later, Shiloh reappeared, a lopsided grin on her lips. Mark hurried to her side. "How is she?"

"Fine, if down for the count."

"Cryptic words," he commented. "Just what do you mean by 'down for the count'?"

As Shiloh began the hike back to the hotel, Mark matched his steps to hers. "It means the cook has pinkeye," she said. "Not particularly dangerous, since I have the correct antibiotic in my case, but definitely contagious."

"Are you saying what I think you're saying?"

"Pinkeye can blaze through your students like wildfire. Rosita must be kept away from the kids."

Mark let out a sigh.

"Whassup, Pastor Mark?" asked the youth with braids, as he extended a hand to Mark.

Mark shook it firmly. "Hey, Quentin. I have a small problem this morning."

"Small?" asked Sandy as she huffed up to them. "I wouldn't call starvation out beyond civilization a *small* problem."

Quentin arched an eyebrow. "Didn't you say on the plane, Sandy, that you were starting a new diet?"

As Sandy's round cheeks blazed with color, Shiloh noticed that Mark bit his lip. She wished she could get inside his head to know what he was thinking.

Then, just as it appeared Mark was about to call Quentin on his comment, Sandy glared at the boy. "Quentin Sharp, you're such a jerk. If you weren't so tall, I'd grab your 'cool' braids and rip 'em out."

Quentin gave a low guffaw. "But you'd have to catch me, and I'm not a running back for noth—"

"Yeah, yeah," Sandy said, cutting him off. Turning to Mark, she asked, "What are we going to do?"

Mark shook his head. "I don't know—at least not about the cook. I do know we're going to gather somewhere and pray for the woman's quick recovery." With a pointed look at both students, he added, "And we'll pray for her sake rather than that of our growling middles."

Quentin's and Sandy's expressions changed. They glanced at each other sheepishly.

"Sorry," both mumbled and hurried toward the hotel.

"I'll get the guys," Quentin called back.

"I'll get the girls," Sandy said.

"I'll head over to the kitchen," Shiloh added. "I'm on duty. I promised Rosita I'd help out while she's in bed."

"Thanks, Shiloh," Mark said gratefully. "I appreciate your offer to help—especially when you have things on your mind. It would be hard for me to work a kitchen, oversee the mission site, and ride herd on my dozen all at the same time."

"An' a lively passel o' beeves they are, pardner," Shiloh said, her large brown eyes twinkling and her coral-colored lips curving in a smile.

Mark responded to her humor with a grin. "You noticed, then?"

Wispy bangs danced on Shiloh's brows as she shot him a knowing look. "Give me a break. I'd have to be dead and buried not to notice. And you know it."

"They *are* energetic, and sometimes they get to me," he admitted. "But they're a good bunch. I'm proud of my flock."

The smile on Shiloh's lips faded to a strange expression. "They seem committed," she said slowly, thoughtfully. "At least the ones I've met. Although they're young—and act like it sometimes—they appear to know where they're going, what God has called them to, and how he wants them to get there."

"You're right. They are young, and right now, Christ is calling them to become faith-filled men and women. They need a lot of guidance from their parents, teachers, and even me. But make no mistake, they ask more questions than we stumbling adults do."

She sent him a sharp look. "What you really mean is that they ask for and accept help, and I don't, right?"

He shrugged, looking uncomfortable.

"I heard you earlier," she said firmly. "And I'd say you have your hands full, Pastor Mark. Besides, I've got brunch to make for a team of hungry kids."

"You do?"

"I already told you I was taking over breakfast—brunch now—for Rosita," she said reluctantly.

"I thought you'd help out, not take charge of a commercial operation."

"I heard the Lord call my name when Rosita begged for help. How could I say no? Besides, there's no one else to do it. But you'd better not expect a gourmet feast."

"As long as you silence my crew's growling guts without poisoning them, I'll be happy," he said, his relief showing.

"Let's hope your happiness lasts *after* you've tasted my cooking," she said, winking at him.

CHAPTER THREE

As MARK forked the last mouthful of Shiloh's killer baked omelet stuffed with tender vegetables, fresh herbs, and melted cheese, he gave his heavenly Father thanks for her cooking talent—and her willingness to share it. Around him, students expressed their appreciation, their hunger satisfactorily silenced.

As long as they were eating, they weren't sniping at each other, he thought with relief. He'd been disturbed by the episode between Sandy and Quentin, since he took God's call to be a peacemaker seriously. He realized the teens were excited about the trip and the chance to do something worthwhile for God. But, because they were between childhood and young adulthood, they were sometimes awkward and indulged in occasional bickering and immature behavior. Mark hated the pain it caused. He wished he had more experience working with kids, but he was only a few years out of seminary. He needed the Father's help with this.

Mark looked up and saw Shiloh begin to clean up. His cheeks warmed as he noticed how attractive she was—with her silky, straight dark hair that framed her cheeks and curved in just below her jawline. *What a woman,* he thought—and then caught himself. He could tell Shiloh was troubled, and he wanted to help. He just wished he knew what was wrong.

Something she'd said, however, niggled at the back of his mind. She'd been unable to refuse Rosita's need. Was that a problem with her? Yes-itis? If so, did it have any bearing on her earlier bout of misery?

Mark knew all about that common condition among Christians. He'd been born as the youngest of six children to parents who, to this day, hadn't learned to say no. This weakness had made life in the Walker home chaotic, and the siblings had practically raised themselves. As far back as he could remember, Mark had always hungered for peace and his parents' attention.

And Shiloh was a nurse, always responding to emergencies. Not quite a cardiac surgeon like his dad, but close enough.

People like his mom and dad—and possibly Shiloh—made warning sirens blare in Mark's head each time they came near. He'd have to be careful around this pretty nurse.

Mark shook off his serious thoughts, then cleared his throat. "Time to help clean up before worship, guys."

The group cleared the table, then sat back down close together.

Mark nodded to Sandy. She'd told him earlier that she'd been the worship leader at her church for two years, so he'd chosen her to lead worship on this trip.

The smiling girl stood, gave her colleagues a benevolent look, and said, "We'll start by singing 'Majesty' this morning." Closing her eyes, she opened her mouth and warbled, "Maaaaaahhhh-ches-ty, woooorship his maaaaaahh-ches-ty . . ." in a voice so atonal it made toads sound like operatic divas.

Fighting his dismay, Mark tried to keep his mouth shut, noting that none of his students had bothered to make any such effort.

A movement at the door to the kitchen made Mark glance away

from the disaster before him. In the opening stood Shiloh, a question on her face. He knew the exact moment when she identified the source of the caterwauling, since her eyes shot straight to his.

The noise continued. How had he gotten himself into this? Why had he named Sandy worship leader without ever listening to her? *I guess I still have a lot to learn,* he thought.

His gaze met Shiloh's, and he tried to communicate his helplessness. With an impish grin, she pointed at him, then mouthed, "It's your party, and you'll cry if you want to."

To his amusement. And further dismay. *Lord? How should I handle this? How should I run morning worship and keep from hurting Sandy's feelings?*

He watched as Shiloh darted back into the kitchen, the grin still on her face. Why did she have to have a sense of humor, too? Even if it were his dilemma she found funny.

Good grief! *It's your party, and you'll cry if you want to.* Well, it *was* his mess, and it *was* up to him how he responded to it. And it was funny . . . sort of. Even though he didn't know how to get himself out of it—yet.

Wasn't it bad enough that Shiloh was pretty, gifted with a compassionate calling, charitable to perhaps a scary extreme? Did she have to be funny as well?

Mercifully, Sandy chose that moment to put all the kids out of their auditory misery. Quentin leaped up and led the group in morning prayers.

Breathing more easily now, Mark glanced at the spot where Shiloh had stood. He couldn't afford to like her any more than he already did. He had a mission here, and it wasn't to find a fellow guest appealing. He'd come to the rain forest on a different kind of vacation—to get away from the stress of his job as associate chaplain at a Christian college, and to do something meaningful while taking a much-needed break. A woman—especially one with yes-itis—was not on the program.

But, he acknowledged, he needed Shiloh's help, so he couldn't alienate her. He *had* to remain focused on the kids and the mission church. He also needed to recharge his own spiritual batteries in preparation for the new school year. He couldn't let himself be distracted by a multitude of other needs, valid and legitimate as they might be.

He'd have to ask Shiloh how long Rosita would need to remain quarantined. If it was for a while yet, he could be in serious trouble. He didn't want to distract the teens from their primary purpose. And he couldn't take over the kitchen duties in addition to his other commitments. If he did, he'd lose his focus and spread himself as thin as his parents did, something he'd spent years avoiding.

Shiloh obviously had an agenda for her vacation, and cooking for him and his minions couldn't be on it. She hadn't seemed thrilled to take over the kitchen. On the contrary, she'd given the impression it was something she would do out of Christian duty.

But she'd proven more than capable in her temporary role. Everyone who'd enjoyed her omelets had offered nothing but praise. Still, if Rosita had to be absent from her job for any length of time, could he in good conscience lobby Shiloh to continue subbing for her? Especially when he suspected she had trouble saying no?

A thought crossed his mind. What if they shared KP duties?

Hmm . . . from the pleasant sense of excitement that idea brought, Mark suspected it was too dangerous to consider. Too dangerous for a man who had to avoid involvement with a yes-itis sufferer. He couldn't expose himself that way.

"We ask this in Jesus' holy name," Brigit Carlsson, the statuesque blonde, concluded. The others chimed in with reverent amens.

He nearly groaned out loud. He'd been so busy thinking about Shiloh that he'd completely missed morning prayers. And he hadn't come up with any answers.

What was he going to do to keep his vacation-with-meaning from falling apart? How was he going to keep a safe distance between himself and Shiloh? How could he justify encouraging her to give more of herself so that he could continue to focus on what God had led him to do?

He didn't know. But the One who knew was only a prayer away.

A few hours later, as Mark was about to take off for the construction site, Rigoberto Rodríguez, the hotel manager, called out to him. "Meester Walker! Pleese wait a meenit."

Mark dropped his heavy backpack on the ground, wondering what the man wanted with him.

"Rosita's girl now also has the red-eye seekness, and they're still *contagiosas*. She can't kook for days. We no know what we do now."

Just then Shiloh left the kitchen and headed toward her *casita*. The two men looked at each other, simultaneously struck with the same thought.

"Mees Morreess!" the manager called out, a shrewd look on his round, olive-toned face.

Shiloh stumbled, then turned their way.

"Can I pleese speek with you?"

Wariness dawned in Shiloh's brown eyes as she strode up to them. "Yes?"

"Everyone loved your *desayuno*. They would steell be hungry if you hadn't kooked the . . . how you say? Oh, yes, the fast-break. But we have a problem. You told Rosita she no return for days. Who will kook then?"

"Breakfast," Shiloh said in correction, then darted suspicious looks from the manager to Mark. Whereas Rodríguez's cajoling expression never wavered, Mark held her gaze for a second, then shifted his weight on his feet. What could he say? He'd already foreseen this very scenario, and he knew what he'd vote for. His kids needed meals, but *he* had to be at the site, far from the very appealing nurse . . . who couldn't say no.

"I'm on vacation," Shiloh objected.

"Yes, yes!" Rodríguez exclaimed. "We give you free *vacación* after Rosita come back. Pleese, Meess Morreess. You kook so good. We are hungry for more than fast-break."

Shiloh again murmured, "Breakfast." Mark could almost see the wheels spinning in her head as she weighed the needs of those at the camp against her own. She shook her head, not saying a word.

She parted her lips, then clamped them shut again. Rodríguez's impatience showed in the expression on his face, the tapping of his foot.

Still Shiloh said nothing.

Mark knew when she made her decision. She drew herself up in a way that reminded him of his mother, took a deep breath, and said quietly, "OK. I guess I can help out. It's the right thing to do."

Mark didn't know whether to allow his exultant group-leader side to cheer or to let his dismayed pastor-counselor side groan. This lady showed all the signs of a serious case of yes-itis. And he had to keep that in mind each time he remembered how attractive she was, how enthusiastic and contagious her laughter was, how admirable her compassion toward others was.

Nurse Shiloh represented nothing but *trouble*. And Mark hadn't come to the jungle to find trouble. He'd come to vacation, direct a team of kids, and help a group of believers build a place of worship. Those were enough things for him to focus on.

A woman had no place in any of those activities. Not even one as interesting as Shiloh Morris, R.N.

"Shiloh!" Mark cried as he ran into the kitchen later that day. "Come quick! Quentin's hurt."

Shiloh spun around, unfastened the bow tied at the back of her waist, and threw the apron in a heap on a chair. "What happened? Isn't the doctor back yet?" she asked as she wriggled past him out the door and hurried toward her *casita,* with Mark following. Mark waited at the door while she grabbed the black case of supplies.

"Still in Caracas," he said, admiring Shiloh's quick, spare motions. "A saw sliced into Quentin's right thigh. I didn't see it happen, but I saw the wound. It's large, deep, and bleeding heavily."

"Oh, no!" She dashed back out, slamming the door behind her. "He's a . . . a running back—football, right?"

"Yes, and evidently he's good. Very good."

"Then this is very bad. Show me where he is."

Mark marveled at her instant concern for the boy she scarcely knew. Then, with a start, he realized he was losing his cook. "Who's minding the kitchen now that you've left?"

"No one, really. But that's OK. I'd already cut the chicken and vegetables for the salad, and the yams are cooked. A week's worth of fresh rolls were delivered by the supply flight this morning."

Admiration again filled him as they jogged to the church site. Shiloh's efficiency was as impressive as her rapid response. But what did her empathy for others leave for herself? For anyone else in her life?

Fortunately for his peace of mind, he had to stop that line of thought because they'd reached the site. Shiloh knelt by Quentin, whose breath rasped in the humid air. Mark sat on the boy's other side.

Pain-stretched flesh sharply delineated the angles of Quentin's face. His eyes clenched shut, more than likely against the formation of un-macho but human tears. His hands squeezed his thigh above the gash, knuckles and tendons in brutal relief.

"Mark," Shiloh murmured after carefully examining the wound, "I need your help. We have to wash our hands with antiseptic. I have Betadine scrub, but we need fresh water. And don't touch anything after washing because we need to keep our hands as clean as possible to suture him. It's going to take layers of stitches to repair the wound."

With a sharp nod, Mark stood and addressed the cluster of locals behind them. *"¿Donde está un baño?"*

After receiving the answer, they followed directions to the nearest bathroom. She turned to Mark, a smile on her lips. "Thank the Lord you speak Spanish."

"I often do thank him for that. It's come in handy a number of times in my ministry, and especially on these trips. The kids and the leader must have a working knowledge of Spanish—no less than one year of instruction in the language—to be effective here."

They scrubbed and waved their hands in the air to shake off the water, Shiloh refusing to let either of them use the less-than-pristine towel provided.

Back by Quentin, she knelt again, took a needle out of her case, and gave Quentin a shot of local anesthetic. Then she popped open a plastic bottle and squirted dark amber liquid onto a gauze pad. "This is a solution of the same antiseptic we used to scrub," she explained as she gently but meticulously cleaned the wound. When done with that swab, she turned to Mark again and bobbed her head toward the open medical kit. "You'll have to pass me what I need."

He nodded, hoping his ignorance didn't get in Shiloh's way.

"How are you doing?" she asked Quentin.

Fear in his eyes, the youth queried, "Will I . . ." He bit back a sob. "Will I be able to run again?"

She doused the ravaged tissue on the powerful thigh with more of the dark orange antiseptic. "I'm not a doctor, so I can't be certain. But if I can suture you well enough, and if we can keep infection from setting in—a real danger here in the damp, hot jungle—then you'll probably be OK after therapy."

"That's cool," Quentin said shortly. "I can work hard. At least it's not all over already. Praise God."

"Amen," Mark said. "One moment for prayer won't be too risky, will it, Shiloh?"

"A very brief one shouldn't."

Nurse and assistant bowed their heads. "Heavenly Father," Mark prayed, "you know Quentin's love for sports, and you know the exact extent of his injury. Guide our sister Shiloh as she works to repair the damage done to his leg. And don't let this makeshift nurse mess up, please."

Quentin smiled at Pastor Mark's intended humor, as Mark had hoped he would, then closed his eyes. "Go for it, Doc Shiloh."

Glancing at the angel of mercy at his side, Mark saw Shiloh take a deep breath. She tore open a foil packet and pulled out a nasty-looking curved needle attached to a long strand of white string. Then she bent closer to the leg she'd cleansed. "Hang in there, Quentin," she said softly as she began her delicate task, hands rock steady.

The carefully patched-up Quentin didn't show for supper, but Shiloh hadn't expected him. After the kitchen sparkled once again, she went to check on her patient, only to find him snoring gently. She smiled. "Thank you, Father, for guiding my hands today," she whispered. "He's so young, and his loss would have been enormous if I hadn't been here . . . or if I'd failed him. I'm glad you put me in this place, at this time, to serve you."

She let herself out of the *casita* Quentin shared with the bleached-white-haired, black-browed boy she'd heard called Kirk, and Moony, the carrottop. As she walked toward her own lodgings, she heard the sound of running water and decided to explore the pool she hadn't yet seen.

She turned at a bend in the path, rounded a huge bush with small white flowers, and came to a stop. She'd walked into a dream. Nothing on earth could look so lovely, so lush, so serene.

Large rocks and boulders sat within the circle of vegetation where the Creator's hand had placed them. A free-form pool, lit by concealed spotlights and fed by a cascade at the far end, beckoned. To her left stood a stone that looked perfect for sitting on and contemplating the richness of the jungle night. It also offered her the chance to soak her tired feet.

Shiloh kicked her shoes off and wriggled her toes in the water with relish. It felt so good to sit. She couldn't believe how tired she was—on her vacation!

She felt almost as if she were still back home, exhausted after a day's work. The coolness of the pool water soothed her sore feet. "Thank you, Lord, for this moment," she said out loud. "This is the peace I was after when I decided to take my honeymoon anyway."

Carrie had been right. Shiloh *had* needed to get away. In the brief time she'd been in the rain forest, Shiloh had already realized what a hash she'd made of her relationship with God. It was something that never should have happened, something she'd never let happen again.

Had her duty-driven overcommitment to work interfered with her relationship with Reg, too? True, they hadn't had much time to spend together because of their busy careers. But they *had* talked every day on the phone. That counted, didn't it?

Or had those conversations been relationship vitamins like her Bible vitamins? Had she and Reg neglected full meals of sharing while trusting too much to those quickie calls?

Oh, Lord, was that what we—I—did? Her eyes grew moist.

A rustle of leaves to her right alerted her to the arrival of an interloper. For a moment, annoyance filled her. She'd found this idyllic spot first. When she saw Mark, she smiled in welcome and surreptitiously dabbed away a tear.

"Pull up a rock and join me," she said.

"Think I will." After he'd collapsed only a few feet from her, he narrowed his gaze and studied her despite the coming velvet dark. "Troubled again?"

When she didn't answer right away, he tried again. "Long day?"

"Mm-hmm," she said, glad for the graceful out he'd given her. "But a good one."

"How so?"

"Rosita and her children have the medicine they need so their eyes will suffer no permanent damage, everyone has eaten, and most importantly, Quentin's leg looks good. I'm pretty sure he'll regain full function. *If* we avoid infection."

"Well," Mark said, steely determination in his voice, "we'll just have to see we do."

Shiloh chuckled. "Ever think of moonlighting as a nurse? You were good out there this afternoon. That was a bad wound, and I was scared—I'm not a doctor. I couldn't have done it without your help."

Pretending horror, he held out one hand, palm out. "Stop! No way. I've been called to heal souls rather than bodies. I'm afraid I'd mutilate someone."

"Nah. You were steady, you listened, and even anticipated what I needed several times. But more than that, you kept Quentin from panicking."

"Yeah, I did all the panicking myself."

Both sat enjoying the silence until Mark said, "Can I ask a question?"

Shiloh's guard shot up. "That depends."

"Well, it *is* a personal one."

"Then I guess it'll depend on how personal it is."

He nodded, clearly satisfied with even that much. "I'll take a stab. I'd like to know why you were crying when I went to your *casita*—and when I got here. You're hurting, and I'd like to help if I can. Sometimes talking, especially with an uninvolved party, helps clarify things."

Shiloh waved vaguely. "I'm not really hurting. I'm sad. I did something kind of stupid. Well, no. It's not like that. I guess I didn't take the time to pay enough attention to some important things, so I wound up in a bad situation. Oh, I don't know. I'm confused. About my work, myself, everything."

"What's wrong at work?"

"Nothing's wrong. It's just that everyone says I'm too consumed by my calling."

"I wonder why anyone would say that about you," he said, smiling and thinking back to her efficiency with Quentin.

Shiloh grinned. "Probably because I *am* committed to my work—maybe *too* committed."

"Sounds as if you're getting somewhere in your thinking. Now, what are you going to do about that excess commitment to work? Do you ever take time off to recharge?"

"I thought I did. Actually, I never thought I needed a lot of downtime since I love what I do. But I've had to reconsider. That's why I'm here—to take a break and think through all of this."

"Good for you. One item discussed, two more to go. Since I see nothing wrong with you, let's discuss that very vague *everything* you mentioned."

"Well, something happened—and don't push me on this. I'm not ready to talk about it—a couple months before I left York. That's where I'm from."

He cocked his head. "York, Pennsylvania? I work at Shepherd's College in Lancaster County. We're neighbors, after all."

"It would seem," Shiloh responded, smiling with relief. At least he'd gotten off the subject of *her*.

He shook a long finger. "Not so fast, ma'am. You have some explaining to finish. What about that something you mentioned?"

Busted! "Well, it shook me badly. It showed me that I don't know myself as well as I thought I did. It also made me question my relationship with God." She paused, not thrilled to reveal the ugly truths she'd learned. But Mark was a chaplain. Surely he'd understand. "I realized I wasn't seeking the Lord as earnestly as I should have been. I wasn't spending enough time in his presence, just listening for his Spirit's voice."

She sat back for a moment, took a deep breath, then continued, "That leads back to my response to God's calling. Have I been working from an overblown sense of duty? From a misguided vision of what commitment to my ministry should be? Before I came here, a friend suggested I was. If she's right, then how much has my desire to heal blinded me to the personal part of my life? Am I meant to continue in nursing? in the ER? Should I change departments? Or should I leave nursing altogether?"

"That sounds drastic. You're good at it, and you obviously thrive on helping people."

Shiloh thought over Mark's words. "You're right. But that's not all. It seems I have tunnel vision. All work and duty and little else. I need to learn to discern where and how best to serve God. I have to do some serious thinking about myself, how I prioritize."

To Shiloh's surprise, Mark tensed his jaw. "Interesting concept, prioritizing."

Shiloh wondered how to pose the question sparked by his statement, but before she could do so, footsteps approached, followed by another set.

"Out for the moonlight?" asked a young female voice.

"Hey, I came to experience nature, raw and untrammeled by filthy man," answered a male who sounded like the redhead.

"To each his own," said the girl.

"It's not mine, it's God's jungle, and we're responsible for protecting—hey!" the boy suddenly cried. "Did you see that?"

"What? That white bird?"

"Right. Before tonight, I'd only seen one on that detective show, *Columbo*. This is the first real cockapoo I've ever seen, and it's flying."

Shiloh stifled a laugh. Across from her, Mark's shoulders shook.

The girl guffawed. "That bird's a cocka*too*. A cockapoo's a dog, a little fur-mop that happens when you cross a cocker spaniel and a poodle. Wait'll I tell the others about your flying cockapoo!" She ran toward the *casitas*.

The boy followed, roaring, "Don't you dare!"

Shiloh let out the laugh she was holding; so did Mark. Both enjoyed the humor of the moment, the beauty of the evening, the pleasant company.

After a while, she stood. "Breakfast will roll around early enough. I'd better get back."

Mark waited while she donned her shoes, then walked by her side to her *casita*. Once there, both felt awkward. Neither knew how to say good night. She didn't know why; it hadn't been a date. *Hmm . . . what would it be like to date Mark?* The idea held great appeal, as did the man. He was funny and capable, had strong faith, and genuinely cared for those around him.

". . . I don't think you should lean so heavily on your own understanding," he said.

Oh, no! He'd been speaking while she daydreamed about him. Shiloh blushed, then winced when his comment registered. She nodded hastily to cover her embarrassment. "I've been told that before. Yet another thing to bring up with the Father before sleeping tonight."

Mark took her hand and looked into her eyes. "I don't want to make you uncomfortable, but you should know that I like you. Very much. I'd be happy to help you sort through your thoughts. Plus, I'm always available for prayer."

Shyness overcame her as did the desire to pray with this man of God. "Could we . . . ?"

"Of course," he answered.

Bowing their heads, they committed Shiloh's concerns to the Father, ending the precious interlude in the best way either knew.

Dreams were sweet that night.

Of each other.

CHAPTER FOUR

THE next morning at breakfast, Shiloh and Mark's patient ate enough for two . . . or four ravenous football players. As the plates began emptying, Mark's stomach churned. What was he going to do about the worship problem? He couldn't subject his kids to another bout of Sandy's tone-free trilling. What should he say to an enthusiastic, devout young woman—who couldn't carry a tune in the proverbial bucket?

He wished he had more knowledge of the workings of the young-adult female's mind. *Lord, help!*

As he uttered his silent plea, Shiloh approached. "May I join you for worship this morning?" she asked the kids with a smile.

"Sure," said Brigit Carlsson.

"Of course," answered Moony Reilly, his red curls springing in all directions like demented Slinky toys.

"Sit next to me, Doc Shiloh," added Quentin, pulling out a chair for her.

She thanked the kids, then turned to Mark. "Is it OK with you?"

He nodded. "Everyone's welcome to praise our God." Then he noticed the sparkle in her eyes. Shiloh Morris was up to something. But what?

"Hey," she said, approaching Quentin and the chair he'd indicated. "How about if we sing 'As the Deer' from Psalm 42? It's one of my favorites." Facing Sandy, she added, "If that's OK with the worship leader."

To Mark's surprise—and pleasure—Sandy smiled at Shiloh and nodded with her usual verve.

Shiloh shot Mark a glance. "On the count of three, then, everyone."

As Shiloh stepped forward in faith, the potential disaster was averted. A grin of reprieve carved itself across Mark's face. He'd been given more time to work out a solution. He gave God thanks for Shiloh's intervention, noting once again how insightful their nurse really was.

One terrific lady.

"But dangerous," Mark said under his breath as he and his young crew tromped to the construction site a short half hour later. He didn't think Shiloh Morris, RN, did it knowingly, but she got to a man. At least, to *this man*.

Who'd have imagined that Shiloh would rescue the team from, as she'd whispered while walking past him on her way back to the kitchen, Sandy's unintentional tympanic torture? To top off her list of attributes, Shiloh had abundant tact and sympathy toward others.

Still, his alarm system was *woo-oo-wooing* loud and clear. Shiloh leaped in where angels feared to tread each time she saw a need, each time someone hinted they needed her. And Mark had yet to see her take a minute for herself.

Did she have the time—or energy—for a relationship?

"Dumb!" he said. Why in the world was he thinking about that?

She *was* dangerous. The absolute worst kind of woman for a man like him: a nurse with yes-itis. He doubted she could offer him the support and refuge a chaplain needed, much less the attention a husband craved.

Just when had he started thinking about what a husband needed?

"Dumb!" he repeated, knowing his thoughts about Shiloh Morris had to end. He couldn't afford to care for someone who'd probably put him at dirt level on her priority scale. In fact, he'd better focus on her cons rather than her pros, or he'd wind up with trouble on his hands and in his life.

That would be the dumbest thing he'd ever done.

He looked ahead, catching sight of the foundation for the future church. He had his Father's will to do; Shiloh Morris had nothing to do with it. So Mark was going to do the only smart thing possible. He was going to avoid her.

"Dumb," Mark stated a third time for good measure.

"You calling me dumb, Pastor Mark?" asked Quentin, who'd insisted on hobbling to the site on crutches borrowed by the hotel manager from the still-absent Dr. Susana Escobar's clinic. This, despite the repair work Shiloh had done on his thigh.

Caught in his reverie, Mark said quickly, "Ah . . . er . . . your decision, yes. You made a dumb one this morning when you chose to come with the rest of us. You have to protect that leg, or your running days will be over."

Quentin's jaw jabbed out, and he wiggled a crutch to make his point. "God called me here this summer, man, and it wasn't to sit under a tree and dodge macaw droppings. Sure, I can't stand or walk much, but I can help while I'm sitting. There's lots of stuff I can do. You'll see."

Against his better judgment, and trying to snuff out the mental image of Quentin evading macaw bombs, Mark gave up. "I won't argue anymore. But I'm telling you, if you even *think* of coming down with a fever, you might want to beg your buddies—you know, Macaw Air—for a ride home, because I'll be turning your vacation into solitary confinement in a *casita.*"

Quentin almost—*almost*—smiled, but then his jaw went rigid. "I won't get a fever. Doc Shiloh gave me an antibiotic from her hospital-in-a-suitcase."

Shiloh again! It seemed Mark couldn't escape the woman, even when he should, for his own good. "Fine. Just be careful. I don't want anything else to happen—"

"Pastor Mark! Pastor Mark!" Brigit Carlsson called as she fastidiously picked her way down the path through decomposing vegetation and damp earth. "Gross," she said, then looked up at Mark. "Please go get Doc Shiloh. That local doctor's still in Caracas, and something's really wrong with Sandy. She's lying on this—" she scuffed a toe on the ground, then scowled at the detritus she picked up—"this disgusting path, all in spasms and crying that she's dying of pain."

That did not sound like the normally ebullient Sandy White. "Where is she?" Mark queried.

Brigit pointed straight ahead.

Mark ran a few yards, hearing Sandy's moans before he saw her. "What's wrong?" he asked.

"Oh . . . Pastor Mark—" Sandy convulsed into a fetal ball, her eyes shut tight against unmistakable pain. Sweat beaded on her forehead. He touched her forehead but felt no fever.

"Do you think you ate something that didn't agree with you?"

he probed, congratulating himself on his even tone while concern flared uppermost in his mind.

Sandy opened her eyes long enough to glare at him, then twisted and cried out again. She lay contorted, whimpers interspersed with sounds of agony.

When the cramping eased for a minute, she gasped, "I'm . . . sick . . . not a . . . glutton. Please get . . . Doc Shiloh." Pain glazed her eyes, and her features were white and drawn. "It's . . . killing . . . me."

"I never suggested gluttony, Sandy. Food spoils easily deep in the tropics," he explained, then rose, struck by the single tear sliding into her light brown hair.

"Please," she whispered as another spasm tied her up in a knot.

"Brigit," he said, "you stay with Sandy." He faced the other frightened students. "Guys, get to work. Armando will show you what needs to be done. And Quentin, stay off that leg. I'm going for Shiloh."

Jogging back to the hotel, Mark figured he'd go home in better shape than he'd come—*if* he and the kids got back in one piece. "If I'd thought Susana Escobar, on whom I counted to help keep my crew healthy, might not be here, I'd never have brought the kids. I'd never have put them in danger. What can I do, Lord?" he said aloud, panic threatening to overcome him.

The only thing he could do was exactly what he was doing: getting Shiloh, the person who could help. But as he reached the midpoint of the path, his heart beating like a conga drum, Mark strengthened his resolve to maintain a safe distance between himself and Shiloh while providing the best care possible for Sandy. It was unfortunate that the reality of the jungle had again forced him to turn to the woman he'd just decided to avoid.

Why, Lord? Don't I have more important things to deal with than an irrational attraction to a woman who's all wrong for me?

No answer came from above. Somehow, though, Mark thought he could hear God's chuckle. He stumbled, pulled to a screeching stop. *No way, Lord. You did not send her into my life. Not a yes-itis sufferer. Uh-uh.*

Once again rich, Amazonian-textured silence echoed beneath the emerald rain forest canopy. Mark's defiance deflated. What if . . . ?

"Oh, Father, please help me," he whispered, feeling more off balance than he had since he'd gleefully fled his teenage years. "I don't like what I think you're telling me, but I want to do your will more than mine. I need your strength here. And your guidance."

The words *I'm always with you, my child* resonated deep in his heart. Humbled by his heavenly Father's love, Mark bowed his head, then resumed his trek to Shiloh.

To another close encounter. Of the dangerous kind.

As she palpated Sandy's abdomen, Shiloh felt sure the girl suffered from a parasitic infection, common among visitors to the jungle. It wasn't life threatening; the disgusting stowaways didn't want to kill their free ride. They just burrowed into their host's body, made themselves at home, and devoured all the nutrients their revolting little hearts desired. Unfortunately, the human host felt miserable, wanting nothing more than to rid herself of the uninvited moochers.

"What other symptoms have you had?" Shiloh asked her pale, clammy patient.

Sandy's eyes darted sideways. "Um . . . oh, OW!" She turned away in discomfort—and Shiloh thought, unexpected relief. She knew the condition caused pain, but Sandy seemed to be milking the situation for all the attention she could get. It was unnecessary but understandable in a sick teen so far from home.

When the girl's cramp eased, Shiloh resumed prodding. "I have to know what else has happened."

"Doc Shiloh, it's . . . too embarrassing!"

Suspecting what her patient didn't want to voice, Shiloh said, "Sandy, I'm a nurse. I've emptied many a bedpan."

"Well, I made it to . . . the toilet, so . . . you won't . . . have to empty one . . . on my account."

Just then a warm hand clasped Shiloh's shoulder for an instant. She knew it was Mark; she turned to meet his gentle gaze.

"How's Sandy?" he asked, hunkering down.

Shiloh smiled, missing the comforting weight of his hand. "She'll live—to a ripe old age."

Sitting back on her heels, Shiloh said to her patient, "I know you feel miserable. I'm as sure as I can be without testing that you have an *Ascaris lumbricoides* infestation. Those are parasites in your intestine. But instead of roundworms, it could also be pinworms or whipworms. I have to get you back to the hotel, so you're going to have to help. We'll go slowly, but you need to cooperate."

Sandy groaned, shut her eyes, and balled up.

Taking a package of Vermox from her medicine bag, Shiloh said, "Since we treat all three with different amounts of the same drug, we'll give you the top dose." She held a tablet out to Sandy. "Take this with the distilled water in this cup, and again tonight, then continue that dosage for three days."

The rest of the group reappeared just then, worried looks on their faces. "It's lunchtime," the rangy redhead named Moony said. "And the cook's not cooking."

Shiloh smiled as she helped Sandy with her drink. "Never fear, the sandwiches are here . . . or there, as the case may be today since I had to leave in a hurry. But I had lunch ready before Pastor Mark came looking for me. We can all go back together, and everyone can take a turn helping Sandy along the way."

"Yeah, Moony," said Quentin, "Sandy's sick. We need to help, not gripe about our bellies. Besides, you're skinny. You don't need the calories us muscular types do."

General ribbing broke out, some kids siding with Quentin, some with long and lean Moony. Brigit scowled and put her arm around Sandy. With a grimace and a swat at the dead leaves that had stuck to her friend's peach-colored T-shirt, she helped the sick girl stand.

"Moony, you should be ashamed of yourself," Brigit said in her throaty voice. "I can't believe I'm saying this, but Quentin's right. Sandy's sick and we should be thinking of her."

"Yes, Martha-the-Perfect," Moony retorted.

Martha-the-Perfect? Shiloh wondered what that meant.

The blonde girl glared. "My name's Brigit, and you know it. You're just being as selfish as a fat, hungry boa, Moonpath Reilly."

"Ah, that reminds me, Moony," inserted Mark, his words sounding to Shiloh a bit rushed and somewhat desperate in his effort to deflect a potential skirmish. "How'd you wind up with such an unusual name?"

"Yeah, *Moonpath,"* added Brigit, ignoring Mark's headshake. "What does it mean—*ooooh!"* she cried, letting go of Sandy to swat at something on her face. "Gross! This place is filthy! Dirt, mud, rotten leaves, bugs, lizards, frogs, and disgusting birds dropping their . . . *stuff* all over the place."

Shiloh couldn't see what had set off the girl's outcry, but she was glad the bleached towhead, Kirk, jumped in and caught Sandy before she landed on the wet path.

"Hey, watch it, More-Martha-Than-the-Original-Stewart!" Moony hollered as he grabbed the squeamish and squirming blonde's shoulders. "The rain forest is a delicate ecosystem full of endangered species, and you're about to trample a perfect specimen of a . . . a . . ." After slapping his pockets, Moony finally found what looked like a pocket text on protecting the Amazon.

"Listen," Moony ordered as he skimmed a page. "It says, 'according to Odum's *Fundamentals of Ecology*—'"

"Hear, hear!" Quentin offered. "It's Dr. Greenpeace himself."

Brigit tilted her chin tree-topward. "So?"

Moony continued as if he'd never been interrupted. "So the fungal mycorrhiza that live in the surface litter—you know, the dirt and mud, dead leaves, and animal droppings—digest it and pass these nutrients to living root cells. That's how rain forests grow such fabulous, valuable species. Some that you're gonna tromp all over and kill in your *ignorance.*"

Kirk, who was still holding Sandy upright, shook his head. "Give it up, man."

Brigit tossed her platinum mane over her shoulder, ignoring everyone but Moony. "What this place *really* needs is a good landscape architect. One who'll weed out this viney stuff." She pointed at the woody vines worthy of testing Tarzan's skills. "And get rid of the tree clutter. Then someone could pave the paths. Plus the grime should be controlled. It's a filthy jungle down here." Waving expansively, she gathered oomph. "Oh, and Orkin wouldn't hurt. The bugs are humongous, and they're sucking the life out of me." She pointed at a mosquito bite on her forearm. "Maybe then we could see what the rain forest is all about and enjoy the flowers, especially the orchids. You know, it might not be half bad with some remodeling and a little decorating . . ."

Brigit's words died off when she realized everyone was staring at her as if she'd suddenly turned into a gecko. Or maybe even an iguana.

When silence threatened to smother her, Shiloh looked at the others. What did one say to *that?*

Mark, too, looked from student to student, clearly hoping for a brainstorm. When none materialized, he began walking. Then he stopped and faced the would-be environmentalist. "What kind of name is Moonpath, anyway?"

As titters of nervous laughter broke the tension, Shiloh glanced skyward. Heaven help her! She'd landed in the middle of a mass breakout from a loony bin—a group of teens and their sincere but emotionally awkward leader.

Just when she'd begun to sort out some of the important things in her head, she'd found herself more attracted to Mark each day. She even found his well-meaning, clumsy efforts around the kids endearing because she knew he cared deeply about his charges.

Suddenly she realized she'd never known Reg's feelings toward kids, much less how he related to them. How well had she *really* known Reg? Maybe, as she was beginning to believe, those telephone vitamins hadn't been conducive to knowing each other well. Especially since in the last six months, she and Reg had counted themselves lucky if they got together for dinner or a movie once a week. And most of those times his beeper went off partway through the date. Phone calls hadn't been enough.

Shiloh stumbled on a root in the path. A hand caught her elbow. Mark.

Noting his concern, she looked up. "I'm fine," she said, smiling, feeling a twinge of pleasure from knowing he cared.

"Good."

She walked for a bit, then stopped. If she hadn't known Reg after two years' time, how could she be so attracted to and seemingly in tune with Mark, whom she barely knew? And after nearly making what she now knew would have been the biggest mistake of her life, how could she trust her feelings for a man again? Especially so soon after the breakup?

Just then Moony marched past her. Thinking of his name made her wonder if *she'd* been the one to succumb to some kind of impending madness. One that struck at the worst possible time in its victim's life. The sort of lunacy that infected perfectly normal, totally sane nurses on their honeymoon.

Or was it something reserved especially for a *single's* honeymoon?

CHAPTER FIVE

"How could I let that mess between Moony and Brigit get so nasty?" Mark asked from his kneeling position by the bed the next morning. "Lord, I hear your call to be a peacemaker, but Brigit's nonsense boggled me so much that I let the situation get out of control." He shuddered with embarrassment, as he did each time he remembered the fiasco of the day before.

"Was my poor leadership your way of making sure nothing personal grows between Shiloh and me? Because if it was, it worked. There's no way she can see me as anything but ineffective now." Which should be fine with him, since he couldn't afford to get involved with a woman like Shiloh.

But it bothered him. A lot. Because that's how much he cared for her.

And he shouldn't. After all, she was the kind of woman who would likely drive him bonkers even before the wedding license ink had dried.

"Wedding license?" he said, disgusted with his train of thought. That was not an acceptable thing to think. Not for him. And not about a woman like Shiloh Morris. She already had him tied up in the weirdest knots. Imagine what she could do to him if he let himself get any more involved with her. He'd lose what little sanity he had left after this trip! And he'd probably wind up as lonely as he'd been in the midst of his large family.

He knew he should feel as if he'd just dodged a bullet. Instead he felt as if he'd missed something crucial, something special, something rare.

At least he'd kept the group from lynching Brigit. "That counts, doesn't it?" he asked his heavenly Father.

As he flipped through the Bible for his daily reading, a familiar and much-loved verse caught his attention. In Galatians 5, Paul had written: "When the Holy Spirit controls our lives, he will produce this kind of fruit in us: love, joy, peace, patience, kindness, goodness, faithfulness, gentleness, and self-control."

Mark chuckled. Clearly he had a ways to go yet, assistant college chaplain or not. Yesterday must have been one of those growing experiences God so often dunked him into. When he bobbed back up, he always knew a little more about himself than he'd known before going under. He wasn't sure exactly what he'd learned from the kids' skirmish, but he knew his Lord would soon reveal it, in his time.

After reading the Ephesians passage he'd originally been heading for, Mark rose and left his *casita,* seeking breakfast. What he found caused him more concern than his grumbling stomach.

A crowd of locals, a sampling of the rain forest's walking wounded, blocked the entrance to the dining room. A little girl sneezed and swiped her nose on her forearm. The mother, in the tradition of mothers everywhere, scolded her daughter, despite the child's flushed cheeks and subsequent coughs.

Irritation bubbled up. What was Shiloh thinking? She'd come to

Venezuela on vacation, clearly with weighty matters on her mind. Then, due to unfortunate circumstances, she'd been called to doctor the cook *and* replace her in the kitchen. Time after time, his own crew had imposed on her for food and medical help. Now it seemed many in the area had heard of the American nurse at the hotel, the nurse unable to turn anyone away.

With determination, Mark made his way through those waiting for Shiloh. Once inside, he caught sight of the makeshift cook zipping by, a harried expression on her face as she tried to balance food preparation with medical care. Shiloh's usually sleek hair looked tousled, and she sported smudges under her eyes. She paused, obviously thinking no one was watching, and pressed both fists into the small of her back. A moment later, she straightened, then let out a troubling sigh.

Anger grabbing hold of him, Mark hurried up to her and impulsively grabbed her arm. "Just who do you think you are? Florence Nightingale? Clara Barton? I don't think even they forced themselves to say yes to everyone and everything until they collapsed! It sure looks as if you're heading down that homestretch."

Shiloh's brown eyes narrowed, a hot light in their depths. Her lips tightened, white edging the usual coral.

Mark dropped her arm as if he'd grabbed one of her kitchen skillets with this morning's sausages still sizzling on the iron. He'd angered her. Well, too bad. He was right, and she was dead wrong.

She fisted her hands on her hips. "What, Reverend Walker, gives you the right to manhandle and tear into me like a blood-scenting piranha? I'm an adult, and I can certainly decide what I will and will not do."

"Yes, but you don't owe the world the kind of martyrdom you subject yourself to."

An ironic smile tipped Shiloh's lips. "Hmm . . . this from the man who's run for my help more than once. Inconsistent, wouldn't you say?"

Mark's cheeks burned. "Ah . . . maybe. But we're not talking about me. *I* haven't taken on every burden someone drops in my vicinity."

"Hmmmmm," she said again, this time speculation drawing out the sound and making her eyes glitter. "Let me get this straight. You're saying I've picked up too many of those burdens."

"Yes."

"And you believe I'm running myself ragged."

"Sounds about right."

"Plus you think I'm on some kind of martyr kick."

"Well, not exactly—"

"But you still come running for my help each time you need it."

Mark reddened again. "Yes, but—"

"And I've helped you and the kids."

He nodded, remembering the value of discretion when it came to valor.

Her brown eyes became mere slits. "Then you have to admit I've taken on some of *your* responsibilities."

"What?" he yelped, sounding, even to himself, like a dog with a tromped-on paw.

"Well, your kids need meals, right?" Shiloh asked, then stared at his charges, clearly warning him against a loud argument in their presence.

Deciding he was better off saying as little as possible, he offered a low, succinct, "Of course."

"And they're your responsibility. Right again?"

Wondering if stapling his lips shut would be better yet, Mark nodded once.

"Then why aren't you in the kitchen making their meals? Or at the very least, sharing the burden of feeding them with me?"

Mark couldn't think of a thing to say as he remembered his reason for avoiding the kitchen—to avoid her. But he couldn't have voiced his thoughts anyway, since Shiloh charged straight ahead.

"What about first-aid supplies? I can't believe you got on a plane with a group of students without knowing the most basic things."

"Now listen here. I have a first-aid kit back in my *casita.* I take it to the site each day, and I use it when I need to. Quentin's leg and Sandy's infection needed a lot more treatment than the most sophisticated first-aid kit could provide, and you know it. You're a trained medical professional with a miniature traveling hospital. That's what those kids needed. But all these others?" He waved toward the door. "Why do you rush to do everything that needs doing? Why can't someone else take over? Why can't these folks wait for the doctor to get back? Why must you always put everyone else first?"

Once again that narrow-eyed glint sliced right through him, leaving him feeling unusually vulnerable. "So what you want," Shiloh stated, "is for me to cook for you and yours, treat you and yours. Only then, in your mind, would I have enough time for . . . who? Me? Is that *really* what you're getting at *Pastor* Mark? A tad selfish, wouldn't you say?"

For a minute, Mark felt sucker-punched. Then he shook his head, a coil of unease releasing somewhere in his midsection. "No. It's just that some Christians tend to spread themselves too thin. They say yes to every good cause, then wind up shortchanging other priorities. And yes, *you* must be a priority for yourself. Your body is the temple of the Holy Spirit, and you're to care for it with respect. That aching back and the shadows under your eyes don't show much respect for your own needs. I know where it's leading. Your health will vanish if you keep on the way you're going."

She had the audacity to laugh. At him! Right out loud. Everyone in the dining room turned toward them, curiosity shining from each face.

"What's so funny?" Mark demanded to know. "My concern for your well-being is hardly the stuff of comedy."

"Just think about it, Mark. You sound pompous, and you're totally out of line. *You're* lecturing *me* on matters of health. Last time I checked, a chaplain didn't need an RN or MD after his name to practice his calling."

He winced. His occasional lack of tact had leaped up and bitten him again—and in front of this intelligent, attractive woman he couldn't seem to stay away from, who was beginning to matter too much.

"I was being neither selfish nor presumptuous," Mark began. "Just think about what I said. You have a real problem saying no—especially when it's in your best interest to do so. You're just like my—"

He clamped his mouth shut. Better not go there. In fact, it was best for him to leave Shiloh to her tasks and go eat the food she'd cooked for him and his students.

He *had* intended to ask her to continue cooking back when she'd ordered Rosita to stay away from her job for a while. But Shiloh had jumped in, relieving him of the need to persuade her.

Discomforted, he wondered if he deserved her accusations. This looked like a good time to seek God on the issue. And it was past time to deal with his feelings of neglect every time he thought of his parents.

Shiloh waited, clearly expecting him to complete his thought. But when he didn't, she stepped forward as if she wanted to say something more. Then she paused, looked around the dining room, and began to move toward the kitchen. But her steps were hesitant, unlike her usual confident stride. She'd been tired before he'd laid into her; now she looked tired *and* shaken.

Dear God, he prayed. *I've added to her burdens and blasted her for the generosity of spirit that makes her such an asset and so admirable. So intriguing. So attractive. So important. To me.*

Mark left without eating. His stomach had gone too queasy to even consider food.

Although Shiloh's first instinct after cleaning up breakfast was to see to the people who'd come to her for medical help, Mark's hurtful words had made her stop and think. She decided to detour past Mr. Rodríguez's office on the way to her *casita.* She found the portly hotel manager behind his desk, a frown on his prominent brow, a sheaf of papers in his right hand.

"May I have a moment of your time?" she asked.

Shoving the papers as far away as he could on the desktop, he nodded. "Sure, sure. *Siéntese, por favor,"* he added, pointing to the black wooden chair across from him.

As Shiloh sat, exhaustion washed over her. Maybe there was some truth to what Mark had said. But this wasn't the time to think about it. *Later,* she promised herself.

To Mr. Rodríguez she said, "I have a problem."

He blanched. "In the keetchen?"

"No. With your neighbors," she answered, pointing out the open window.

He spun around on his swivel chair, which squawked loud enough to rival a howler monkey, then got up and stuck his head outside. A stream of race-car-rapid Spanish followed, none of which Shiloh could decipher.

"I see," he said, collapsing into his chair. "They're seeck, and *la Doctora Escobar* is gone for two or three more days." A downtrodden look appeared on his features. "I no know about medicine. No one else does, too. Meess Morreess, could you maybe help—"

She held her hand out to stop the upcoming lobbying. "Fine. I'll see them, but lunch will be late today. I just hope nobody else gets sick tomorrow. I need a break."

"Bien, bien," he said with obvious satisfaction. "No more seeck peeple tomorrow. And you break then."

Shiloh nodded, not even considering his words as any kind of promise—which he couldn't reasonably make. But after the argument with Mark she felt as if all her energy, her usual strength, had abandoned her. Just when she needed it most.

She'd hardly had a minute to herself since she'd arrived. Too little time to think back on her cancelled wedding. Had she been this busy back home, too? Could Carrie have been right? Had her busyness led to all the disappointment and pain of her failed engagement?

She couldn't help remembering the family reunion a few weeks ago. She hadn't wanted to go, knowing how awkward it would be with all her relatives mincing around the "tragedy." But she hadn't known how to tell Grandma Zoe that she wouldn't be there.

As she'd feared, halfway through her hot dog, Amy, her cousin, had asked the absolute worst question of all: "Do you think you can patch things up with Reg now that some time has gone by?"

That had been enough to send Shiloh fleeing for her car. But things had gotten worse. As she'd rounded Grandpa Matt's barn, she'd heard Uncle Bert's booming voice. "So, Steven. How much did Shiloh's wedding—ah, nonwedding—set you and Rachel back? I know a bunch of those deposits, like for the hall, the flowers, the food, aren't usually refundable. Will you need help this winter?"

The pain had made Shiloh gasp. Mom and Dad had insisted on paying for the reception and the flowers, even though they were still trying to recover from the recent drought. The farm had been hit hard.

Her troubles had added to theirs.

Could Mark be right and not just preposterous, pompous, and presumptuous? Selfish? Overbearing?

More importantly, could he really be concerned about *her?*

After Shiloh saw to her line of patients, none of whose ailments were serious, she served a hastily prepared lunch of fruit salad and sandwiches, demolishing her supply of fresh rolls. A new batch wasn't due to arrive until the doctor did on the next flight in. So the delicious *cachapas,* a slightly sweet, Venezuelan flatbread made of ground yellow corn, would just have to do for all of their upcoming menus.

She thought of adorable Elenita with her bad cold . . . of Raúl with his broken toe . . . of frail-with-years but sassy-with-life Tomás, whose grin told tales of pranks and antics despite the infected gash on the palm of his hand. She couldn't have withheld her help from those who needed it. Jesus had said, "When you did it to one of the least of these my brothers and sisters, you were doing it to me."

Just as she couldn't have said no to Mark and his kids. As she knew she wouldn't say no to them if they needed her again.

When the prep for supper was done, she headed for her *casita*. A cool shower and a nap sounded like the right prescription for this hurting nurse.

As she burrowed into the comfort of her bed, she thanked God for the merciful inspiration that led to the invention of the spring mattress.

Bang, bang, bang!

Shiloh bolted up from her pillows, shocked awake by the knocking on the door. The fact that the light knocking sounded deafening to her ears showed how tired she'd been, how deeply she'd crashed. Finally.

After zipping on her terry-cloth robe, she answered the door. To her surprise, Mark Walker stood before her, looking distinctly uncomfortable.

"Did you need something?" she asked.

"Yes—to apologize for my earlier outburst. You were right. I was out of line with my attack and my attempt to tell you how to manage your health. You're also right about my selfishness. Please forgive me."

Shiloh accepted his apology with a simple "Of course." But she had plenty to say on her part, especially after spending time with God under her shower.

"You weren't the only one in the wrong," she said. "I do overcommit, take on too much. I have to change. I just don't know where to start."

A smile brightened Mark's face as he held out an orchid plant still on a branch. "How about starting with a truce?"

Shiloh caught her breath, stunned by the beauty of the plant. Purple and violet petals unfurled with ripe elegance, the velvety softness of the flower exquisite, its frills and curves lush and feminine, rich and opulent. Here was her Georgia O'Keeffe moment, courtesy of Mark Walker. "Thank you. And a truce sounds good to me."

He wiped his forehead in exaggerated relief. "Whew! And just to show you I've repented of my selfishness, you and I are the new co-chefs. We should be able to get the work done in half the time."

An impish light went on in her eyes. "Ah, but can you cook?"

"As you told me two days ago," he said with a mischievous wink, "you'll have to see how you feel *after* you taste my cooking." Then he shuffled his feet. "I really would like you to come and meet the people we're helping. I know you need time to yourself, and the kitchen's a burden, but we'd love to have you join us when you get a chance. Besides, we're not too far from a spectacular view of Angel Fall. You can relax there."

Shiloh arched an eyebrow. "And you have no ulterior motive behind this invitation?"

Sincerity shone in his eyes. "None, other than wanting your company at the church site."

"Hmm, a woman has to seriously consider such an offer. After all, you still have a dozen kids out there. They haven't taken a vow of silence recently, have they?"

He laughed. "Unfortunately not."

"They're good kids, Mark. You were right about that. And I'd love to come out and see the progress you've made."

"Wonderful! If you'd meet us tomorrow afternoon after we're done with lunch, that would be great."

"Sounds good to me."

"Then it's a date."

As Mark jogged toward his *casita,* probably to wash off the grime of the day, Shiloh watched him, her jaw gaping.

A date? She wasn't ready for a date.

Lord? she asked. *What's this all about?*

God, however, kept his peace, leaving Shiloh with a distinct lack thereof.

CHAPTER SIX

FOR the next two days, Shiloh found herself drawn to the building site. She was glad Mark had invited her to come, since by watching him in action—and pitching in wherever she could—she'd come to know a great deal about him. She liked what she'd learned.

It was yet another thing to think about. Should she be so attracted to a man she'd only just met? And only a little over two short months after her engagement had ended?

No matter how often she asked God those questions, the answers still escaped her.

Mark was more than physically impressive. His genuine interest in and concern for those around him shone through his every action, his every word. All the kids were crazy about him and went out of their way to earn his praise, which he gave lavishly.

When the recovering Sandy drove in her first *straight* nail without smashing a digit, Mark made so much of the event that one would have thought the girl had defanged a puma single-handedly.

His rapport with the locals amazed Shiloh. At any given moment, he'd drop what he was working on, wrap an arm around the man he was speaking with, and join him in prayer. When any of the women came to visit or deliver a meal to their husbands, he'd hurry to help with the infants or toddlers who invariably accompanied them. He'd earned the genuine respect of all the locals.

Shiloh felt that same respect each time she remembered how he'd helped her cope with Quentin's hideous gash, how he'd helped the boy remain calm even though he'd said his every inner urge was to panic.

And Sandy . . . although Mark constantly had to rein in the girl's exuberance, he did it in such a gentle way that Sandy had become Mark's greatest cheerleader.

If Shiloh didn't yet qualify for the post.

Was it wrong for her to feel so much respect, admiration, and attraction for Mark so soon after Reg?

She mulled over the question as she again approached the construction site. Mark had invited her this Sunday morning to join the congregation of students and locals for the worship service. She'd spent Saturday anticipating the opportunity to praise God in their company. She couldn't help the excitement she felt when she thought of listening to Mark preach a sermon.

Then it had occurred to her that she might not understand a word he said. It was all going to be in Spanish. Why on earth had she agreed to join them? him?

Because she really liked him. She wanted to spend time with him, wanted to watch him in every situation he faced. She wanted to support his efforts to improve the lot of these fellow Christians, whose worthy goal was to have a house of worship of their own.

She liked Mark Walker so much she feared she could fall in love with him.

Then what? After all, she'd fallen in love with Reg.

Or had she?

Now that God had shown her a few unattractive things about herself and her current habits, Shiloh had the sneaking suspicion that she'd never really loved Reg. Not as she should have to consider marriage. They'd been initially attracted to each other, had a lot in common, and felt affection for each other, but it now seemed to her that they'd never truly *known* each other. They'd spent so little time together and had rushed into an engagement.

Had she given herself the time needed to know whether a future with Reg was right for her? Shiloh didn't think so now. Had she waited on God? It didn't seem she had, since she now suspected that her engagement had failed because she'd moved ahead toward marriage without knowing if this was God's time for her to love and to marry.

Shiloh's fingers went cold; her stomach tightened. How would she know if she loved Mark? Really and truly loved him? How would she know if *he* loved *her?* They'd known each other for less than a week. Most important, how would she know, deep inside the most secret places in her heart, that Mark was God's will for her? *If* he was?

She stepped into the clearing where the worshipers had gathered, and her breath snagged in her throat. Mark wore navy linen trousers, a brilliant white shirt, and a dark red silk tie. His brown hair had been tamed, and the waves flowed smoothly away from his chiseled features. Intelligent and compassionate eyes found hers the minute she stepped forward.

"We're waiting for only Brigit and Moony now." Mark smiled. The look in his eyes said it was meant for her. "Did you see them on your way here?"

Shiloh blinked. She'd been so wowed by his appearance that

she'd only caught some of his words. "Ah . . . no. I didn't see anyone. Do you want me to go back and check?"

Mark shook his head. He gave her an appreciative head-to-toe look. "You look wonderful, and I'd hate for the jungle to ruin your dress."

Shiloh flushed with pleasure. She'd chosen the simple cotton carefully, trying not to look as if she'd primped for him, but she had wanted to look good. In the last two days, they'd begun dating. And he'd invited her to picnic after the service at that spot he'd said offered a spectacular view of the fall. The tallest waterfall in the world. In a lush, tropical rain forest. The two of them, surrounded by flowers, serenaded by exotic birds, watching God's majestic creation rush down a rock-faced cliff with the kind of power man only wished he could generate.

She could hardly wait.

Suddenly the tromping and bickering that usually preceded Brigit and Moony cut into her anticipation. She glanced toward Mark. As usual, their discord etched a frown on his brow. She knew the kids' behavior troubled him, and he obviously hadn't yet found a way to change it. *Lord, if there's anything I can do to help him, show me, please.*

As they came closer, Moony exclaimed, "Hey! Get a load of that!"

"What?"

"That spiky-looking plant. It's a bromide. I read about them in one of my books last night."

Brigit laughed loud and hearty.

Shiloh fought her own chuckle. A bromide? Last time she checked, *bromide* was an antiquated way of referring to the medicinal form of *bromine*.

In between chuckles, Brigit said, "You're not as smart as you think, Moonpath Reilly. And maybe we need to give *you* a good dose of my great-granny's bromide. She took it to sleep."

Shiloh glanced at Mark, whose green eyes mirrored his mirth.

Moony's words came closer. "No way, Brigit. Bromides are plants. The pineapple's one of them."

Brigit snorted. "No way, Moony. Pineapples are *bromeliads.*"

"Bromides, bromeliads. Same difference. They're special kinds of plants. Some of them grow on the trunks of others. You know, they're . . . epithets!"

No matter how hard Shiloh and Mark tried, both lost their battle against laughter. As they roared, together with the rest of the students, Brigit and Moony finally broke through the cover of vegetation that blocked the path. Brigit wiped tears—the laughing kind—from her eyes. "Epiphytes, Moony. Get it right, will ya?"

"What makes you think you know so much, Martha-the-Perfect-Stewart?"

"I worked part-time at a nursery, Mr. Greenpeace Wanna-be—"

"Welcome," said Mark, his voice strained at the resumption of sniper warfare. "We were waiting for you to begin our Sunday service. If you would care to join us, I believe everyone else is ready."

Brigit and Moony scooted onto a pair of scarred wooden chairs, chastened expressions on their young faces.

Mark returned to his makeshift pulpit and nodded to Kirk, who began strumming his guitar. Within a minute, voices soared to the heavens, praising almighty God.

Later, when Mark took up his Bible, Shiloh noticed it looked as worn as her own.

"Good morning, Doc Shiloh," whispered Quentin as he dragged

his chair closer to hers. "Pastor Mark asked me to translate, since you don't speak Spanish."

Mark's thoughtfulness—and Quentin's willingness—brought a warm glow to her heart. "This is very nice of you. I appreciate it."

"I appreciate my leg. So we're both happy."

Shiloh reached her hand out to the boy, and he clasped her fingers. She knew she'd made a friend for life by doing nothing more than what the Lord had equipped her to do.

"Ahem!" At the sound, both swung their attention to the pulpit. "I trust I can begin today's sermon?"

And Quentin translated.

"I'd prepared a specific passage," Mark began, "complete with examples to illustrate the lesson. But something has come up since, so I'm throwing out this man's plan." He dropped his notes to the ground. "I'm following our Father's leading instead.

"Turn to 1 John, chapter 4, verses 11 and 12. This is a very familiar passage, often ignored for that very reason. But I want us to examine it as if this were our first time reading it.

"'Dear friends, since God loved us that much, we surely ought to love each other. No one has ever seen God. But if we love each other, God lives in us, and his love has been brought to full expression through us.'"

He set down the Bible, then looked at his flock. "How is this love to be manifested? With pure emotion? With grand actions? I don't think so. I think God wants his children to recognize that, since he created all of us, every one has the potential of accepting his Son. *That* is what we should see in others, and what should determine how we treat them.

"What about our love for fellow Christians? In the preceding chapter, John wrote, 'Anyone who hates another Christian is really a murderer at heart.'

"Does that mean the kind of hate that leads to war? to murder?"

Not a sound breached a mouth—except Quentin's whispered translation.

"I'd like to tell you what I think," Mark continued. "I think that God sees the petty jabs we call jokes—which really aren't, if you think about it—as evidence of hate, lack of love. I think the competitiveness we indulge in is a form of hate. I think silly arguments, constant bickering, and faultfinding are all variants of hate. They are meant to demean another child of God, not to love him or her as God calls us to love. In other words, it's hate in God's eyes. And his Word calls *that* murder in the heart.

"I invite you to examine your hearts this morning. Repent and confess your sins. Ask God's forgiveness, then that of your victim. In closing, let's sing 'They Shall Know We Are Christians by Our Love.' "

"Wow," mouthed Quentin as he stood to sing. "We're up a creek."

Shiloh hadn't taken her eyes off Mark. His words had been powerful, pointed, yet undergirded by faith and his love for the kids. He hadn't scolded or reprimanded them; he'd used the Word of God to make his case, and he'd presented it eloquently. He'd encouraged them to examine their own actions, words, and deeds.

She could easily come to love this man—and she had a date with him for a picnic lunch at quite possibly the most romantic spot on earth.

Is Mark why you brought me here, Lord?

A short time after the subdued students trudged back to the hotel, Mark took Shiloh's elbow, silently leading her away from the construction site.

After his impassioned sermon, she didn't know what to say. She was too busy thinking about her own actions. After a while, Mark's hand slipped from her elbow to catch her fingers, and they continued on their way, hand in hand.

Then Mark disturbed the quiet by blurting out, "I was too harsh, wasn't I? The kids walked away like puppies who'd just met the end of a rolled-up newspaper."

Shiloh shook her head. "You weren't too harsh. I've noticed their attitudes. Even when one of them was hurt or sick, they still found reason to pick on each other, as if it were a sport. It bothered me."

"It drove me right up the wall! I had to do something."

"And you did it very well. I was moved to examine myself, to question my so-called jokes, to consider the motives behind my words. Even without the full scrutiny I intend to put myself through, I know I need to ask some people for forgiveness."

"Me, too. I just hope I haven't turned these guys against me. I can't afford it."

"You haven't. They respect you too much."

Mark turned his gaze from the path to her face. Shiloh wondered what he saw there.

"How about you?" he finally asked.

"Me?" she squeaked. How was she supposed to answer *that?* Should she give him a polite evasion? Or should she go with complete honesty? A nudge in her heart urged her to do the latter. "I admire you a great deal, Mark. You're a man of conviction, and your actions show it."

He stopped. Setting the basket he'd packed on the ground, he faced Shiloh. "We're here," he murmured, never taking his eyes from hers, placing gentle hands on her shoulders.

As much as Shiloh wanted to see the falls, right now that spectacular view held less appeal for her than the man before her.

The man she *knew* was about to kiss her. The man she wanted to kiss.

As Mark drew her closer, she tilted her face upward. His lips came down on hers, warm and tender.

Infinitely moving.

Happiness surged through Shiloh. When the kiss ended, she felt disappointment at the loss of that caring touch.

But the light in Mark's eyes promised more at some future time. For the moment, he pointed toward the waterfall, keeping his arm around her. "Like it?" he asked.

As her emotions bubbled inside her, Shiloh drank in the resplendent vision. The water rushed down the rock-faced mountain, frothing as it fell, churning when it hit the river surface, misting into rainbows on its way down. Along the cliff, the unmistakable emerald of the Amazonian rain forest framed the stark beauty of the falls, while puffs of cloud floated among the trees. The song of the water both invigorated and humbled Shiloh.

"*Like* is too wimpy a word," she said softly. "This is more like walking in God's footsteps to witness his work firsthand."

Mark squeezed her waist. "I felt exactly like that the first time I saw it."

"Is this where you come when you need a break from the kids or your work?"

He nodded. "And when I need to pray or think. I've come here for a nap or to read awhile. It soothes me, even though the sound of the falling water rushes excitement right through me."

"I'm so glad I came on my honeymoon after all."

Mark pulled away. "Your WHAT?"

"Oops. I didn't mean to say that." A blush seared Shiloh's cheeks. "But it's true. This is my honeymoon. Or it was supposed to be. And since I needed time away, I decided to take it anyway."

Disgust flared on Mark's face, and Shiloh suddenly realized what he thought. She chuckled.

He frowned more ominously. "There's nothing funny about this. You agreed to date me when all along you're—"

"Single, Mark. My fiancé called everything off a couple of months before the wedding. I'm on a *single's* honeymoon."

His eyes narrowed as he studied her. "Are you sure about that?"

His doubt bothered her, but she could understand why he'd be troubled. "I haven't lied to you. I wouldn't. I—I like you too much."

"But you'd lie if you didn't like me?"

Shiloh rolled her eyes. "Of course not! I don't lie. Period. It's a stupid thing to do, ruins friendships, makes everyone miserable. Why would I want to do that? I *am* a Christian, you know."

He grinned. "I know. But your words shook me up. I didn't expect to meet someone here, especially not someone like you, but here we are."

It was Shiloh's turn to study him. "What do you mean, someone like me?"

Shiloh watched as Mark began the shuffling dance he did whenever he felt uncomfortable. It was amazing how well she'd come to read this man in such a short time! Imagine how much more she'd learn if they continued to date, perhaps ma—NO! None of that.

"Well," he started, drawing out the word, "I didn't mean it to come out like that."

"How *did* you mean it to come out? What did you mean?"

"Well, you're not what I expected. I mean, I never thought I'd be interested in a woman like you."

Shiloh's temper, usually well banked, began to boil. "You said it again. Exactly *what* do you mean?"

Mark's rough fingers rumpled his brown waves of hair and his green eyes darted from plant, to path, to falls—everywhere but to her.

"I'm waiting," she prodded.

"You're . . . a lot like my parents."

Shiloh's jaw gaped.

"Yes. The three of you suffer from the worst cases of yes-itis I've ever seen."

"So we're back to the you-take-on-too-much bit again."

He nodded, keeping—wisely—silent.

"Why do you bring that up again?" she queried, giving him points for his silence.

"Because you never say no. Mom and Dad did the same, and as a result, they were never there when we needed them."

Mark turned his back to Shiloh and continued.

"Dad's a cardiac surgeon. He's always been at the mercy of the phone. I understand that, but it left a void at home. Then Mom, as the good doctor's wife, hasn't met the worthy cause she can't embrace. Everyone knows that Miriam Walker drops whatever she's doing to help those in need. Even if it means letting down her kids, missing important moments, not being there when disappointment hits. Those calls have always come first with them. It's hard to . . . care for someone like that."

The old anger and pain in Mark's voice caused Shiloh's irritation to vanish. She placed a hand on his shoulder. "I'm sorry," she whispered.

"Don't get me wrong," he said. "I'm not interested in a mother. I have one already. I'm interested in you as a woman, a friend, a companion, and after that kiss, as a whole lot more than a friend, too."

Shiloh smiled. He was honest, she had to give him that. "It seems we're both interested in the same thing."

He turned around. "You're not mad?"

"No. But that doesn't mean you're right. About me, that is. I don't neglect people—"

But you didn't nurture your relationship with Reg, and it died.

The uncomfortable thought cut off Shiloh's words. Self-realization hit hard. She hadn't given enough importance to her engagement. Would she have done the same to her marriage? Surely she wouldn't do so again in the future. Would she?

"Are you all right?" Mark asked, as he cupped her jaw in his hand.

She nodded, then shook her head. Finally, she shrugged. "I will be, I guess. It seems I still have a lot of thinking to do."

"About . . . ?"

"My failed engagement, me . . . and now, you."

"We're in the same boat, then. I have a lot of thinking to do about my parents, me . . . and you, too."

Wrapping her arms around her middle, Shiloh stepped away and gazed back toward the waterfall. "I want to be sure."

With the deliberation that refused to accept the distance she'd imposed between them, Mark moved closer and put his arm around her. "Me too."

The warmth felt good at her side. *Mark* felt good at her side.

Each deep in thought, together they watched the endless ribbon of water crash to its destination. The peaceful scene lent itself to contemplation, especially in the company of someone who cared.

Sometime later Mark tapped Shiloh's shoulder. "How about some food?"

"Won't turn it down."

Mark walked to where he'd left the basket. "If you'll wait a moment, I'll spread our tablecloth and you can sit."

Shiloh peered into the basket, but couldn't identify the contents. "What's in here?"

"A tropical feast. Just for you."

Pleasure shimmered through her. He'd spent time planning their date. He'd shown her that she mattered to him, as he did to her.

He'd given their budding relationship priority, despite his many responsibilities. She could learn to do the same. *Couldn't I, Lord? With your help?*

And maybe Mark's.

Shiloh felt as if someone had lit a bulb in her heart. She smiled at the man who'd done it. "And for you."

CHAPTER SEVEN

As Mark and Shiloh packed up the remains of their tropical picnic, the sound of a scuffle put an end to their serene moment.

"What on earth?" Shiloh asked.

"I don't know, but I don't like what I'm hearing." Mark grabbed the basket's handle and extended his other hand to Shiloh.

She took it and hurried to keep up. To her surprise, instead of heading for the hotel, as she'd expected him to do, he took off toward the disturbance.

They arrived at the source quickly. A small-scale but violent riot had broken out. Among the combatants, Shiloh saw men and women she'd come to know from her time at the new church site. A group of strangers pitched battle against them, the insults and cries of pain crashing in a cacophony of horror.

Blood stained the clothes of some, while faces bore evidence of scratching. Rocks flew from upraised hands, and children at the edges of the fray cried for their mothers. A rocky missile found its mark on the head of a tiny moppet whose fist was stuffed in her mouth. A wail burst from her plump lips.

Shiloh shook off Mark's grasp and ran to the little girl. She wished she had her medical supplies.

"What are you doing?" Mark roared.

"What do you think I'm doing?"

"Jumping to meet a need before thinking about it."

Ignoring Mark's words, she moved a hank of the child's black hair to get a better look at her injury. Her patient whimpered when Shiloh's gentle probing found blood.

Shiloh turned to Mark and was stunned to see him pulling apart two enraged men who were intent on doing each other harm. "And what do you think *you're* doing? Those two are going to mash you to a pulp!"

"I'm trying to stop them from killing each other."

"Well, do something quickly because this little girl's bleeding too much. I need my medicine case."

"Then get out of here! Take her with you. Just don't take on more than you can handle."

As Shiloh's temper began to rise, someone touched her elbow.

"Señorita, por favor."

Shiloh turned and saw a woman with what looked like a vicious bite on her forearm. Oh, dear. If she didn't clean that up, the infection from the human bite could endanger the woman's life.

Then a guttural howl at her right made her turn that way. A knife! Someone had sliced into a young man's shoulder and then had run away. *Dear God, I can't handle all this. Help us, please.*

She stood and ran to the youth. "Come with me," she said, leading him toward her two other patients.

Although he grimaced with every step and didn't understand a word she said, he seemed willing to follow.

"Shiloh, you can't take care of everyone!" Mark yelled. "Get out of here before you can't help anyone, including yourself."

"I can't just leave these people like this! They're hurt. They need me—"

Then a rock flew toward her, and a piercing pain shot through her head. Everything went black. Her knees gave way. "Mark . . ."

Before she lost consciousness, she heard a woman bark, *"¿Qué está pasando aquí?"* followed by a masculine, "Shiloh? *Shiloh?* Dear God, help her!"

From a short distance away, Mark watched in helpless horror as Shiloh lay on the ground, a large gash on her forehead drenching her hair with blood. Dr. Susana Escobar, a boxy woman with a no-nonsense look, knelt beside her, taking her pulse, lifting her eyelids, examining the wound.

"Doctora Escobar!" called Armando, Mark's construction foreman. *"La senõrita . . ."* Armando's words died off as he indicated where the rumble no longer raged. The shamed fighters had approached and now stared at the unconscious woman who'd been caught in their discord.

His legs suddenly finding their strength, Mark ran up to the woman. "Susana! Praise God, you're back. I've missed you, and we really need you now. The injured lady is my . . . friend. Please help her."

The godly woman he'd come to like and respect over the years gave him a sharp look. *"Claro.* Of course, I'll help her, Mark. But I have to radio from home for the airplane to take her to the hospital in *Ciudad Bolívar.* I don't have the equipment to treat head injuries."

Mark's face blanched. "Is it . . . serious?"

"All head injuries are, but I can't tell how serious here in the jungle. She needs more help than I can give."

"Do it, then. Please."

After another penetrating stare, Susana said, "Since you're so worried about her, go to the hospital with her. I'll take over your *muchachos*. It's only fair, since you've had to watch them alone while I was gone."

With relief, Mark watched his co-chaperone leave to go back toward her combined home and doctor's office. Her patients followed her, the child carried by her worried father. As Mark held Shiloh's hand, a church member told him the tale behind the riot.

The family who had donated the land for the church was divided over the decision. Tensions had risen as the building took form. Trouble had broken out. The opponents of the project had begun to dismantle what the proponents had built. As church members tried to protect their future house of worship, tempers flared. Someone threw a punch. Then a rock. Finally the disaster that led to Shiloh's injury had erupted.

As Mark studied Shiloh's pale features and shallow breathing, his own anger was roused. Fighting over a house of God. Hurting others for the right to use a piece of land to worship the Father.

And Mark hadn't been able to speak God's peace. He hadn't been able to help the two groups come to an understanding. He'd been so busy worrying over Shiloh's resemblance to his parents that he'd failed to pay sufficient attention to what was brewing among his temporary flock.

So Shiloh got hurt.

But she bore her own bundle of guilt in the matter. She should have listened to him. Her yes-itis had led her into trouble again. And if that plane didn't arrive in time, he feared her "yes" this time might lead to disaster.

Mark couldn't stand to think that he'd found Shiloh, only to lose her.

"Señor Walker?" asked the man in green scrubs.

"Yes," Mark answered, standing.

"La Señorita Morris needs more tests. I'm afraid it might be a subdural hematoma. That's bleeding inside the skull. It can cause pressure on the brain."

"That's bad, isn't it?"

"It's not good, no."

"Will she . . . ?" Mark couldn't bring himself to finish his question.

"I don't know. I hope she'll recover, but it's too soon to tell. That's why I have to run the tests. I need a signature from you, since you accompanied her."

"And she needs the tests to recover?"

"I think so."

"Then bring the papers," Mark said, catching his breath.

"Good. I'll send a nurse out for your signature."

Mark watched the man return to the Emergency Room, recognizing the irony in the situation. Shiloh, who worked in an ER, now depended on the skills of those who worked in another one.

He dropped back into his chair to resume praying. A short time later a harried-looking young woman darted out the same doors the doctor had used and thrust a bunch of papers at him. "Mr. Walker?"

"Yes, yes," he said impatiently, signing as fast as he could.

The loudspeaker crackled overhead. "Marielena Rojas.

Marielena Rojas. *A la Sala de Emergencias, por favor!"* Turning on her heel, the young nurse ran toward the ER, her shoulder thudding against the heavy metal door. The last Mark saw of her, she was rubbing the tender spot, never slowing her pace.

She'd left Shiloh's crucial papers behind.

Horrified, Mark scribbled his name on the last one and hurried to the waiting room receptionist. "The nurse didn't take these. They're very important. Shiloh is seriously injured and these give the doctors permission to care for her. But the nurse ran off without these papers. How could she do that? Shiloh's condition is desperate, her treatment of utmost importance. She needs immediate attention—"

"Marielena was called to an incoming heart attack, sir," the woman said in a calm, understanding voice. "Dr. Moreno spoke with you already, and you gave him permission. The papers are only for our records. Your *compañera* is in good hands, receiving the care she needs."

With those words from the receptionist, Mark lost the last of his steam. Once again he'd let old memories of his parents' neglect rob him of his common sense. Embarrassed, he at last realized the truth. The nurse had to see to a patient who could die if she didn't run. And the doctor had set the wheels in motion for Shiloh's treatment. Marielena *hadn't* abandoned Shiloh for another cause, another project. She'd run to save another life.

As his father did daily. As Shiloh did, too. As she'd done to save Quentin's leg, relieve Sandy's pain, treat the cook's eyes. In the same way she'd run to help the child who'd been struck by the stone her uncle threw. To treat the woman who'd been bitten by a cousin and the man whose brother had stabbed his shoulder.

As he'd fought for peace when he'd come upon a fight.

At last Mark recognized his pettiness. He'd wanted Shiloh's attention from the moment he met her on the flight to Caracas. But she'd turned to a book, putting an end to their first conversation.

To be perfectly honest, *she* hadn't kept them from speaking during the long flight. His students had surrounded him, and he'd never found the opportunity to talk with her again.

He'd had to turn to another matter that time.

Then at the hotel, he'd been thrilled to find her there—until she'd been called to help.

Once again, he'd felt pushed aside, unimportant. He'd always longed to come first for someone, to not be shuffled into a lesser position for the sake of something—anything—else. An immature need, he conceded, but one that had always gone unmet.

He remembered six-year-old Marky, whose mom was the only one who hadn't made it to the first-grade play; she'd been running a soup kitchen that day. He remembered twelve-year-old Mark, who'd missed his father as he was named Little League MVP; Dr. Walker had been chairing a Cardiac Department meeting at the hospital. And he'd never forget twenty-one-year-old Mark Walker, whose college graduation dinner with family and friends was cut short when Mom received a call to help flood victims in the next county. Dad had gone, too, just in case.

His parents loved him; they loved all six of their children. But they'd been too busy to give Mark the attention he desperately needed. He'd never felt important to them. As the last of six kids, he'd always felt he brought up the rear in their list of priorities. And although the elder Walkers took on each good cause because they truly loved people—as Shiloh did—and felt called by

God to help those less fortunate, their children had become unfortunates, too.

Mark's need to come first to someone still battled with the knowledge that his parents had done God's work when they'd left him alone.

Lord, help me. I'm a grown man, a chaplain. You've called me to care for others, too. Why do I still struggle with the need to be first?

As he clasped his hands and prayed, a verse memorized in childhood came to him. Jesus, in speaking with his disciples, had said, *"Many who seem to be important now will be the least important then, and those who are considered least here will be the greatest then."*

Then he knew. Tears welled in his eyes. In his wise and wonderful way, the heavenly Father was saying that while Mark might not come first with his earthly parents, during his earthly life, when he reached heaven, he'd hold a position of importance in his heavenly Father's kingdom. A position that became his when Jesus died on a cross for him.

O Lord, forgive me. I've known the truth of faith all my life, but even though you held it out to me, I never fully claimed it. Until now.

As Mark waited for a very special woman to pull through, he felt that void he'd always known close and fill with God's healing love. The love of a Father who gave his child's need of salvation the greatest importance. The God who had never shuffled him aside.

Forgive me, Father, for my blindness, for not seeing where I truly stood in your eyes, he prayed, the knot in his throat preventing any sound. As he prayed, Mark confessed his resentment toward his parents—and his need to forgive them. For his own sake.

And for his future.

If he and Shiloh were to have one.

Shiloh was sure someone had set loose a band of busy cobblers inside her head when she began to wake up. She'd never had a worse headache in her life.

The air smelled funny—like an ER. So what was she doing napping on the job?

Then she remembered. She was supposed to be in the rain forest on her honeymoon, her single's honeymoon. With Mark . . . or had it all been a weird dream?

She pried open one eye and wished she hadn't. Light stabbed into her, hurting even worse, if possible, than the nails in her skull. If it weren't too absurd for words, she'd swear she had a whopper concussion.

But at work?

When she was supposed to be picnicking with Mark Walker at Angel Fall?

OK. So maybe Carrie was right. Maybe she *was* nuts. Nothing made sense.

Shiloh tried to open her eyes again, and again the light shot pain right through them. Her head continued to pound, and her middle didn't feel particularly trustworthy.

Since determination had always been one of her qualities, she put it to use. Little by little she managed to lift her eyelids enough to see that she was in a hospital, but not York Hospital. The green walls were of a bilious shade she hoped wouldn't gain popularity soon. Something tickled her forehead, and she lifted her hand to see what it was. To her surprise, she couldn't move her arm.

Craning her neck, she saw that she was restrained to keep her from dislodging the IV in her hand. Well, at least she hadn't forgotten what she'd learned back in nursing school. She *did* have a concussion, which explained why she felt so crummy.

But where was she? And how did she get hurt?

With a flash, she remembered. She remembered Mark's sermon, the picnic, and especially their kiss. But what she couldn't come up with was an explanation for her condition.

"What happened?" she whispered. Taking care not to jostle her head, Shiloh looked around the room. Utilitarian, and . . . well, green. Just not the beautiful green of the rain forest or the gorgeous green of Mark's eyes. Then she saw him in the corner of the room. His eyes were tightly shut, and his breathing was deep and even. She knew he'd feel lousy when he woke up since he'd scrunched his long, powerful frame into a regulation-issue hospital armchair. She should wake him up and tell him to go home. To the hotel. Wherever he was supposed to be. She was awake, and she was going to be fine . . . eventually.

That he'd stayed and put himself through the torture of sleeping like that spoke volumes. What he'd said by the falls must be true. He must care for her. A lot.

As she'd come to realize she cared for him.

How could it have happened so soon after the debacle with Reg?

She didn't know. What she did know was that God had brought her to Venezuela, and here she'd found a man with whom she wanted to build a life. A man who'd never let her cheat their relationship by letting it become less important than the tyranny of the urgent. A man she found attractive, intriguing, challenging. A man with whom she could share her faith and the rest of her life.

How had it happened? She didn't know. God had brought it to

pass. She had no intention of questioning his judgment, much less letting this opportunity pass her by.

She also knew now that Carrie—and Mark—had been right. She'd been driving herself too hard these last few years. She was only one nurse, and no matter how many hours she worked, she couldn't personally care for everyone who needed attention.

She needed to pay attention to herself, to her personal life, and especially to her relationship with the Father. Thinking back, Shiloh could see where her Lord had tried to catch her attention—when her desire to spend time with Reg had begun to wane, when Reg's canceling dates had meant only the chance to take on another shift at work—to warn her of the danger that lay ahead. But she'd spent so little time sitting still and listening to God's leading that she'd worked herself right into a mess.

Her heavenly Father, in his mercy, had worked it out in the end.

Or so she hoped.

Her honeymoon in the jungle was almost over. She and Mark would soon go their separate ways. What would happen then? Would they find and use well the time she now knew a relationship needed to grow as God intended?

Shiloh took a deep breath and pressed the nurses' call button. They should know she was awake. Suddenly, even though she felt horrible, she wanted to leave the hospital as soon as she could sign a release. She wanted to get back to her life—a life she was now going to treat with more care.

A life in which she hoped time with Mark featured prominently.

When the nurse ran into the room and straight to Shiloh's side, she asked in accented English, "How you feel?"

Shiloh twisted her lips wryly. "Terrible."

"Sí, sí. That good, very good. Here, I look in eyes."

Before Shiloh could brace herself, the nurse flashed a light into her right eye, then her left. What she saw must have satisfied her because she let Shiloh close her searing, tearing eyes.

Through the haze of pain, Shiloh heard rustling from Mark's corner. "Wha—?"

"I woke up."

"Praise God," he said, his voice coming closer to her side. She tried to look at him, but tears still blinded her. The pain was too great.

"Go back to your *casita,"* she urged him. "You're going to hurt everywhere after sleeping in that thing."

"Hush," he answered, covering her lips with his finger, making them tingle with the pleasant warmth. "I'm not leaving until you come with me. Susana Escobar—the absent doctor—returned a day earlier than I expected her, but just in God's good time. She's watching the kids."

"Then for her sake and yours, let's pray they spring me soon."

"Amen to that."

As the nurse left the room, the door closed partway, still allowing the shaft of light that had initially pierced Shiloh's eyes to enter the room. The shadows around the bed provided privacy.

"You and I have a lot of talking to do," Mark said.

Shiloh smiled, easier this time. "I was thinking the same thing before the nurse arrived."

He took her free hand in both of his. "Good things, you know. Deep things, important things."

She nodded. "You-and-me things."

"Exactly." He rubbed her hand tenderly. "How soon will you be leaving Venezuela?"

"What day is today?"

"Monday dawn."

"Tomorrow was supposed to have been the last day of my honey—"

"Your vacation, OK?"

"OK."

"You shouldn't travel right away, though, should you?"

"Not on that long a trip."

His feet shuffled beneath the bed. She smiled. "Out with it!"

"Um . . . would you . . . that is, is it possible for you to stay longer? I'd like to spend more vacation time with you. Besides, you shouldn't go back to work so soon."

Her smile widened. "It can be arranged. How much time would you like?"

"You want the truth?"

"Of course."

"All. Every bit of the rest of your life."

Shiloh gasped. Her eyes flew open. She ignored the throbbing in her head. "Are you saying what I think you're saying?"

"Yes."

"But it's so soon—"

"I'm only stating what I want. Then there's what you want, and most importantly, what God wants." He squeezed her hand. "I'm asking you for the time we need to discern the Father's will."

"How can I say no?"

"You can't."

"But I'm recovering from yes-itis."

"And I'm overcoming last-child-itis. We both have to work through these things, and I see no reason to do it alone when love will make our efforts easier."

"Hmm . . . love? I see a certain appeal in that."

"Love. I hoped and prayed you would."

Shiloh savored the vision of the future that Mark had just painted. She liked it. A lot.

"So," she said, "you say I'm no longer on my honeymoon."

"No way. You're on vacation, a summer vacation. Your honeymoon, Shiloh Morris, is yet to come. When the time is right before God."

EPILOGUE

ONE YEAR LATER . . .

One morning, on a deserted beach in the Bahamas, a couple lay on a blanket, water beading their skin and darkening their suits. As they treasured the moment, they remained oblivious to the seagulls soaring overhead. The sun kissed the sand with glitter, and the two vacationers soaked in the warmth, peace, and each other's company.

"I just thought of something," said the woman as she rubbed the emerald ring on her left hand.

"What's that?" asked the man, opening eyes that matched the emerald.

"Did you ever learn the story behind Moony's name?"

"Um-hm. His parents met in a commune once upon a time. They were following the moonpath—whatever *that* means."

"They don't anymore, do they?"

"Nah. They met the Lord along the way."

Silence returned.

"It's good to know there's been no more trouble at the Church of the Falls," the woman said some time later.

"Um-hm. Good we could help bring peace again. I'm glad we were able to stay a couple extra weeks."

"Amen."

Peace reigned between them, too.

After a couple more waves drenched the thirsty sand, she added, "And that the medicine pipeline to the missionaries is keeping them well supplied."

"Um-hm," he murmured. "I'll never forget how happy they were to see you bearing those first much-needed gifts after you got out of the hospital and could get back to your *casita*."

As the sun hit its zenith in the brilliant blue sky, the man asked, "So, what do you think about honeymoons now?"

She laughed. "Let's just say I'm glad the other was my summer vacation after all. Honeymoons—the married kind—are the only kind to take."

"Thank you, Nurse Walker."

"You're welcome, Pastor Mark."

A NOTE FROM THE AUTHOR

DEAR Reader,

Vacations are *grrrreat!* When Tyndale House mentioned tioned the plan for a *Dream Vacation* anthology, I immediately remembered a very special one our family took nearly fifteen years ago.

At the time, we had two sons—one four years old and the other eighteen months. For Christmas that year, we went to visit my parents, who for business reasons had returned home to Caracas. While there, my husband and I decided a trip to Angel Fall would be the perfect, unforgettable adventure—even for the boys!

We backpacked the younger one and hung tight to the older one, and flew in over the waterfall on a very tippy prop plane. To say I don't fly well is to greatly understate reality.

When we finally arrived at the motel, we found . . . the setting for "A Single's Honeymoon"! The cabins were wonderfully simple and rustic and isolated, the vegetation gorgeous in its intense coloring, the birds spectacular, the orchids breathtaking. We followed paths through the rain forest, rode the river in a native's dugout canoe (we have the pictures to prove it!), and gloried in our Lord's magnificent creation.

The memories of that family vacation remain particularly precious to us. None of us could ever forget the power and beauty of that waterfall—not even our then-eighteen-month-old son. He vividly remembers that and the toucan he befriended. (Picture that, will you? A diaper-clad toddler chatting with a wild toucan perched on the branch of a massive, white-flowered shrub.)

Only God could paint that picture. I hope he helped me bring a bit of his majesty into your life, too.

Blessings,
Ginny

ABOUT THE AUTHOR

A FORMER newspaper reporter, Ginny Aiken lives in south-central Pennsylvania with her husband and four sons. Born in Havana, Cuba, and raised in Valencia and Caracas, Venezuela, she discovered books early and wrote her first novel at age fifteen. (She burned it when she turned a "mature" sixteen!) That first effort was followed several years later by the winning entry in the Mid-America Romance Authors' Fiction from the Heartland contest for unpublished authors.

Ginny has certificates in French literature and culture from the University of Nancy, France, and a B.A. in Spanish and French literature from Allegheny College in Pennsylvania. Her first novel was published in 1993, and since then she has published numerous additional novels and novellas. One of her novels was a finalist for *Affaire de Coeur*'s Readers' Choice Award for Best American Historical of 1997, and her work has appeared on various best-seller lists. Ginny's novellas appear in the anthologies *With This Ring,*

A Victorian Christmas Quilt, A Bouquet of Love, and *Dream Vacation.* Watch for her new novel, *Magnolia,* coming this spring—the first in a series called Bellamy's Blossoms.

When she isn't busy with the duties of being a soccer mom, Ginny can be found reading, writing, enjoying classical music, and preparing for her next Bible study.

LOVE AFLOAT

by
Jeri Odell

You made all the delicate, inner parts of my
body and knit me together in my mother's womb.
Thank you for making me so wonderfully complex!
Your workmanship is marvelous—and how well
I know it. How precious are your thoughts about me,
O God! They are innumerable!
PSALM 139:13-14, 17

CHAPTER ONE

A CRUISE?" Calder Nevyn hoped he didn't sound as unappreciative as he felt. "You're sending me on a cruise?"

"Yes, Curly! Won't it be wonderful?" Katie, the wife of his boss and best friend, Rick, answered. Her brown eyes danced with excitement.

"Wonderful? I guess that's one way you could describe it." *Personally, I'd choose horrible.* He looked from Katie to Rick, trying to fake a smile. *What in the world are you two thinking? Cowboys and cruises don't mix.*

Walking over to where Curly sat, Rick stretched out his hand to shake Curly's. "This is our way—" Rick winked at his bride of several months—"of saying thanks for the five years of hard work and dedicated service here on the ranch. Also, I won't ever forget the time you invested in discipling me." Rick's voice cracked with emotion.

"You don't have to send me on a cruise for doing my job. Why don't you two take my place?" Curly begged.

"Too late," Katie said. "Everything's in your name."

"And you leave in three days, buddy," Rick added, as if that were some sort of perk.

"Three days?" Stunned, Curly thought, *How will I ever get out of this in only three days?* Aloud he only said, "I don't know about this. We've got those cows up—"

"Curly, I'll handle everything here. You go and enjoy yourself," Rick insisted.

"But—"

"No buts," Katie instructed.

"This gesture means the world to me," Curly said, shifting uncomfortably in his chair. "But I'm a ranch hand. Somehow a cowboy setting sail on one of those big fancy ships just don't seem right. It's like sending a cow to vacation in an aquarium. I don't even own a suit."

It took only one look into Katie's hurt eyes to wish he'd never said a word.

"This is something we really wanted to do for you, but if you don't want to go . . . ," she said sadly, shrugging.

There went his hope of getting out of this crazy mess. How could he disappoint them when it seemed so important? "No. I'll go. I'm just not sure which fork to use once I get there."

Katie laughed. "You'll have a great time. The ship is owned and operated by a Christian man, so there's no drinking, gambling, or half-naked dancing girls. He books top Christian entertainment and an excellent speaker for the nightly chapel service. Dress is casual—there's only one formal dinner the entire cruise, and that's optional. Best of all, you get to tour the Holy Land, walk where Jesus walked! It's a fifteen-day trip, and during that time you visit ten ports and five different countries—Turkey, Greece, Israel, Egypt, and Italy," she exclaimed, the sparkle back in her eyes and voice.

"Well, guess I'd better get packing." *I can do this—for them,* Curly thought, trying not to dread the trip too much. It might actually be interesting to see another part of the world, but he wasn't so sure about a ship full of strangers. He didn't make friends easily or mix well in crowds.

"My friend DeDe is going on this trip, too. That's how we found out about it. You remember her from the wedding, right?"

Yes, he definitely remembered Danika Sutherland—in fact, too well. "Does she know I'm coming?"

Katie blushed slightly. "Not yet, but I'll call and update her."

"Please tell her I don't expect to tag along with her the whole time. She's probably traveling with friends."

"No, she's traveling alone, and I'm sure she'd enjoy your company." Curly doubted that; he and Danika were in different leagues. "Here's all the information," Katie said, handing him a folder filled with papers. "And a list of what to pack."

"I don't know what to say. Thank you, but this really isn't necessary."

"It's our pleasure," Katie assured him. Both she and Rick gave him a hug as he left the big house to head for his little trailer nestled down the hill next to the barn. Thoughts of Danika invaded his mind.

He'd just helped a mare deliver a breech foal. He squatted next to the mama horse, tenderly stroking her neck and telling her what a great job she'd done. Then a sniffling sound caught his attention, and his eyes met beautiful blue ones. A blonde leaned on the gate, gentle tears rolling down her cheeks. As she'd smiled, something inside him responded for the first time in years.

"Hi, I'm Danika. I'm a friend of Katie's—her maid of honor actually. Anyway, she had to make some phone calls, so I'm taking a self-guided tour of the barn. I heard your voice and wow! I just witnessed my first birth." She brushed the wetness from her cheeks with manicured hands.

Then, in a southern drawl just above a whisper, she continued, "That was the most amazing thing I've ever seen. You were incredible. If you hadn't been here, would she have died?"

Incredible? No one had ever called him "incredible" before. "Possibly, but she might have made it on her own." He smiled at her and stood up. "I wonder how anyone can ever witness the miracle of birth and then question the fact that there's a God in heaven."

"You're a Christian?" she asked, her smile widening and her eyes changing to a bluer shade.

"Yes, you?"

"Absolutely! I'm sorry, but I didn't catch your name."

"Curly." Suddenly his childhood nickname sounded silly. "Ah, Calder Nevyn." He held out a birth-stained hand to shake hers, and they both broke into laughter.

"I think I'll pass on that handshake, Curly, but it's a pleasure to meet you. I've heard terrific things about you from Rick. You have his utmost admiration and respect."

Unused to hearing his own praises sung, Curly felt his face grow warm. "And he has mine."

"Well, I'll let you return to your work. I guess we'll see each other again. You are the best man, right?" At his nod, she continued, "So you'll have to put up with me at all the prewedding hoopla over the next few days, and then you'll have to walk me down the aisle. Think you can manage?" As her radiance lit up the barn, he was drawn to this cute, perky blonde like a horse to a sack of grain.

"Guess I'll manage, somehow," he said, grinning, his heart lighter than it had been in years.

Crazy as it seemed, he'd relived that scene, and all the others from his week in Danika's company, many times over the past four months, and he'd never forgotten how she looked at the wedding.

Unable to take his eyes off her, he'd spent the day mesmerized by her charm.

He'd sworn off women years ago, but now he wanted to renege on that self-made promise. The thought of spending countless hours in Danika's company again caused panic to rise within him. Maybe he'd miss the boat—and thus avoid this whole unnerving mess and those amazing blue eyes.

"Katie, how *could* you?" Danika said, her anger with Katie growing in spite of the fact that she usually avoided confrontation.

"DeDe, I know you're interested in Curly."

"How can you possibly think that? It's absurd!" Danika said, her tone clipped and short.

"I don't think it. I *know* it! I saw the way you looked at him the week you were here. You can't fool me. I know you too well."

"Apparently you don't know me at all because other than thinking Curly is a very nice guy—"

"DeDe, you talked about him nonstop. Curly did this. Curly said that. You and Curly are the only two people who are clueless about your feelings for one another."

"So you admit this is a matchmaking scheme?" Danika said, gripping the phone receiver more tightly.

"Only if you admit Curly intrigues you."

She couldn't admit that even to herself, let alone say it aloud. "Katie Laramie, the only thing I'm admitting is that you and Rick crossed a line here that shouldn't have been crossed. You have no right to meddle in my life or Curly's. He's a really great guy and very tender. What if he ends up getting hurt by your well-meaning plans?"

"He'll only be hurt if *you* choose to hurt him," Katie said ominously.

"Now it's my fault? I resent your interference in my life. I saved for two years to afford this cruise. How can you put me in this position? How can you expect me to baby-sit your livestock foreman? It's not fair, Katie. Not to me. Not to Curly."

After a moment of silence, Katie conceded. "I'm sorry, DeDe. You're right. I should have stayed out of it. It's just that I love you, and Rick loves Curly. We want you both to fall in love and be as happy as we are."

"Katie, I'm not free to fall in love, and you know that. I'll never be able to get married, at least not as long as my mother's alive. Why torture me with what I can't have? Don't you understand it's taken me *years* to be content with singleness? And yes, Curly intrigues me. He's a gentle cowboy with incredible inner strength. He's chivalrous and kind; the things dreams are made of—" Her voice broke, giving away her deep emotion.

"Even if I *were* free to marry—and I'm not—he lives in Arizona in a world of horses and cattle. I live in Tennessee in the world of gospel music and PR work. We don't have any history to bridge the gap like you and Rick did. You two had a lost love to build on. You also had Kasey, the daughter Rick knew nothing about until she was five years old. We have nothing. It's hopeless, and you're only kidding yourself if you think otherwise."

"You're right," Katie said solemnly. "Would you at least watch out for him? I know the thought of taking a cruise isn't exciting to Curly. You know how quiet he is."

"Yeah," Danika said resignedly. "OK, I'll watch out for him if you will promise *never* to play matchmaker in anyone's life again."

"I'd like to find Rick's sister—"

"Anyone's, Katie! Promise?"

"Oh, all right. If you promise to forgive Rick and me."

"Agreed. I'll talk to you when I get back, and I'll try to make sure Curly's not too miserable."

"Thanks. I love you, DeDe." With a click Katie disconnected.

Danika sighed and hung up the phone. *Oh, Curly, if you only knew how much I dread seeing you again. I guess it's a good thing you don't, since we have to get through the next two weeks.* But deep inside, a little part of her heart didn't dread seeing him at all. "Traitor," she said softly, laying her hand against her chest.

Danika spotted Curly across the airport at the gate where she'd catch her flight on Turkish Airlines to Istanbul. Katie obviously had managed to get him on the same flight. Danika stopped and watched him for a minute—the man who felt more at ease in a pen with a wild bull than in a crowded airport. He must have sensed her eyes upon him, for his wide-set brown ones found hers and he began to smile.

Danika moved toward him, feeling the chemistry she wanted to deny. Curly looked great, and she loved the flecks of gray that highlighted his temples and dotted his otherwise dark beard. But it was more than his rugged looks that captivated her: she was attracted to the quiet, godly man inside like a compass needle was drawn to the North Pole.

"Danika, hello." He seemed reserved, as if uncertain how to greet her, but his burnt-almond eyes glowed with what she hoped was happiness at their meeting again. Part of her wished he'd welcomed her with a hug.

"Hey there, cowboy. Delivered any foals lately?"

"No. The season's over. Most breeding is done in the spring, so the foals are born early in the year."

A voice over the loudspeaker announced the preboarding of their flight. "What's your seat assignment?" Danika asked.

He held out his boarding pass.

"Right next to mine," she said, pleased. "Looks like you're stuck with incessant chatter all the way across the Atlantic. I'll try to control myself. The bad thing is that when I'm nervous—and flying makes me nervous—I tend to talk nonstop. Do yourself a favor," she joked, "and request a new seat assignment."

"I'll take my chances with you. At least I've been forewarned and know what I'm in for," he replied, reaching out to take her carry-on bag off her shoulder. "Let me get that for you." He left her carrying nothing but a purse.

She wanted to object, but his thoughtfulness was so endearing that she just smiled at him and said, "Thanks." Turning, she led the way to the line of people who waited to board their flight. *God, please don't let him be so appealing.*

Once settled in their seats and buckled for takeoff, Danika sensed Curly had something pressing on his mind. Finally he cleared his throat. "Danika, please don't think I expect you to be my escort on this entire trip." He glanced past her toward the window. "I'm sorry you've been unfairly saddled with me. I'm sure you were as astounded as I was by this—gift."

She laughed at his phrasing and candor, knowing it was hard for him to be so straightforward, and admiring his need to set her free from this obligation. He was so honorable and likable that spending two weeks with him suddenly felt like anything but a burden. She laid her hand over his large, calloused one and patted it a couple of times before returning hers to her lap.

"Yes, I *was* astounded by Rick and Katie's clumsy matchmaking attempt, but I can't think of a person I'd rather spend the next two weeks with, as a friend, of course. That is, unless you're gracefully trying to tell me to get lost. If that's the case, you'll have to say so, because I'm a little dense."

"No, that's not it at all," Curly said quickly. "I just don't want you to feel you're stuck with me."

"Nor do I want you to feel stuck with me, so if either of us needs space, we'll just say so. Deal?"

"Deal."

As she shook his hand, the power that passed through his touch rocked her very soul. Telling him good-bye in two weeks might be the second hardest thing she'd ever have to do. The first was deciding never to fall in love at all. *Would that decision soon be null and void?* her traitorous heart wondered.

CHAPTER TWO

"WOW!" Danika exclaimed.

Curly watched her stop, trying to take it all in.

"I had no idea it would be so big. Did you? It's a floating city."

They stood on the dock, staring at the monstrous ship before them. Well, actually, *she* stared at the boat, and he stared at *her.*

"Majesty," she said, reading the ship's name aloud. "Come on. We've got decks to explore," her gait changing to that of a fireman headed for a fire. Curly trailed after her.

Soon they had their room assignments and were riding the crowded elevator toward the two lowest decks. "Did you notice that each deck is named after a fruit of the Spirit? I'm on Joy Deck, and you're on Love Deck," Danika blurted out as she continued to glance over the ship's map. "How funny—the dining spots are on Goodness Deck, and the gym, jogging track, and weight room are all on Self-Control Deck." Curly sighed, realizing Danika obviously didn't follow the unspoken elevator rule about silence being golden.

The elevator dinged. "Well, here's my deck," she said. "Want to meet at the very top in an hour and explore this thing?" At his nod, she called, "See ya then," as the elevator doors closed. All he could do was smile. Where did all that exuberance—about silly things like deck names—come from?

"She's a cutie," an elderly man commented as he and Curly exited on the bottom deck.

"That she is," he agreed, making his way to his own room. He thought back to their flight. Danika had chattered much less than she had threatened to. He was amazed—once again—at how easy it was to spend time with her. When he slipped his key into the door and opened it, *small* was the first word that came to mind. Very small and no window. Oh well. Who needed sunshine with Danika around?

"You've got to stop thinking like that, old man," he said aloud, chiding himself. Laying his suitcase on the twin bed, he unpacked, trying not to think about the vivacious blonde with blue eyes who called to the lonely spot in his heart. A spot he'd forgotten existed until a February day in the barn. A spot he'd decided years ago not to fill, knowing he'd never be worthy of a woman or her love.

An hour later, Curly found Danika on Hope Deck, the tenth and highest deck of the ship and the only one not named after one of the fruits of the Spirit in Galatians. Her short locks blew in the breeze as she stood at the rail. He approached quietly, not wanting to spoil her pleasure.

"Can you believe this?" She spotted him and held her arms out, as if trying to embrace everything her eyes beheld. She spun around a couple of times, her arms still outstretched. He loved watching her expressive face. "Well," she said, motioning with her head, "what are we waiting for? This deck awaits our inspection." Then she was off.

Curly observed that Danika rarely did anything at a slow pace.

He felt as if he'd enrolled in an aerobics class rather than taking a leisurely stroll to get acquainted with the ship. The volleyball and basketball courts passed by in a blur, and he caught only an impression of an exercise course and blue-cushioned deck chairs awaiting sunbathing enthusiasts.

As they headed for the stairs to begin their race around the next deck, he grabbed hold of her arm. "Whoa, slow down there, Dani-girl. Take time to smell the roses."

She stopped dead in her tracks. "What did you call me?" she queried, her look and voice so serious that he feared he'd made a grave error.

"Dani-girl," he said again, watching intently for her reaction. Tears sprang into her eyes.

"No one's called me that since my dad died twenty years ago." Long tapered fingers wiped a few stray tears away. "Sometimes he'd call me his little morning star. That's what Danika means."

"I'm sorry. I didn't know. I won't call you that again."

"Of course you didn't know. It's OK, really. It's kind of nice to hear after all these years. I was fifteen when he died in a car accident—a drunk driver ran a red light. Can you believe I still miss him after all this time?"

"I miss my dad, too. He left home when I was three. He never looked back, that I know of." Why in the world did he tell her that? He'd never shared his personal life with anyone except Rick—once; so he quickly changed the subject. "Shall we continue at a rose-smelling pace—" he paused, wondering if he dared—"Dani-girl," he tacked on softly.

She smiled up at him and nodded, but her eyes still held sadness. "We shall."

As they walked, he asked, "Why does Katie call you DeDe?"

"It started when Kasey was a baby. Shortly after she learned to say 'mama,' she started making de-de-de–type noises. Katie insisted she was saying my name and started calling me Aunt DeDe. It sort of stuck."

He and Danika toured the rest of the ship at a snail's pace, compared to their tour of Hope Deck. Neither wanted a big dinner, so they opted for soup and salad at a small, inviting deck-side café with blue-checked tablecloths. By now Curly was much less intimidated by this adventure at sea. Danika had a way of making him feel comfortable, even when he wasn't. He remembered that from the wedding.

"This is an amazing place, isn't it?" she asked between bites.

"Yes. It really is a floating city."

The wind played havoc with her hair as they admired the view of Istanbul's lights from their table by the rail. "It's so gorgeous."

And so are you. He cleared his throat, hoping to clear his mind as well. "This has been a much-longer-than-normal day."

"It has. Shall we call it a night?"

"How will we ever see the entire city of Istanbul in ten short hours?" Danika questioned Curly the next morning as they left the ship.

"With the breakneck speed you use in approaching life, I don't think it'll be a problem. We'll probably be back on board ship in time for an afternoon nap," he said, with another slow and easy grin spreading across his face, as it had often during their breakfast. She loved the way his eyes crinkled when he smiled. The fact that she was hard-pressed to find something about this man she *didn't* like just made her resolve to avoid appealing men that much more important. *Why did Rick and Katie do this to me? Oh, Curly, if only things were different in my life, I'd fall for you in a second.*

Once inside the taxi, Curly directed the driver to take them to Topkapi Sarayi Palace. At breakfast they'd realized there was no way to even come close to seeing everything (according to the information they'd read, they needed two days instead of one), so they picked three major attractions to visit in the morning. They decided to save the afternoon for the Grand Bazaar.

The driver told them in his broken English, "Istanbul, Turkey, straddles the Golden Horn between Europe and Asia and is home to ten million people and four hundred mosques. Though we embrace religious freedom, most of our residents are Muslims. We are the city of two continents."

Unbelievable, thought Danika, excited. *In one day, we'll visit both Europe and Asia.*

The driver continued, "Ferries and suspension bridges link the city together." As he pointed out Old Town and New Town, she marveled at the differences. "Old Town holds a treasure chest full of ancient buildings and ruins. New Town is as modern as any metropolis in America," he proudly informed them, stopping in front of the first attraction on their list.

Curly paid the man, took Danika's hand, and helped her from the taxi. "Sounds like he memorized a brochure," Curly whispered and winked, as they followed other tourists toward the great palace of the Ottoman sultans. When Curly stopped and stared, she grabbed his arm. "We've got to get through this thing in two hours. No time to smell any roses today," she joked.

"It's huge. I could spend all day here," he informed her.

"Not with me as your guide," she assured him, pulling him through the Imperial Gate where they entered the First Court or the courtyard.

"Wait—I'm the guide," he replied.

She stopped. "Says who?" she asked, with hands on her hips in a mock challenge.

"Says me. I'm the one who did the homework," he reminded her, taking a crumpled brochure from his pocket.

He held out his hand to her. Should she take it? One glance at his shy, almost embarrassed eyes, and she knew she couldn't reject him. She grinned up at him, placing her hand in his. Her heart jolted at his touch.

He took charge, following his brochure and leading her through the many exhibits. The sights and sounds made her head spin, but the constant nearness and chivalry of Curly made her heart spin. She saw—as she had at the ranch—a strong, competent man.

As they crossed through the first court, Curly pointed out the Byzantine Church of Haghia Eirene. Passing through Orta Kap, the middle gate, and into the Second Court, they entered what's considered the "inner palace," though they were still not inside any building.

Curly and Danika heard the haunting call to prayer that resonates through the city five times each day. "Too bad we Christians aren't as dedicated to our prayer times," Curly lamented.

"That's for sure," Danika agreed, feeling guilty for not making Christ and prayer a bigger priority in her life. "Especially when you consider that they don't even pray to anyone real, or to anything with the power to answer. They're more faithful to Allah than I am to the living and holy God."

"I know what you mean."

They rushed from sight to sight. Danika could tell Curly longed to read and examine everything, but there just wasn't time. They practically ran through the three museums on their way out.

"Next is Haghia Sophia," he informed her as they left the palace behind.

"What is it exactly?"

"It was a church, then a mosque, and now a museum. Aren't you glad I stayed up late reading up on all this stuff?"

"Yes, Mr. Brochure, I am. You and the taxi driver both," she teased.

"One of us has to know what's going on," he informed her smugly. He grabbed her hand, surprising her by taking off at a jog. "It's only a few blocks, and you're wasting my sightseeing time!"

"I'm glad I wore my tennies." This was crazy, and obviously the downside of trying to squeeze ten ports into two weeks. At least Curly made it fun, though their jog was short lived. The streets were way too crowded.

Arriving at the museum, both halted to admire the architecture. "Everything is so big and old," Danika commented.

Once inside, she heard Curly's sharp intake of breath. "I've never seen anything like it," he said in awe.

Neither had she. Huge columns supported the gold, ornate building. They stood staring at the domed ceiling for what seemed like hours until she whispered, "We have to keep moving." This time she took his hand and led him on.

"They turned this from a church that honored Christ into a temple to worship Allah," Curly said sadly.

As they inspected the mosaics in the South Gallery, many of

which included Christ, Danika felt the same sadness as Curly over the fact that most of the people in the city worshiped a false God.

Finally Curly looked at his watch. "Time to head on over to the Blue Mosque."

"Tell me about yourself, Curly," she encouraged as they moved toward their next destination.

"Not much to tell," Curly said reluctantly.

During their week together at Katie and Rick's wedding, Danika had tried several times—unsuccessfully—to turn the conversation to personal matters. Curly would talk about the ranch, riding, hunting, fishing, and God, but never about himself. This time she decided to push. "Were you hatched, or did you have parents?"

He chuckled. "Hatched."

"Well, tell me about the woman who laid the egg."

"You're not gonna let me off the hook, are you?"

"No."

"Why?"

"Because I want to get to know you."

"It's not a pretty picture."

"It rarely is. Did you grow up in a Christian home?"

"No. You?"

"Kind of," Danika offered after a pause. "My dad definitely was, and my mom thinks she is. I'm not convinced though. I don't see any evidence in her life."

"You were closer to your dad than to your mom?"

"By far. Are you close to your mom?" she asked, again turning the subject to him.

"No. We once were. I don't even keep in touch with her anymore, though. I left home about twenty years ago and never looked back."

"Curly, that's so sad. Why? If you don't mind my asking."

"My stepfather."

"Did he beat you?"

"Only verbally. He hated me from day one, even as a four year old. I left home as soon as I finished high school. I'm sure he's relieved I never came back." When a glum silence settled around them, Danika wished she'd kept her curiosity to herself. She made a mental note to avoid future conversations of such a personal nature.

Now she understood why Curly felt more comfortable with animals than people. *Animals can't break your heart the way humans can and do. Animals give love and acceptance, not criticism and anger,* he'd told her that week at the ranch when he'd taken her on a horseback ride. Because of a harsh, unkind stepfather, Curly's heart must have been broken many times over. No wonder he lacked confidence with people!

Hearing his sad story only drew Danika's heart more completely toward him—and reconfirmed her need to build him up. *I want to help him see how truly wonderful he is,* she thought.

CHAPTER THREE

HERE we are, milady." Curly bowed at the entrance to the mosque, motioning for Danika to enter first. He hoped to lighten the mood to where it had been before he shared his unhappy history with her.

She sent a tiny smile his direction as she entered the spacious courtyard. Curly pulled her against his side and out of the way of foot traffic. "Don't let twenty-year-old news ruin our day," he spoke softly against her ear. "It was a long time ago, and God's done a lot of healing in my life since then."

"I'm glad." Relief settled on her features. He liked knowing that she cared. An urge to hold her close welled within him, but instead he grabbed her hand and starting moving quickly into the crowd of tourists.

The inside was covered with over twenty-one thousand blue porcelain tiles. "We have to take off our shoes," he informed Danika, "because of the Turkish rugs covering the floor."

Barefoot, they admired ivory carvings of emperors, bronze gateways, white marble statues, and wood-inlaid shutters. Carpets, kilims, and stained glass all exhibited exceptional craftsmanship. Again, they rushed by much of it because of the time factor.

"Let's have lunch before we go to the Grand Bazaar." Curly

pulled out his information on Istanbul from his back pocket, turned to the right page, and handed it to Danika. "Pick a place."

She studied it. "How does this sound? The Yesil Ev Restaurant is only a block from here and has a splendid garden to lunch in during the summertime."

"Sounds perfect." As they strolled together through the crowded streets, he often placed an arm around her shoulder to keep from losing her in the swarm of people.

"This is such a different world. The people, their clothes, the buildings, even the smells," she observed.

He agreed as a swirl of exotic images played through his mind. The sights, the sounds—everything was foreign.

At the restaurant, Curly struggled to tell the host that they wanted to eat in the *bahce.* Finally, the man nodded in understanding and led them to the garden.

"Oh, Curly, I love it!" Danika stopped on their way to the table and spun around, as if trying to take it all in.

Curly just grinned at the astonished look from the man who was leading them to their seats. Danika was just too irresistible to annoy anyone. Soon they were seated in a beautiful spot between a lush tree and a gurgling fountain.

"This place is terrific," she said with her usual zest.

"It has very good international and Turkish cuisine," Curly replied, quoting the brochure in a deep broadcaster-type voice.

"I'm going with something Turkish. That way I can experience some real Turkish cooking firsthand."

"You just take life by the horns, don't you?" Curly said, realizing she never seemed to shy away from new things—not on the ranch, and not here either.

"Is that a bad thing?"

"No. Not at all. Just an observation. Now tell me about yourself."

She chose an impersonal route. "I'm half Norwegian and half English. You probably figured that out already by my looks. My blonde hair is from my father's Norwegian genes, and my long nose, from my mother's English heritage."

"Your nose isn't that long."

"Quit being nice. It's a typical English nose, long and narrow."

"Whose eyes do you have?"

"My father's."

"They're beautiful. Even if your nose is long—which it isn't—no one would ever see past your eyes," he said, his voice husky. Since he'd never received any praise growing up, he felt a little awkward complimenting her. It was hard to know how to give it—and sound sincere.

"Thank you, Curly. What a sweet thing to say. Now what shall we order?"

I think I'll have one of you. Curly surprised himself with that thought. One cute, pert blonde sounded perfect. Then he shook his head slightly. *I must be delusional or something.* He'd decided years ago to avoid any and all entanglement with marriage material, and yet here he was thinking about a relationship. It must be the sea air and the fact that he was so amazingly comfortable with her. Danika was so different from other women that he couldn't quit thinking crazy thoughts about them—him and her—and there was no them.

Once they'd ordered, Danika asked, "Have you ever been on a cruise before?"

"No."

"Me neither, but I've decided this is the way to travel. I wish they weren't so expensive. I'd take one every year. Think about it: we're going to visit three different continents—Europe, Asia, and Africa—in just over two weeks. Doesn't that amaze you?" He loved watching her eyes when she talked.

"Yes, but it's all happening so fast I wonder if I'll actually remember anything I've seen." *Except you—you I'll never forget.* "The Topkapi Palace is a maze of several hundred rooms, and we barely made a dent."

She smiled widely. "Oh, yes, you're my rose-smelling friend. You'd rather spend the whole day exploring one place thoroughly, and I'd rather catch a glimpse of the big picture."

"Well, we did catch a glimpse," he said with a twinkle in his eye. "Finish telling me your story. After all, you owe me after dragging my sordid childhood into daylight," he said nonchalantly, not wanting her pity for his pain-filled past.

"Mine isn't a very pretty picture either." Her eyes grew sad, and her smile died away. "My dad was a vibrant, life-loving man."

She paused, and Curly knew she took after her father.

"My mother, on the other hand, is a hypochondriac. She uses her illnesses to manipulate. She's controlling." Danika bit her bottom lip. "I'm slowly learning to break free from her, but it hasn't been easy. Old habits die hard. I normally just give in to her because it's easier than a fight."

He reached across the table, taking her hand in his, hoping to offer comfort. "Sounds like she'd pair up nicely with my stepdad." He was glad his words brought a slight smile back to her lips.

"Yes," she said, nodding, "yes, she would."

When the waiter placed their plates in front of them, Curly asked the blessing. Then, changing their topic of conversation, he said, "Tonight, when we leave port, it will be thirty-seven hours before we dock in Kusadasi. We'll spend tomorrow morning sailing around Mt. Athos Peninsula."

"Then I may sleep until noon tomorrow. I'm so tired. It'll be a great day to recover from jet lag."

As they ate, he wondered if she'd already grown tired of his company. She did look exhausted, though. "I guess we lost a whole night's sleep with the huge time change."

"Except for what little we got on the plane. This is really good. How's yours?"

"Different. I'm more a steak-and-potatoes kind of guy."

"I'd have guessed that about you, cowboy," she said, laughing. "So, tell me what I need to know about the Grand Bazaar."

"We saved the best for last," he assured her, rather proud of himself. "It's filled with over four thousand shops. Just your kind of place. I remember how much you and Katie like to shop."

Her smile joined his, and he knew she too was reliving the memory of her and Katie dragging him and Rick through every little shop on Mt. Lemmon when they'd gone up there to enjoy the snow during that week before the wedding. She'd nailed him good with a firm, well-made snowball, and he'd wrestled her to the ground, shoving snow down her back. As they'd laughed together there on the ground, he'd almost kissed her. But instead, he'd jumped to his feet, pulling her up with him, and the moment had passed.

The tender look on her face right now told him she, too, remembered their first not-quite kiss. "Let's forget history this afternoon," he said in a low voice, "and make sure you get a shopping fix."

"Thank you, kind sir. I might be much more cheerful tomorrow because of your thoughtfulness."

"I sure hope so. Your moods *are* pretty hard to take," he joked back. In truth, she was one of the most easygoing females he'd run across. Not that he'd run across that many, but he'd heard other guys talking about moody women.

After lunch they caught a taxi to the crowded and hustling Grand Bazaar. Again he hugged her tightly against his side. "This way I won't lose you." But even as he did so, he wondered. Was that his true motive, or was he only looking for excuses to be near her?

But she didn't seem to mind. "Thanks for being my gallant knight." They strolled together through the hordes of people. "I've never seen anything like this."

"If you look at the ceiling, this place goes on forever," Curly said, following the line of the high arched ceiling. "This is the largest *souk* in the world."

"Where do you come up with these words?"

"Hey, I studied my brochure!"

On each side of them were vendors in small shops. Whenever they walked into one, they were invited to sit down, sip apple tea, and bargain for the merchandise.

He followed her from shop to shop. This was the one thing Danika didn't rush through. She touched, admired, and enjoyed. Late that afternoon they caught a taxi back to the dock, with a Turkish carpet from Baghdad and several other souvenirs in tow.

When they got back on the ship, Danika told him she'd decided to skip dinner and take a nap. "If I wake up in time, I'll see you in the chapel service at 9 P.M. Thanks for a memorable day," she said, quickly kissing his cheek before exiting the elevator.

"Good night, Danika."

Why did hearing Curly say her name bring such a rush of pleasure to Danika's heart? It had to be the reminder of her dad, she decided. Her dad's voice had rumbled a low bass much like Curly's, and he'd been strong and kind like Curly, too. Maybe that explained her attraction to Curly. Otherwise it didn't make much sense. After all, they lived in two worlds that were poles apart.

"Bye," she'd said and kissed his cheek.

"What am I doing?" she asked herself aloud, once inside her room. She shook her head at the woman in the mirror and sighed. "Face it, he's your dream man, and you're not allowed to dream." Her vision blurred, and she turned away from the mirror.

She threw her pillow across the room. "I'm so mad at you for doing this to me, Katie," she muttered in a tortured voice. "And I'm mad at you, Mother, for making it easier to avoid relationships than to constantly fight with you." A tear glided across her cheek and dropped onto her blouse.

As she prepared for her nap, she contemplated Curly's attributes. She loved his shy, sweet manner, so unassuming, so gentle. Her heart ached for the mistreated little boy he'd been—and for the uncertain man he'd become. But as she'd spent time with him, she'd realized, oh, how wonderful he was!

She no longer dreaded his company. In fact, that was the problem: she liked being with him too much.

Curly decided to take the elevator to the top, to Hope Deck. As he stood there, watching Istanbul grow smaller, he wondered about his past choices. At eighteen, he had thought he made the right one, focusing his energy and love on God and animals, but he was no longer so sure. After growing to care about Rick and his family for the past five years, then Katie and Kasey, and now Danika, he realized that many people were worth the effort of maintaining a relationship.

When darkness filled the sky and Istanbul was nothing more than a row of lights far off on the horizon, Curly took the elevator to Love Deck. He hopped in the shower, hoping to wash away past memories. But in his heart, he knew it would take more than soap and water.

Later, as he headed toward the chapel on Faithfulness Deck, he opted to take the five flights of stairs, thinking it would be faster than joining the crowd waiting for the elevator. He wondered if Danika would make it to chapel. Why did being near her do crazy things inside his heart?

Finding an empty chair near the back, he sat down. Within a couple of minutes, a young man who didn't look a day over twenty-five began leading them in a few praise songs. He ended with Curly's favorite, "I Stand in Awe of You." When he left the stage without a word, a middle-aged man limped out to the podium. His legs were twisted, and he struggled even with a walker.

"I'm Howard Danby, and I'm here to tell you that I'm fearfully and wonderfully made. Some of you may want to laugh at that statement, but let me assure you, it's no laughing matter. The doctor said, 'birth defects.' My mother said, 'There's nothing defective about my child. He's exactly the way God designed him.' The Bible says God knit me together in my mother's womb. Now I ask you, does God make mistakes?

"I think not. The psalmist said God's workmanship is marvelous, that I'm wonderfully complex. How many of you think I look marvelous? Complex, maybe. Wonderful, never. But I'm here to tell you, as my dear, sweet mama said, there is no mistake or defect about me. I stand before you exactly how God designed me.

"Do I have the right to quibble with my Maker? I think not. He tells me to be content, joy filled, and not grumble or complain. So what are my options? I could sin by not accepting this body, or thank God for it. I opted for acceptance and even appreciation. What about you, my friend? Are you willing to accept yourself, just as you are, and offer yourself back to God for his service and for his glory?"

Curly swallowed hard. His greatest struggle in life was self-acceptance. He knew he was worthless. How could God value a man whose father left, whose mother didn't love him enough to defend him, and whose stepdad hated him with a passion? How could God value a man whom few valued, including himself?

After all, he'd been told he was worthless every day from age four until he left home fourteen years later. He could still hear his stepfather's voice echoing through his head: *You're good for nothing. Your father must have had defective genes. No wonder he left. He surely felt ashamed that you came from his loins.*

The pain from those words could still draw tears to his eyes, but tonight the memory didn't hurt quite so much. He heard another voice, a still, small voice, affirming that there were indeed no defective genes, for God designed him inside and out.

It was all there in black and white in Scripture. God didn't just save him. He loved and treasured him. The news was more than Curly could bear. A tear slid down his cheek as he pondered the cost of the cross—for him. Jesus had suffered because he, Calder Nevyn, was worth it.

CHAPTER FOUR

DANIKA had slept through the first chapel service and much of the previous day while they were at sea. She had made it to last night's service, though, and had seen Curly there. This morning they had docked in Kusadasi and had traveled by land to Ephesus. After spending the day there, Danika and Curly decided to try one of the more formal dining rooms back on the ship. While she waited for him, Danika thought back over their day together. The marbled streets and Curly. The ruins and Curly. The amphitheater and Curly.

She smiled, remembering his pleasure at the ancient ruins, remembering her pleasure when he'd taken her hand again and again. Together they'd discovered the treasures that lay in what was once the first and greatest metropolis of Asia. They'd walked the colonnaded streets and inspected each ruin.

Curly had touched and read everything. As he'd appreciated each relic, she'd enjoyed watching him. He was an outdoorsman, muscular with a rich, dark tan. Even his well-trimmed beard and mustache added to his rugged look. His nose was straight, nicely shaped, and masculine. Heavy dark brows and thick lashes framed his burnt-almond eyes. His mouth was firm. . . . For a minute, she wondered how his lips might feel against hers.

Danika! Appalled by her own traitorous thoughts, Danika remembered the only time she'd kissed a man—Ron, her old boyfriend. *And that's the way I plan to keep it,* she concluded. Again she struggled with anger toward Katie—and her mother. Her well-ordered, busy life now seemed empty. Her hard-earned contentment with her singleness had fled. Each time Curly took her hand in his leathery one, her resolve chipped away.

She'd fallen for this soft-spoken, gentle-hearted man before her week in Arizona had ended. Now each moment tasted bittersweet. The worst part, unless she'd lost her ability to read men, was that the feelings were mutual. When he looked at her, his eyes said he adored her. His smile said he felt enchanted, and his touch said he held her with a hope in his heart.

"Hey, you look a million miles away," Curly commented upon his arrival.

She jumped. "I was just thinking about Ephesus." *And you.*

"Two for dinner," Curly informed the host, who led them to a small, linen-covered table in the corner. The host held out Danika's chair, and she settled into its padded comfort. After inspecting their menus, Curly ordered a T-bone. She chose lobster.

"What did you think of Ephesus?" he asked when the tuxedoed waiter departed.

"I enjoyed watching you. You loved it, didn't you?"

"I did. Couldn't you almost hear the apostle Paul delivering his letter to the Ephesians? Couldn't you almost picture twenty-four thousand people sitting in the amphitheater with us, listening to him?"

She nodded, again touched by his passion for the place.

"Did you tire of smelling the roses?" he asked.

"No. I marveled at how amazing man was, even before modern technology."

"Maybe even more so. I doubt anything we build today will be standing two thousand years from now. And to think Paul passed through there, walked where we walked."

Their salads arrived. "What do you think of Howard Danby?" she asked.

"He's really got me thinking. The night you missed he spoke of God's amazing love for each one of us . . . and how, if God is mindful of the smallest sparrow, think how he feels about us."

"I've always been amazed that the God of the universe knows the number of hairs on my head," Danika responded.

"Me, too!"

Danika thoroughly enjoyed her dinner and her dinner companion.

The next morning Curly woke with a smile on his face. In his heart he felt a deeper love for Christ, a greater appreciation of the cost Jesus paid for his salvation, and a joy in the knowledge that he was special to almighty, most holy God.

And yesterday with Danika was as close to perfect as a day could be. He closed his eyes, remembering her hand in his as they meandered through sites of Ephesian history. He probably shouldn't have held it at all, but once he'd touched her, he never wanted to let her go.

He'd spent years with little physical human contact. He'd almost forgotten how wonderful it felt to touch another human being. Her hand—soft, warm, and small—fit perfectly in his, almost as if God had designed her just for him.

That thought brought a twinge to his heart. He crawled out of bed and pulled on a pair of blue jeans. What if his vow to avoid relationships wasn't God's plan but his own? No, that couldn't be. He had nothing to offer a woman, especially a woman as terrific as Danika.

"Good morning, sunshine," he said to Danika as he joined her for breakfast. She looked up from her bagel, her blue eyes glowing when they met his.

"Hey, you. I thought you decided to ditch me."

If he had any sense at all, he would. "Naw, just moving slowly this morning."

"You'd better eat quickly. We dock in Athens in fifteen minutes."

"You're not going to let me have another slow, easy day, are you?"

"Not on your life," she promised with a smile.

She picked up the Athens brochure he laid on the table and looked it over while he ate a chocolate doughnut and drank a cup of black coffee. Her interest in the pamphlet gave him an opportunity to memorize her face. One day he'd want to remember every detail, after she returned to her PR work in Tennessee, and he was back working on a ranch halfway across the country.

Her blonde hair was short and bouncy, like her personality. Her cheeks glowed rosily, and her wide mouth smiled often. Her eyes—those he'd never forget. Sometimes when he looked into them, he felt as if he were drowning.

Suddenly those eyes were on him, and a slow heat crept up his neck and face. "You ready?" he said quickly, taking a last gulp of coffee and hoping to hide his embarrassment.

"Sure."

An hour later, hand in hand, they were climbing the Acropolis, the hilltop site of ancient Athens. "I sense the history," Curly commented.

"Me, too." Danika turned and looked back down the hill. "Look at the smog. How sad."

"I read this city houses 25 percent of Greece's population. No wonder it's smoggy."

They continued on up the hill and stopped when they reached the Propylea, a huge gateway with five doors and marble ceilings. "Can you believe it? We're standing in Athens, Greece!" she proclaimed, excitement threading through her words.

He couldn't help but smile. "Capital of this fine country and named for Athena, goddess of wisdom," he informed her in his tour-guide impersonation.

"OK, Mr. Brochure. For someone who didn't want to take this cruise, you've sure gotten into it. Hey, let's visit the Parthenon first. It's considered the most majestic of the Acropolis ruins. If I let you go at your pace, that's probably all we'll have time for," she teased.

"And at your speed, we'd already have been done five minutes ago," he joked back, his heart soaring with the pleasure of her presence.

They stopped in front of the remains of the Parthenon. "Can you believe those massive columns?" she asked.

"It was the first building constructed here. What's left of it is over twenty-four hundred years old."

"Did you know we have a "parthenon" in Nashville?"

"Really?"

"Really. It houses an art gallery. It was built in 1897, I think, for Nashville's centennial celebration."

"Guess this one is a few years older," he replied, laughing.

Holding hands, they strolled through the ruins. According to the brochure, the building didn't have one straight line in its entire construction. Every inch was curved to achieve perfect proportion and harmony.

"Next, the Erechtheum," he informed her.

"Is that the place with the porch?"

He nodded. "They used caryatids as columns to support the building."

"Cary-a-what?"

"They're carvings of draped maidens."

"They're incredible," she said when they came into view.

"Imagine the work that went into those."

"I'm more awed by the ancient world with each passing day."

"I agree."

They spent the morning touring the north side of the Acropolis. "Let's go have our lunch at the Odeon. It's on the south side of the Acropolis." They'd brought a picnic lunch from the ship, which Curly had carried in his backpack.

"You spend too much time with your brochure. What's the Odeon?"

"It's another word for theater. This was built in A.D. 160," he informed her as they climbed down a few rows. "The theater of Herodes Atticus seats five thousand people. Now, without its roof, the Greeks use it for summer festivals."

They settled onto a stone bench, and Curly unpacked their lunch. "Thanks," she said when he handed her an apple and a ham and swiss on rye.

They ate in silence for several minutes. Finally he worked up the courage to ask her what he'd been wondering about since Arizona. "Have you ever been in love?"

"What?" She nearly choked on a bite of apple.

"Sorry, random thoughts."

"I'll say."

"It's just there are many women your age—"

"My age! Hey, buster, I'm not that old."

"I just wondered . . ." He gave up trying to explain gracefully. He'd been stupid to ask.

He barely heard her quiet answer. "Once—a long time ago."

"What happened?" Not normally a meddler, he really needed to know.

"My mother happened." She wadded up her half-eaten sandwich in its wrapper and shoved it into the empty paper sack. "She doesn't want me to find anyone because then she'll be alone." A sadness settled over her face.

Great, he'd deflated her jovial mood.

But she surprised him by continuing. "After that, I gave up. Ron ended up being hurt. I ended up being hurt. I won't give her another opportunity to ruin the promise of love. It's easier to settle for singleness than to fight her at every turn."

"So you never date?"

"Never. Ron found someone else without a psycho for a mother. He still goes to my church, so I run into him and Debbie occasionally. They have a couple of kids now and seem happy." She swallowed hard and looked off into the distance.

He took her hand, stroking the back of it with his thumb. "I'm sorry," he whispered. More sorry than she'd ever know. This new information assured him there was no future with her, and even though there was no future with him either, he felt saddened by the news.

It still hurt to talk about Ron. Not that she had any feelings left for him, but the anger at her mother welled within her. Danika closed her eyes and took a deep breath, releasing it slowly. Upon thinking about it, having this conversation with Curly could only be a plus. Now he knew for sure where she stood and wouldn't carry false hopes about them.

Curly apparently heard the message loud and clear, for he avoided touching her again the rest of the day. Still the country gentleman, his manners remained impeccable, but she wished he'd take her hand again. With her hand in his, she'd felt his strength and his protection. Now she sensed distance.

When they arrived back at the ship Curly seemed anxious to be rid of her. "Maybe I'll see you in chapel. Thanks for keeping me company in Athens." He tipped his hat toward her, forced a smile that came nowhere near reaching his eyes, and was gone.

In the wake of his departure, he left a host of feelings for Danika to deal with. What had begun on this cruise as a project to rescue Curly and teach him to believe in himself now left her needing someone to rescue her from her own heart. Unknowingly, Curly had captured it and moved straight in without so much as an invitation.

Was she wrong to spend all this time with him, knowing there could never be a future? Would she do more damage by sharing the next ten days with him or by ditching him? Thinking of his expectant eyes, she knew she'd treasure all the time she could with him. She'd ponder each moment in her heart; then she'd spend countless years missing him.

She didn't think she'd see Curly again that night, so she decided to eat in the charming little pizzeria they'd passed several times on the Goodness Deck.

Soon Danika was settled at a small table, quaint with its red-checkered tablecloth, and looking over her choices. *I wonder what Curly's doing,* she thought, inhaling the wonderful scents of oregano and garlic.

"How about a large with everything?" Curly's low voice pulled her out of her musing. His forlorn-looking smile tugged at her heart. "Mind if I join you?"

Hoping her smile told him how welcome he was, she replied, "A large with everything sounds great."

"And how about a moonlight stroll when we're done? The full moon out there is breathtaking."

As they wandered around the decks later, Curly still seemed to avoid touching her. "I wrote my mom a letter when we got back today," he said nonchalantly, as if it held no importance.

Danika stopped dead in her tracks. "Curly, that's great! I know that must have been hard for you after how many years?"

"Twenty." He settled on a bench, and she joined him. "I asked her forgiveness."

Danika took his hand and held it between her two. "I'm proud of you," she said, finding it difficult to get the words past the lump in her throat.

"I've struggled with believing I had any value at all because of the way my father and stepfather treated me. Even my own mother—who should have loved and protected me—sat like a bump on a log while her husband verbally cut me down.

"Last night, for the first time, I clearly saw her predicament. Caught between my stepdad and me and being a meek woman, she did the only thing she knew how to do. Forgiving her came easier than I expected. Forgiving my stepdad will take more time."

"You'll get there," she assured him, knowing he would.

"I always interpreted my mom's lack of help as a statement that I wasn't worth the effort. I thought she just didn't love me enough to stand up for me."

"Oh, Curly, how could she not love you?" Tears rolled freely down her checks as his pain became her own. "How could anyone who knows you not love you?"

Startled brown eyes looked into hers, and she knew she'd said too much. His years of hurt and longing lay naked in his face for her to see. Barely a whisper, his question pleaded for honesty. "Even you?"

How could she deny him the words he so desperately needed to hear? "Even me," she said softly. "You're the most incredible man I've ever met."

He touched her cheek with his fingertips, his eyes telling her much more than he dared put into words. She knew he yearned to kiss her but lacked the courage.

She moved toward him, and his hand slid from her cheek into her hair. Her lips touched his for only a brief second, but it was enough to meld her heart with his for eternity; she knew she'd re-live that moment in time again and again. The look of wonder on his face confirmed how he felt about her.

CHAPTER FIVE

THE following morning Curly woke again with a smile on his face. *This is getting to be a habit,* he thought, grinning. He could hear Danika's voice in his head saying, *Even me. You're the most incredible man I've ever met.* That was the second time she'd called him *incredible.* Boy, was it an amazing feeling to have someone believe you're wonderful!

He'd backed off after she'd told him that, because of her mother, she avoided relationships. He'd even stopped holding her hand, knowing that, with each touch, his heart cared more deeply. Discovering she felt the same way sent his emotions soaring somewhere into the heavens.

Today they'd spend the day at sea, so he'd slept a little later than usual. Now he jumped out of bed and dressed, not wanting to wait another minute to see her. He hardly dared to believe that God had

z0/ brought such an amazing gift as her into his life. Finally, he'd accepted himself as God's special design, and now he was free to give himself to another.

Unable to find Danika in any of the dining rooms, he went to her cabin. When a teary-eyed woman opened the door, his heart instantly fell. She must have realized her mistake in thinking him incredible. "Danika, what's wrong?" he asked, standing in the open doorway, uncertain if he really wanted to hear her answer.

She turned away and walked over to her bed, grabbing a Kleenex from its box. He saw her suitcase lying open and most of her clothes neatly folded inside. Was he so bad that she had to get away?

Sniffling, she picked up an envelope off the nightstand and carried it over to him. A dread settled over him. Telegrams always meant bad news. He unfolded the paper and read, *I'm ill. I need you. Please come home. Mom.*

Watery gray eyes looked up at him, and a selfish relief flooded him. This had nothing to do with him or them. He pulled her into his arms, where she sobbed against his chest. He held her until the storm passed. Finally, she stepped away and returned to the box of Kleenex across the room.

"Why can't she ever let me live my life? She does this every time I do anything she doesn't want me to." Her eyes begging for his understanding, Danika leaned against the nightstand.

"She didn't want you to take the cruise?"

"Of course not! Who would take care of her?"

"Is she an invalid?"

"No. She's a healthy sixty-five-year-old woman who wants me to be as miserable as she is."

Curly rubbed the back of his neck. How could he help her? "Do you think she's really ill?"

"It's doubtful. She never is. She did this to me when I was at the ranch for Katie's wedding. Turned out to be nothing—at least nothing the doctor could find," she said, shrugging defeatedly.

"Do you think you need to go home?" he asked, hoping not. He couldn't imagine this cruise without her.

"I don't know," she said in a flat, lifeless voice.

Lord, I pray that her mom is OK. Please show me how to encourage Danika and comfort her.

"Her mysterious pains always subside once I get home. Her doctor says she's healthier than most forty year olds."

He decided to be honest. "I don't want you to leave . . . I know that sounds selfish, but I'm really enjoying your company." He swallowed hard. Should he tell her? *I'm in love with you. And I'm sure you're perfect for me.*

Danika rested her head against the wall. He knew they had a long way to go. Neither of them ever planned to find love, but love had found them—or at least him—anyway. No, it had found her, too. At least, she had said so last night.

She sat on the edge of her bed. "Maybe this is a test. I know I need to break free from my mom's manipulation of me. God's been dealing with me about running from conflict."

Both were quiet for a few moments. Then she stood, raising her chin in a determined fashion. "I won't let her do this to me!" She marched over to where he stood in the open doorway.

He drew her into his embrace. Surprised by his own boldness, he hugged her for the second time that morning. She smelled of citrus. "I'm glad you're staying."

"Me, too. I'm starved. Let's go eat."

He took her hand and led her to the elevator. Her nose had a red hue, and her eyes looked bloodshot from crying, but she was still the best sight he'd ever seen.

Hands intertwined, they rode in silence up to the Goodness Deck. When she leaned her head against his shoulder, Curly wondered if the rest of his life would feel as terrific as this moment did. *Thank you, God, for this amazing woman. I can barely believe she loves me.* He knew he wore a goofy, ear-to-ear grin and didn't even care.

When the elevator opened, Curly draped his arm around her shoulder. As she laid her aching head against him, she felt his strength seep into her.

They sat down at a table, and Curly's tender gaze rested on her. *Father God, I love this man,* she thought, amazed by how much he comforted her. *I love the way he takes care of me. No one has done that for a long, long time.* She was surprised that she, Miss Independent, enjoyed his protective attitude.

"Tell me about your mom," Curly said softly, once they'd ordered and their coffee had been served.

"My mom . . ." Danika sighed, stirring her coffee. "She's difficult. As long as I'm in her will—so to speak—she's likable and we get along fine. If I cross her . . . " Danika's eyes looked off into the distance. "Well, let's just say she makes sure I regret that decision."

"How did she break up you and Ron?"

"She accused him of coming between us. She called him at work, at home, sent letters blaming him for her health problems. She said horrible things and finally wore him down. She's sort of like a pit bull; she clamps on and never lets go."

The waiter placed steaming plates before them.

Curly spoke in low tones once the server walked away. "Nothing against Ron, but I'd never let her drive me away. Not if I really loved you." And his eyes told her he did.

"It's not that easy. He took it for months."

"She'll never come between us. I promise you that," he said, taking her hand.

"But Curly, there is no us," she said, his declaration causing her heart to ache. "Not now, not ever." She wished there were a kinder way to say it.

"You said—"

"You are the most incredible man I've ever met, and you are. If things were different . . ."

"Danika, I love you."

She closed her eyes. Hearing him say the words only increased her inner struggle. "I know. I feel the same way about you, but there is no us. There is no future."

"But—"

"I'm sorry if I led you to believe anything else." A stunned Curly sat back, looking wounded. "I vowed to myself that I'd not get involved with anyone as long as my mom's alive because I promised my dad I'd take care of her."

"Danika, you can't be serious," he said quietly. But, instead of the hurt or anger she expected, a gentle love resided on his face. "I love you, and I'm not giving you up without a fight."

"And I love you." She couldn't leave those words unsaid any longer. "But my mind's made up."

The tiniest smile had touched his lips when she'd announced her love, but she noticed it disappeared quickly at her determination.

Why is life so hard? She touched his beard, surprised by its softness. He wrapped his hand around her wrist, and turning his head, he kissed her palm. His eyes melted her heart. *If only . . .*

"Don't shut me out. I've waited *years* for you." Hope glimmered in his eyes.

"Curly—"

"We have eight more days. Spend them with me. Then let me be the one to take care of you. Let me be the one to help take care of your mother."

"If only it were that easy . . ."

"It can be if you let it."

"I can't make you any promises."

"I only want two promises: that you'll pray about us, and that you'll spend each day with me until we get to Rome."

She smiled. Having someone love and admire him had changed him. He acted bolder, more sure of himself. "All right—if you promise you'll accept my decision when we get there."

She saw the hesitation on his face. "Only if it's the right decision," he said, winking at her.

"Curly, I'm serious."

"So am I." He stood, helped her to her feet, and planted a quick kiss on her lips.

"For a shy man, you're becoming awfully daring."

"Love must do that to a person." *He sure uses that word freely all of a sudden,* she thought. "Are you agreeing to my plan?" he said, pressing her.

"Only the part about spending the rest of the cruise with you. I'm telling you right now the rest is impossible."

"With God all things are possible," he reminded her.

"Maybe with God, but not with my mother."

They started walking toward the elevator. "You couldn't resist my charm. Maybe she won't be able to either."

"You're becoming obnoxious," she teased. "Suddenly you think you're God's gift to all women."

"Not to all women, just to you."

His words stabbed at her heart. She'd never considered the possibility that God had sent him to her; she'd just assumed the reverse. He needed someone to believe in him, to encourage him. But maybe she needed him just as much—if not more than he needed her.

"I can't believe our trip is half over," he commented the next evening as they strolled around the deck after chapel service. They'd spent the day in Nazareth and at the Sea of Galilee. "Just think, I didn't even want to come, but I would have missed all this. I would have missed you . . ." He squeezed her hand. "I might have missed my future."

"I'm *not* your future," she said, her voice tinged with frustration.

"Not yet, but I'd like you to be someday."

"Don't count on it," she said hopelessly and stopped at the rail.

Curly stood next to her. "You promised to pray about us."

"What's the use? It'll never work."

"Danika—" He grabbed her arm, turning her around to face him. "I love you. Don't give up yet."

"I've been down this road before, full of hope only to be crushed. I know my mother. Nothing is ever going to change. I promised my dad I'd care for her. I can't break that promise."

Curly gathered her into his arms, holding her tight, vowing somehow to find a way to hold on to her. He kissed the top of her head. "I love you. I don't believe God brought us together for nothing. Do you?"

"God didn't bring us together. Katie did. And every time you hold me or kiss me, it will make it that much harder to say good-bye next week. Don't you see that?"

He never would have guessed that inside this upbeat, happy-go-lucky woman lived a pessimist. "I've spent most of my life without hugs or any human touch. It's hard—now that I've found you—not to hug you at least a hundred times a day. I'm trusting God to work this out somehow."

"I wish I could believe that," she said sadly, despairingly.

He wanted to lecture her on faith and God's amazing power, but he didn't. Instead he asked, "Do you mind if I hold your hand?" In answer, she shook her head, so he took it and they started walking again. "I'll try not to hug you anymore, if that will make you feel better," he promised. "Tell me about your life in Nashville," he said, switching the subject.

"I'm very busy between my job, church, and volunteer work."

"That doesn't surprise me." He grinned down at her. "No time for smelling roses, huh?"

"No—or thinking," she confessed.

They stopped to watch a volleyball game. "How does your mom feel about you being so busy?"

"I guess we found an unspoken compromise. As long as there are no men in my life, she doesn't fight my crowded schedule."

"What kind of volunteer work do you do?"

"I donate some weekend time at Mercy Ministries of America. That's how I met Katie. Then I became her spiritual mentor and discipled her for a couple of years."

He nodded, remembering that was where Katie had ended up when she fled Arizona as a pregnant teen. "Does your mom go to church with you?"

"Not often. Maybe once or twice a month."

"Are you involved in the singles' ministry?"

"No, why torture myself? I teach a ladies' Sunday school class. I avoid men as much as possible. It's easier that way because then I don't become tempted by things I can't have."

"You must have been thrilled when Rick and Katie sent me here to tag along."

"I had mixed feelings."

"Mixed, how?"

"A part of me—the insane part—really looked forward to seeing you again."

"Really?" The news somehow increased his hope. Surely, it was no accident they ended up on this cruise together. Certainly, Katie had something to do with it, but couldn't she have been part of God's plan?

"Really. Don't think because I can't love you that I don't. I'd like nothing more than to be part of your ever-after. I'm not rejecting you because I want to, only because I have to. If there were ever a man in my life, it would be you."

Boy, was she stubborn. *God, I need a miracle—and I need it in the next seven days,* he pleaded. *I really believe Danika is part of your plan for my future. Please convince her, if that's true.*

CHAPTER SIX

LORD, please get me through the days ahead. Help me to enjoy this time with Curly, instead of thinking about when it will end. One day at a time, that's all you ask. Please get me through today, that's all I ask. Thank you, Jesus.

Danika found Curly waiting near the information desk where they always met before disembarking. "We have less than eleven hours to take in the sights and sounds of Jerusalem. Let's start with Old City, so we cover that first," he said, reaching for her hand. Then, dropping it like a hot coal, he mumbled, "Sorry."

She ignored the incident. "Old City? You stayed up all night reading those brochures again, didn't you?" she said, laughing, as they made their way down the stairs and onto the dock.

"Who me?" He grinned. "Well, not all night," he assured her. "We'll catch a bus from here, but according to my handy-dandy information—" he waved the brochure in the air—"walking is the best way to see the city."

They boarded the bus to take them from Ashdod to Jerusalem. "So fill me in on the agenda for today." She took a seat next to the window. Curly slid in next to her.

"The Old City is the historic, walled area in East Jerusalem. It's only a small district, but well preserved. So it should take us a good portion of the day to tour. It's divided into four quarters: Jewish, Muslim, Christian, and Armenian. I thought we could take a couple of the mapped-out walks in this book I picked up from the tour desk this morning."

Danika nodded and looked through the information. Once they arrived, they traveled down a narrow street bustling with bazaars and markets. "This has a real oriental feel," she commented. Modern buildings towered off in the distance, a stark contrast with the old Arab and Jewish structures surrounding them.

"Yes, it does." They entered Old City through the Jaffa Gate. "Do you realize this place has been continually inhabited for the past four-thousand-plus years? It's been rebuilt and destroyed more than any major city."

"Look at these old pictures of what the gate looked like in earlier times." They paused for a moment, then continued on.

"What's that huge building with the gleaming gold dome?" She pointed straight ahead. "Its presence dominates Old City."

"That's The Dome of the Rock, built in the seventh century. It stands on the very spot where Solomon built the first temple to house the ark of the covenant in the inner sanctuary or the Holy of Holies. These stairs—" he pointed to the left—"lead to the Promenade on the Old City Wall. Right over there across the street is the Citadel of David."

They walked a short way, and she paused in front of The Gate.

"Gotta stop, right?" Curly joked.

"It's the first shop we've seen." As they meandered through the first floor, her shoulder briefly brushed his arm. She felt him tense at their contact and briskly move away. "It's so sad that The Dome of the Rock stands where the temple stood," she commented. "It must grieve God's heart to have people living in his Holy City who don't know or have a relationship with him," she whispered, climbing the stairs to the second floor of the store.

Curly nodded. "I'm sure it does. Jerusalem is the cornerstone of the world's three great religions: Christianity, Judaism, and Islam. But it fell under Muslim rule in the early 600s. Since then it's changed hands many times. Then in 1967, after the Six Day War, Israeli troops won control of the entire Holy City once again."

She admired the necklaces, rings, and earrings while Curly shared his knowledge with her. But she didn't buy anything, and soon they continued along their walk through the Christian Quarter. Curly brought up Howard Danby. "That man can preach. Every time he speaks, God does a work in my heart."

"I know." They passed by the New Imperial Hotel.

"His message on God adoring me and me needing to love others with that same love spoke volumes. I've been afraid of love all my life."

Guilt stabbed her heart. Here she was giving him one more reason to avoid love in the future. "What spoke to me the most was his message on forgiveness—the one three nights ago. What was it he said?"

"Forgiveness frees you, not them?"

"That was it! I loved the little poem he shared. How did it go?" She paused, trying to remember. "I got it! 'When I forgive, I set the prisoner free; Only to discover, the prisoner was me.' I realize I have a lot of issues with my mom because she acts so helpless and needy."

Her heart wished she could run off with Curly and forget the heavy burden her mother had become. But her dad's last words to her as he lay dying in the ER were *take care of your mother for me. She's frail. . . .* How could she disappoint him?

They'd stopped walking. This time he did squeeze her against his side. "It wasn't fair of your dad to put that on you. You were just a kid."

As Curly held her, Danika's mind was a million miles away. It wasn't the first time Danika had wished her dad had told her mom to take care of *her,* instead of the reverse. She could hear Howard Danby's voice floating through her head: *Now that you've gotten rid of the baggage that saddles you when there is unforgiveness, you're free to run the race God has for you. He has plans for you, plans to give you a hope and a future.*

She'd prayed. She'd fasted. But her mother never changed. When would her future begin? Where was her hope? The only thing Howard said that she could identify with was about running the race. She'd gotten good at running. She kept herself so busy that she fell into bed each night too exhausted to think or wish or dream. Her future looked grim.

And therein lay the problem with this vacation. With way too much time on her hands, she thought and wished and dreamed. And the rugged man standing next to her—the one with the gentle touch and eyes that pleaded with her heart to let him in—filled those thoughts and wishes and dreams.

Curly's heart ached for Danika. Surely her dad hadn't meant for her to sacrifice her whole future because her mom didn't want to be alone.

As he and Danika walked on, they discovered Old City was

crowded with churches, synagogues, and Jewish study houses. The streets were an ever-changing collage of people, images, colors, and sounds. Graceful Arab women carried large baskets on their heads. Hasidic Jews wore the same costumes they'd worn for over a century.

They walked by the eastern edge of Omar Square. "I'm tired of just walking. Let's have lunch at that little deli. Then we'll check out some of the main attractions." He hoped to get her mind off her problems. He missed his perky little friend.

After lunch, they walked to the Western Wall or the Wailing Wall. Many people gathered there, wearing prayer shawls. In accordance with Jewish tradition, a partition separated the men from the women. "This is all that remains of Herod's temple," Curly said. "It's only a remnant of a wall that once supported the Temple on the Mount."

"Herod's temple? I thought it was Solomon's temple."

"Solomon built the original, but Herod the Great rebuilt it, using the same plan as Solomon's. It was said to be even grander, which is hard to picture since Solomon spared no expense, employing the finest materials and craftsmen. Notice that every head is covered, and no food or drink is allowed at the Wall. The Jewish people consider this a sacred place. Behavior and dress are considered of the utmost importance."

Danika nodded.

"Next, we'll visit The Dome of the Rock. We'll have to take off our shoes like we did in Istanbul.

They climbed the cement steps to enter what was considered one of the most splendid buildings in the world. After removing their shoes, they began their tour.

"According to belief, beneath this building lies the rock upon which Abraham planned to sacrifice Isaac. It's also on this spot that Mohammed is said to have ascended to heaven." Curly spoke in low tones as they passed through the mosque. "For nineteen centuries the Jews have prayed daily to return to a restored temple in Jerusalem."

"It's all so heartbreaking, isn't it?"

Curly had to agree. "It is, but it's beautiful inside and out. It's just built to honor the wrong god."

"Now where?" Danika asked later as they left The Dome.

He removed his brochure from his back pocket. "How about the Via Dolorosa?"

"The way of the cross," she interpreted.

"It has fourteen Stations of the Cross, each marked for prayer."

They walked the Via Dolorosa in silence. The thought of Christ carrying his cross along this route seemed to impact Danika as much as it did Curly. He found himself humbly worshiping his Lord and King with a grateful heart. God had done so much for him on this cruise.

Whatever happens with Danika, Lord, I'm glad I came. I'm thankful I finally realize the depth of your love for me. I'm so grateful my value doesn't come from the way others see me or treat me. My worth comes from you alone.

Father, please set Danika free from the things that bind her. Set her free from her promise to her dad and her mother's selfish expectations. Lord, if our future is meant to be together, you have a lot of obstacles to overcome. I'm glad none of them are too big for you. I lay my hopes for us at the foot of the cross. Do with them what you will.

Along the Via Dolorosa Curly let go of his future and placed it in

God's hand. He realized that God had used Danika to show him he was capable of loving and being loved—and that may have been her sole purpose in his life. He had to let go of her . . . and them.

In his heart he wept over the price Jesus paid to redeem him and all mankind. Jesus gave his life, and God gave his one and only Son because of his deep, abiding love for all men. Curly was glad that, over a decade ago, he'd accepted God's free gifts of salvation and eternal life.

As Danika and Curly walked the Via Dolorosa, she couldn't help thinking of Christ carrying his own cross. He'd forgiven her for every little thing. How could she refuse to forgive her mom? It must have been hard to have her husband snatched from her in one fatal evening.

God, I will choose right now to forgive her. Maybe she doesn't even deserve it, but neither do I. And I need to forgive my dad, too. A part of me is angry that he left me, and another part's angry that he strapped such a heavy burden to me when I was so young myself.

Howard Danby was right: Danika felt a weight lift. She'd been a prisoner of her own doing. Knowing the old anger might return and that sometimes forgiveness is a process, she prayed she'd just keep giving it all back to the Lord.

After they left the Church of the Holy Sepulchre, believed to be on the site of the crucifixion, it was getting dark. As they made their way back to the ship, both were quiet, contemplating the significance of the sites they'd seen and of their growing relationship.

CHAPTER SEVEN

"GOOD morning," Danika said, sounding unsure if it really was or not.

"Hello," he greeted her as he took a chair at their little table by the rail. "It's a pretty morning."

She nodded, then gazed toward the horizon.

"I'll just have black coffee," he told the waiter.

"Aren't you hungry?" she asked, pushing the food around her own plate with a fork.

"No, not really." Letting go of his hope for a future with her had robbed him of his appetite.

"Me either." She pushed the mostly uneaten food away. "Shall we go?"

He followed her out to the elevator.

"So, tell me about Port Said, Egypt," she requested as they left the ship.

He felt relieved that they had something to talk about that didn't revolve around them, her mother, or their future. "Port Said is located at the northern end of the Suez Canal. There's actually not much to see there, so I thought we could take the tour to Cairo, if you're game. The downside is it's a three-hour bus ride to get there."

"Time to catch a nap," she said lightheartedly, the dark circles under her eyes convincing him she needed one. "I put my day in your hands, Mr. Tour Guide."

Why couldn't she put her future in his hands? Why couldn't she trust him to protect her, even from her mother, if need be? He cleared his throat, hoping also to clear the downward spiral of his thoughts, and took the brochure from his back pocket.

Flipping open the pamphlet, he read, "Cairo is the largest city on the African continent. It's actually a thousand villages pushed together. An amazing combination of sights, sounds, and people awaits our arrival." He directed her to the place where they'd catch the bus. A large group of people already waited there. "Too bad our time is so limited."

"We'll just have to race to take it all in. No turtle pace for you today," she joked.

Her teasing elevated the mood. "Yes, ma'am," he agreed with a salute.

"What will we do once we get there?" she asked as they boarded the bus.

He carefully took his place on the seat next to her, avoiding touching her. "I thought we'd tour the famed Egyptian Museum, grab a bite, and cross the Nile to reach the pyramids at Giza. Then we'll either take camels or horses the rest of the way."

"Camels? That sounds intriguing."

"Not to this cowboy. I'm voting for horses."

"Ah, come on. You ride horses almost daily. When will you get another chance to ride a camel?" Some of the sparkle returned to her dull, lifeless eyes. He could tell her smile was genuine and that she'd relaxed.

"Your wish is my command," he said as a joke, but his words rang true. He knew he'd never deny her anything that was in his power to give her.

As her gaze locked with his, countless emotions crossed her face: sorrow and joy, hope and fear. He raised his hand to touch her cheek, then remembered. Halting the gesture in midair, he dropped his hand to his lap and turned away from her, looking out the window across the aisle. The rest of the trip was deadly quiet.

They toured the museum without much enthusiasm, both lost in their own pain. Curly found the whole place distasteful. Filled with stacked mummy cases, statues, and death masks, it felt eerie. He was glad when they exited into the busy, noisy city.

"If we walk this way, we should run into a street café." He nodded in the correct direction, allowing Danika to lead. But the dense traffic seemed endless, and waiting to cross the street felt like a death wish in itself. Finally, at a small break, he grabbed her hand, and they dashed to the other side.

He planned to let go when they reached safety, but he didn't. Instead, he found his thumb tracing the outline of hers. They stopped at the first place they saw. He pulled out her chair, and once she was seated, took his place across the table.

After they ordered, he read facts to her from the brochure. It provided a safe distraction from conversation. "Cairo is filled with mosques, mausoleums, huge cemeteries, and churches."

"They seem obsessed with death," Danika commented. She took a sip of tea and made a face. "This tastes bitter."

"That's the way they like it, according to the brochure. Cairo is a cosmopolitan city rich with Islamic tradition. It's 85 percent Muslim."

When lunch arrived, they ate without further word. He hated this tension between them—and seeing her tired, worried, burden-filled eyes. He was beginning to feel defeated and hopeless too.

After eating, they made their way to the camel rides, each choosing the one they'd take to the pyramids. Soon both discovered that camels didn't possess the sweet dispositions many horses did. They'd just as soon spit on you as look at you. And they swayed so much from side to side that even Curly, a born horseman, felt nauseous.

"Have you ever seen so much sand?" Danika asked once they were on their way. "It seems to go on forever."

"It feels desolate." *Just like my heart,* Curly thought. "And hot. Giza houses the largest and most famous of the pyramids. Each took twenty years to build, and they are the most massive stone structures on earth." *How much easier it is to recite facts than examine feelings,* he decided.

"Don't you feel like we're viewing pieces of lost stories from another world?"

"Yeah. An ancient, mystical world."

The pyramids stood even bigger than Curly had imagined. The astounding monuments rose out of the ground, reaching toward the heavens like a bleak world without color or life. They didn't speak of hope or Christ; instead, they were reminders of man's inability to take his earthly possessions with him into eternity.

He glanced over at Danika, straddled across her camel. She looked his way and wrinkled her nose in distaste. "Touring Egypt has been my least favorite day," she whispered for his ears only. "All this sand . . . I feel dirty and gritty."

It was his least favorite day, too. He wondered if it was the strain between them or the place itself. Probably both.

The next morning, Danika noticed that Curly had already ordered their coffee by the time she joined him at their table. He was still so very sweet, even when feelings were strained between them. But the sadness residing in his eyes never seemed to go away anymore, nor did the sadness in her heart.

"What's on our agenda today?" she said, hoping to sound light and bubbly. But her effort didn't quite make it.

"Alexandria, named for Alexander the Great," he said, quoting from the brochure. "This second largest city in Egypt lies on the Mediterranean Sea and is filled with Greek and Roman history. Known for its beautiful beaches and breathtaking turquoise water, it's considered the best resort city in all of Africa."

"Let's spend the day at the beach. Wouldn't it be nice to relax instead of fighting the crowds?" she asked eagerly. "I still haven't recovered from all that walking we did in Jerusalem."

"Sounds good to me. If we get tired of that, we can always take their streetcars and catch an overall glimpse of the city."

Within the hour, they walked along the beautiful blue green sea. "This is much nicer than where we were yesterday. I love the water," Danika commented.

Curly smiled at her but didn't respond. She'd noticed that his confidence was wavering. She was angry at herself for hurting and disappointing him, yet she refused to let this gorgeous day on a peaceful beach be ruined.

"Don't you feel sorry for those women?" she said, realizing they needed to find a safe topic of conversation. "Can you imagine being fully dressed in this heat and even having your head covered with a scarf? I'm glad I'm not bound by their culture just because I'm a female."

"I read that the country is on a return to conservatism." Curly spread out their towels and sat down. She joined him. "A few years ago their women came to the beach with less attire."

"It must be hard to make progress, only to lose it again. . . . Hey, let's go in the water." She jumped up, hoping he'd join her. She shrugged off her T-shirt, then untied her wraparound skirt and dropped it on her towel, revealing a modest one-piece swimsuit.

He removed his shirt, wading into the water in his jeans shorts. As they played, splashed, and swam for the next hour, Danika's tension faded with each minute. They just enjoyed the time, unconcerned about the past and the future, concentrating only on the here and now.

After their frolic in the warm Mediterranean, both lay on their towels and napped in the sunshine. Then they sauntered along the sun-baked, sandy beach for what seemed like miles. The serenity and joy of the day flooded Danika's soul.

"What were your dreams as a child?" she asked when they finally turned around to retrace their steps along the beach. Both carried their shoes, and waves lapped over her bare feet as they walked along the edge of the water.

"That my stepdad would love me and treat me the same way he did my half brothers and sisters. I longed to be part of their family. I never was."

Again, the image of that lonely, left-out child broke her heart. "What were you like as a little boy?"

"Quiet and awkward. I spent as much time as I could in the barn. I felt safe there—and loved."

"You grew up on a ranch?"

"A farm in Ohio. My stepdad worked me hard, but I'm thankful for the knowledge I gleaned. It enabled me to survive on my own when I left home."

"Where'd you go when you ran away?"

"I hitchhiked my way west. I worked at many farms and ranches along the way. I've been with Rick's family the longest—five years."

"You seem close to them."

"I am, especially Rick."

"Is that why you stayed so long?"

"Yeah. We're friends. My last real friend was Buddy, an eleven-year-old kid who planted the first seeds of the gospel in my life. He spent his summers with his grandparents on the farm next to ours. Then when we turned thirteen, his grandparents sold the farm and moved to town. I never saw him much after that."

Curly's life was filled with people leaving him or rejecting him. Now her name would be added to that long list of folks. "Do you plan to stay on with Rick until you retire?"

He stopped and picked up a shell, examining it closely. Then his eyes looked out over the sea. "I've saved a little nest egg over the years. I thought that someday I'd buy a little spread of my own." His gaze now turned to her. "A few days ago, I was thinking Tennessee. Now that doesn't look too promising." With those few words, he moved on toward their towels.

Danika stood frozen, stunned. She never imagined he'd move to Tennessee to be near her. She assumed she'd have to quit her job and move to the desert. Tears dampened her eyes. He was the kindest person she'd ever met. Denying him her love proved excruciating over and over again.

She saw him down the beach, waiting for her. She did want him, with all her heart. If the choice were hers alone, she'd never reject him—not ever. But her impossible situation made it hopeless.

When she was only a few steps away, she took a deep breath. Although it was audible, he didn't look in her direction; he kept his eyes on the jewel-like beauty of the Mediterranean. It wasn't until she placed her hand on his arm that he looked down at her. But his eyes weren't welcoming.

She swallowed her dread and forced the words out. "I love you. Please believe me."

"But not enough, Danika. Not enough to fight. Not enough to pray. Face it, I'm not worth it to you," he said, disappointment echoing through his words and etching itself on his face.

"You want me to fight God?" she said defensively.

"No, I want you to consider the possibility that God brought us together, and only your mother and a promise you made twenty years ago keep us apart. I want you to love me enough that you won't give up on us." Then he laughed harshly. "Why would I even expect that? No one's ever been willing to fight for me. Why would you?"

Again he walked away, leaving a confused Danika in his wake. She followed behind but didn't try to catch up. She couldn't please him, or her mother, or even herself. Every choice seemed to be the wrong one. Could she go back to her life of busyness now, denying the love in her heart?

Was he right? Was her love selfish and self-centered? Did she love him enough to fight for him, for them—even if it meant breaking a childhood promise?

She *longed* to be married and have a family. Why couldn't he understand that? Why didn't he believe she wanted him as much as he wanted her? Didn't he know she was in as much pain as he was?

CHAPTER EIGHT

THE next morning it seemed as if a bull sat on Curly's chest. To his amazement, his heavy, broken heart still beat. He felt certain he wouldn't see Danika again. When the going got tough, Danika seemed to run.

How ironic that he'd spent all these years guarding his heart and avoiding women. Then she'd come along and drawn him out. She'd even convinced him he was worth something. Yet, when he was most vulnerable, she'd denied him her love.

I love you, Curly. Her watery eyes begged him to take her words at face value. *Please believe me,* she'd pleaded. How could he believe her? Her actions spoke volumes louder than her claims. He'd never walk away from her—*never!* Real love didn't take the easy way out, but Danika did.

He thought of the little spread he planned to buy—maybe even in Tennessee. He'd actually started thinking in that direction when Danika left after the wedding. He'd never admit that to a living soul; he'd even refused to believe the idea had anything to do with her. But now he knew better.

He'd even done a little research. The rolling, green hills outside of Nashville would provide the perfect spot to raise horses and cattle. He'd convinced himself that he was ready to try a new corner of the country. Somewhere he'd not been before. All the while his heart yearned to draw closer to Danika, even if she never knew he was there. And this past week, he'd imagined a little place with a guest house for her mother.

He picked up the phone and followed the directions to make a ship-to-shore call. He knew the cost was outrageous, and he was not a spendthrift, but he *needed* to talk to Rick or Katie. He needed somebody in his court, praying for him. Unfortunately, he forgot about the time change.

"Rick, I'm sorry I woke you. What time is it there?"

"Hey, Curly. It's OK. We haven't been in bed too long. It's 11 here. Hang on."

Katie's excited voice came over the line. "Are you calling to tell us there'll soon be a wedding?"

"No. I'm calling to tell you that Danika is the most impossibly stubborn woman I've ever met. She won't even try." His voice cracked, giving away the emotions stirring within him.

"I'm so sorry. Have you tried talking to her?"

"I've tried everything this side of a shotgun."

Katie chuckled. "I guess it's time to just give it to the Lord," she said softly.

"I'm trying," he said, with grief. "Easier said than done."

"I know," she said, pain and regret in her voice. "We'll be praying . . ."

"That's why I called."

"I'm so sorry, Curly. This is my fault."

"I know you meant well. I don't want you to feel bad, just pray."

"I will. Here's Rick."

"Curly, we're both sorry, and we love you, buddy."

"Thanks. I'll see you in a few days." As Curly hung up the phone, the pain in his heart throbbed like an unhealed knife wound. After a shower and his quiet time with the Lord, he wandered restlessly around the ship.

He had no intention of coming between Danika and her mother. He loved Danika, and he would have loved her mother, if only she'd given him the chance. Since he had no family, he appreciated their value. He wanted to *join* Danika in caring for her mother.

Why would a loving father ask his daughter to give up her own life and happiness to care for her widowed mother? *Lord, help her understand that her father couldn't possibly have meant for her to never marry.* Saying the words, "Oh well, it's too late for us," aloud caused his voice to break with emotion. He wished she weren't quite so honorable. Yet, the truth was that Danika's feelings for him weren't strong enough to overcome her obligation to her parents. He had to swallow back his hurt.

Curly wandered restlessly around the ship for two days. The idea of being stuck at sea made him feel cooped up. He wasn't good at idleness. He had no desire to play shuffleboard with strangers. He'd stood outside Danika's door several times but never summoned the courage to knock. The hour chapel services each night were his only reprieve from misery. Even during prayer and his time in God's Word, he couldn't concentrate. The only prayer that made sense was, *Lord, heal my broken heart.*

He'd been wiser at eighteen when he'd decided to avoid friendship and emotional intimacy with a female. Why, now in his thirties, had he weakened his stance and let an amazing woman steal his heart and his contentment?

His eyes searched for Danika as he entered the chapel service at the end of the second day. He knew she wouldn't be present but longed to see her one last time. Tomorrow they'd dock in Naples for another day of sightseeing, but he felt certain she'd not meet him at their usual spot.

The worship time lifted Curly's spirits. He was able to focus on God and even forget his own misery for a while. Then Howard Danby took his place behind the podium, sharing with them from God's Word.

"In Philippians 3:12-14, Paul throws out a challenge that I pass along to you today. 'I don't mean to say that I have already achieved these things or that I have already reached perfection! But I keep working toward that day when I will finally be all that Christ Jesus saved me for and wants me to be. No, dear brothers and sisters, I am still not all I should be, but I am focusing all my energies on this one thing: Forgetting the past and looking forward to what lies ahead, I strain to reach the end of the race and receive the prize for which God, through Christ Jesus, is calling us up to heaven.'

"Are you *working, focusing, straining* to be all God created you to be? Forget the past. Lay it down. Move forward today with one goal in mind: Christlikeness."

That was all Curly heard from the sermon, but it was enough. With God's help, he could do this. He could lay Danika and his broken heart down and move forward. Another hint of hope stirred his heart. God didn't bring him this far to leave him hurting and in pieces. He wasn't looking forward to the future, but in time God could change that. At last, peace enveloped him.

Danika slipped out of the chapel when Howard Danby started his closing prayer. She had sneaked into the last row just as he began his message. She avoided running into Curly, but then spent the entire service with her gaze riveted to his bowed head and stooped shoulders.

Guilt-ridden, she took the stairs back to her cabin where she'd hide out until tomorrow. Seeing him only brought doubt to her resolve and made them both feel worse. She wanted to be mad at Katie and her mother but ended up mad at herself. Why did she allow this to happen when she knew better? How could she have so easily forgotten her responsibility to her mom and her promise to her dad?

She'd spent the past two days locked in her tiny cabin, and she desperately wanted out. She'd prayed, fasted, and read the Word, but felt no closer to an answer. Was God even there? It sure didn't feel like it.

She sat in an Indian-squat position on her bed, opening her Bible to the passage Howard had just read. She'd spent so much of her life staying busy that she'd failed to work toward being all Christ saved her to be. Her focus was survival as the self-righteous daughter who gave up everything for her mom.

God, forgive me. I've lost sight of you in the battle to please my dad by putting my mom first. I've been far too busy to hear your voice. I turned to busyness to avoid the loneliness in my heart instead of allowing you to fill the spot. A tear slid down her cheek, dropping onto the Bible in her lap. "Some vacation! I've spent half of it miserable," she chided herself.

She reached for a Kleenex and dried her eyes before continuing to read. The time had come to focus her energy on Christ, to forget the past and look forward to whatever God had for her in the future. The time had come to forget Curly. With God she could do it, but it might be the hardest thing she'd ever done, except maybe forgiving herself for causing more pain and rejection in his life.

His warm, brown eyes came to mind. Eyes that would barely look at her when they first met. Eyes that warmed to her and slowly trusted her. Eyes that began to believe in his self-worth and even fill with hope. Eyes that said *I love you* and begged her to love him back. Then came sad eyes, disappointed eyes. Would those eyes haunt her forever?

They did plague her dreams that night. Finally, at 4 A.M., she gave up tossing and turning. Taking the stairs to Hope Deck, she watched the sun slowly light the sky. The picture brought to mind another sunrise.

She sat on the Laramies' patio, waiting for the sun to show its face. Katie and Rick had left on their honeymoon, and the wedding was only a memory now. During the ceremony, her gaze had remained locked with Curly's. Against her better judgment, she'd imagined them as the bride and groom.

They'd spent the evening together, helping Mrs. Laramie clean up after the guests left. Then they'd walked to the barn so she could see the foal one last time. They'd talked until way after midnight. Nothing special, just small talk. When he told her good night, she'd seen the longing in his eyes and felt it in her heart. After three fitful hours of trying to sleep, she'd given up.

As the sun peeked over the Catalina Mountains, she found herself wishing she never had to leave. Wishing she were as lucky as Katie to have a man to love for a lifetime.

"Danika?" She'd jumped at the sound of Curly's voice. "I thought you'd still be asleep for hours."

His disheveled look confirmed that he, too, had found no rest that night. Her fingers yearned to brush his hair into place. "I couldn't sleep," she confessed.

"Me either."

Together they watched the sun paint a kaleidoscope of colors across the sky and heard the sounds of the day waking around them. Tranquillity enveloped them, and she knew their hearts were irrevocably bonded.

When he drove her to the airport later that day, she desired to share her feelings with him. But wisdom won out, and she didn't. Instead she flew back to Nashville and squeezed more activities into her life to avoid the memories of Curly and the brief touch of love.

With a start, Danika's mind came back to the present. She rushed back to her room, not wanting to chance an encounter with Curly. She couldn't stand another day in her "prison cell," so she decided to go ashore in Naples late, hoping he'd be long gone.

An hour later, Curly was nowhere in sight as she made her way off the ship. This time she had to carry her own brochure and do her own reading. She refused to think about the what-ifs. That would only make her more miserable. She knew they would say good-bye in Rome, anyway. It would just happen a few days earlier than she'd planned.

The pamphlet claimed that Naples, in the south, was Italy's third largest city and Italian to the extreme: home to red sauces, red wines, and pasta. It was also the birthplace of pizza and organized crime. Her heart dropped at that fact, wishing she didn't feel so alone. *Guard your possessions closely,* the paper warned.

The brochure presented an earthy place with a zest for life, but her heart sank lower at the sights before her. Myriad mopeds and scooters darted here and there, even on the sidewalks at times. Trash blew everywhere, and graffiti-covered buildings lined the cobblestone street.

Lonely and uncertain, she walked from one tourist attraction to another. This day was even worse than Cairo had been. She stopped for lunch at a pizza place, but their pizza wasn't quite the same as back home. She wandered down streets lined with fresh-fruit and vegetable markets. Someone passing by told her that when the shop fronts close, they become private homes at night. "And hold tight to your camera," the pedestrian warned. Danika tightened her arms around it.

She watched, amused, as an Italian grandmother tossed her fresh fruits to the market owner and he caught and bagged them. Then Danika's quest led her to Cappella Sansevero, a small chapel. After that she planned to return to the ship early—again to avoid Curly.

Once inside the chapel, she saw a statue like none she'd seen before. It was Christ's body after his death on the cross, laid out on a soft pillow. Carved from marble sometime in the eighteenth century, it looked so real. You could still see his features, the crown of thorns at his feet.

Danika began to weep, remembering the cost Christ paid for her soul. He had died in her place, so she, upon confessing her sins and need for him, could spend eternity in heaven. She stepped outside, leaning against the wall. She was so moved by Christ's sacrifice that she forgot the world around her.

A yank on her neck brought her back to reality. A man ran off with her camera as the broken strap dangled from her neck. Her gentle weeping turned to sobs as she watched him carry away her pictures of Curly—the only part of him she had left.

CHAPTER NINE

AFTER reading the brochure on Naples the night before and learning about the high crime rate, Curly had decided to keep an eye on Danika. But what good was he? Helpless from half a block down and across the street, he'd just watched a man flee with her camera. Then, running toward her, he was almost hit by a moped. The angry driver yelled at him in Italian.

Finally he reached her, and taking her into his arms was the most natural thing in the world. She grabbed onto him. "Curly, a man just—"

"I know. I saw him," he said and kissed her temple.

"You saw him?"

"I was down the street a ways when you came out of the chapel, but I was too far away to be of any help." Great protector he was. She could have been hurt, and he wouldn't have been able to stop it. He was as angry with himself as he was with the thief.

She no longer cried but still trembled slightly. "Would you walk me back to the boat?" she asked, seemingly embarrassed by her request.

"If you'll let me spend the day with you tomorrow in Rome."

"I don't know, Curly . . ."

"No expectations. I just want you to be safe. No personal conversation. No guilt. Just an escort."

"I'd like that. Thank you."

With his arm supporting her, they walked back to the ship. She leaned heavily against him, as if she didn't possess the strength to carry her own weight. "Have dinner with me tonight," he said, surprising himself by stating his wishes aloud.

She looked up, and he saw a mixture of uncertainty and longing battling within her. He figured good sense must be telling her to refuse even while her heart pleaded to say yes.

"It's our last night on board. I don't want to spend it alone. Do you?"

"No, but nothing's changed. Do you still want to spend it with me?" she asked.

"Nobody but," he assured her. When they parted at the elevator, he said, "Dress up, and we'll go to the formal dinner. I'll pick you up at seven-thirty, so we can make chapel afterward."

She nodded, and the hint of a smile curved her lips. "See you then."

Curly rented a tux. For some reason he wanted their last night to be extra special. Maybe so she'd remember him fondly. When she answered the door wearing a black gown, he shoved his hands into his pockets rather than pulling her into his arms.

"You look great." Her glowing eyes confirmed the sincerity of her words.

"And you look—breathtaking," he told her as he extended his arm to her. She rested her hand in the bend of his elbow.

Dinner was quiet and slightly strained. What did a guy say to the love of his life on their last date?

After dinner they went to their last chapel service together. He would miss hearing Howard Danby teach. Not as much as he'd miss

Danika, though. Their time together came closer to the end as each minute ticked away. How would he ever say good-bye to her, to them? He knew he'd never see her again once she boarded that plane. He felt certain nothing could drag her back to the ranch as long as he resided there.

He barely heard a word in chapel. His mind was full of good-byes. He remembered saying good-bye to her just months before at the Tucson airport.

He stood next to her in the line, waiting to check her luggage. He held her suitcase in a death grip to avoid giving in to the desire to touch her. He wanted to say something, anything, but no words came. Finally, her turn arrived to check in, so he carried her bags forward, placing them on the scale.

Once she had her boarding pass, they walked to her gate. The passengers were already loading. She stopped and turned to face him. "I had a wonderful time. Thanks for everything." Her wide smile flipped his heart upside down.

He nodded, grasping for something witty to say. But nothing came. She squeezed his hand.

"Good-bye, Curly. I enjoyed meeting you and every minute we spent together."

He nodded again like a silly fool. "Me, too."

In a flash, she walked away to board her plane. As she moved forward in the line, she glanced back once and waved. Then the boarding tunnel swallowed her up, and she disappeared from sight.

This time he held no secret hope of seeing her again. This good-bye was forever.

After chapel they took a moonlight stroll around each deck. She shivered, and he draped his coat around her shoulders. Finally she said, "I'd love to do this all night, but I'm beat. I haven't been sleep . . . anyway, let's call it a night."

At her door, she laid his jacket over his arm. "Thanks for joining me tonight," he said, smiling, hoping to alleviate the tension between them.

"Thanks for asking. I'll see you in the morning."

"Night, Danika. Sleep tight, my love," he whispered to her already closed door. Back in his room, he lay across the top of his bed. His tux jacket smelled like Danika, so he held it close. He fell asleep that way.

The next morning they disembarked for the last time. They caught a taxi to the hotel where both had rooms reserved. They checked in, stowed their luggage, and agreed to meet in the lobby fifteen minutes later.

One last day in Rome, and tomorrow they'd fly back to the States separately. Katie had only been able to get Curly on Danika's flight to Istanbul. She'd leave first thing in the morning. He'd catch a plane a few hours later.

When he came down, Danika was already waiting in the lobby. Her smile looked almost genuine. "Ready?"

"Ready," she agreed.

"Where to?"

"I thought you were our tour guide. Did you forget to read up on Rome?" she said, tilting her head to one side.

"The problem is, way too much to see, way too little time," he said, producing a brochure. As she moved in close to share it, he found himself wondering more about this sudden change in her attitude than what they might see in Rome.

"Why don't you pick the sight you want to see the most; then it'll be my turn. We'll do that until we run out of time," she said exuberantly.

"Ladies first," he insisted, handing her the brochure.

"I knew you'd say that." She smiled up at him again. "I want to see the Sistine Chapel." She handed the brochure back to him, then startled him by taking his hand and leading him out the door of the hotel. Hope bloomed in his heart like a fragile flower. Dare he believe something had changed her mind about them? He decided he'd wait for her to tell him what was going on. He'd not push her.

Danika hoped she wasn't making a huge mistake, but she couldn't bear another somber, gloomy day. She longed for the easy camaraderie they'd shared during the beginning of the cruise. She wanted their last day to be their best, not their worst. She decided to re-create a time when there'd been no tension between them—a time when being together had been as free and easy as a summer breeze. She knew Curly longed for that time as well, so for today they'd erase the strain, forget she had a mother, forget she'd made a promise to her father, and pretend they really *were* going to last forever.

Hand in hand, they toured the famous chapel. Her idea worked; the strain between them disappeared. When Curly smiled down at her, all felt right in her world. She loved this man. If only her mother weren't so unreasonable. If only she'd get to know Curly, Danika knew her mother would love him, too. *No thoughts of her today,* Danika reminded herself.

"Your pick. What do you want to see?"

"The Colosseum. Do you want to stop for an espresso first?" he asked as they passed a sidewalk café.

"Sure."

After ordering, Danika asked, "Was it a coincidence that you happened by just as my camera was taken yesterday?"

He squirmed. "No. I was keeping an eye on you. With all the warnings about thieves and muggers, I was worried."

Touched by his protective attitude, she asked, "How'd you know where I'd be?"

"I followed you off the ship," he confessed.

"I didn't see you."

"I was careful. I knew you didn't want me around, but my conscience wouldn't allow me to let you wander around Naples alone."

She placed her hand on his. "Can we forget all that? I want you around now."

"And there's nowhere I'd rather be." He turned his hand over, wrapping it around hers. Contented, they sipped espresso, held hands, and watched the people pass by.

After touring the Colosseum, they ambled to a church ten minutes away to see Michelangelo's *Moses*. "Seeing this was worth the walk," Curly commented. He hadn't let go of her hand since their stop at the sidewalk café.

They spent the day holding hands and touring Rome's most splendid sites. Danika decided this was her favorite of the cities they'd visited. They picnicked near the Piazza Navona and then toured the Vatican and St Peter's Church in the afternoon. Both built in the Renaissance period, they were Rome's greatest monuments to Christendom.

For dinner they veered off the main path to the district where rustic *trattorias* claimed to serve the best pasta besides Mama's. They ducked into a little place where spaghetti was served in bowls.

After dinner, they made their last tourist stop at Trevi Fountain. Curly handed Danika a coin, and she threw it in, wishing that tonight never had to end. Curly tossed a coin also, and his eyes told her his wish was similar.

Slowly they made their way back to the hotel. He drew her against his side, holding her close. She rested her head against his shoulder. "Tired?" he asked in a low voice.

"Yes. My plane leaves early tomorrow."

They'd arrived back at the hotel. "May I walk you to your room?"

She nodded, and they walked across the carpeted lobby to the elevator. "It was a wonderful day. Thank you for sharing it with me. The eternally beautiful city of Rome captured my heart."

"And you, pretty lady, have captured mine," he informed her when the elevator doors closed and they were alone inside. His kiss assured her the words were true.

At her door, Curly took her key. "What time do you need to leave in the morning?"

"Why?" A dread settled in her stomach as he pushed her door open. Maybe he didn't realize that nothing had actually changed between them. Tomorrow was still good-bye, and there were no more tomorrows for them after that.

"I'll go with you."

What should she do now? Fight with him here in the hallway, or leave a Dear John letter at the desk? Rather than cause a scene, she opted for the coward's way out. "Meet me in the lobby at eight."

"I'll be there," he promised. "Sleep well," he said, placing one last tender kiss on her cheek.

She wouldn't sleep at all. As she watched him retreat down the hall, she was ashamed of herself. Once again she'd hurt this dear man. Tears of regret blurred her vision. "God, please forgive me," she said in a tortured voice, entering her room.

Lord, why is honoring a promise so difficult and costly? Why is it so painful? Help me understand. She wanted to ask God to give her the words to tell Curly, but she couldn't bring herself to ask him to be part of her deception. No, she'd have to write this note on her own. She settled on her bed with paper and pen; through tears she wrote the note she knew would break Curly's heart one more time.

Danika cried herself to sleep sometime after midnight. Then her alarm woke her at five. She checked out, leaving Curly's note at the front desk. She explained to the man behind the counter how important it was for Mr. Nevyn to get it. Thankfully her plane would be in the air before he discovered she'd gone. Part of her felt relieved to never have to see him again. Another part mourned the loss of the person she now knew she loved most in all the world.

CHAPTER TEN

THE next morning Curly wasn't positive how everything would play out, but he looked forward to sending Danika back to Nashville with the promise of a future in their hearts.

He decided to take a surprise to her room before their eight o'clock meeting in the lobby. Wanting her to have a memento of their time together, he'd cleaned and polished the shell he'd found on the beach in Alexandria.

Rushing up to her room, he was surprised to find her door ajar. A maid's cart stood in the hall. Inside he noted the bed was made. No sign of Danika remained. Puzzled, he checked the closet and then the bathroom, startling the maid as she cleaned the toilet.

"Where's Danika?"

The Italian woman only shook her head and mumbled something he couldn't understand. He dashed back down the hall toward the elevator.

She must be waiting in the lobby. That was it. He wondered why she'd gone down so early. That didn't make much sense. *What if she's gone?* "She'll be there," he told the empty elevator. But he couldn't chase away his dread.

When the elevator doors separated at the bottom floor, he didn't see Danika anywhere. He hurried into the coffee shop and looked around. Would she leave without saying good-bye?

Tapping his boot impatiently, he stood in the checkout line, not wanting to believe she'd ditched him. There must be some logical explanation.

Finally he made it to the front of the line. "Can you tell me if Miss Sutherland has checked out?" he asked the man behind the counter.

"Yes, sir. Almost an hour ago."

Curly's heart dropped with a thud. *Why? Why would she do that?*

Somewhere in his brain it registered that the hotel clerk was asking him something. "I'm sorry? What did you say?"

"Your name, sir? I asked your name."

"Calder Nevyn." He wondered what that had to do with anything.

The clerk handed him an envelope. "Miss Sutherland left this for you."

He took it and numbly made his way back to his room. Grasping feebly for some excuse, he thought, *Maybe she had an emergency*. Once settled on the edge of the bed, he tore open the envelope. Fearing the contents, he unfolded the piece of hotel stationery.

My Dearest, Dearest Curly,

These past fifteen days with you will be my fondest memories. I shall hold you and our time together in my heart forever. I will never forget you. I will never stop loving you, I promise.

I pray you'll understand that I have no choice. I must lay you and our love aside for my mother's sake. I know these words hurt you, and I'm dying inside as I write them—please know that. If there were another way, I'd take it.

You truly are the most incredible man I've ever met. It is with tears and sorrow that I walk away. You are everything a girl dreams of—and more. Hurting you is killing me because, believe me, you are worth the fight. But I can't fight God. He considers our word and our promises sacred.

I beg you to forgive me. I beg you to try and understand. I love you.

Now and always,
Danika

Tears formed in his eyes. He *didn't* understand. He hurt even worse than he did as a child when his stepfather shot cruel words and accusations at him. Wadding the letter, he threw it across the room. "I loved you, Danika. I believed you when you said loving people was worth the risk. You lied to me because nothing is worth the pain I feel right now."

Danika settled into her middle seat on the plane. She dreaded the long flight home, already feeling exhausted. She hoped to sleep most of the trip to block out her guilt and anguish. She didn't want to think. She didn't want to pray. She only wanted the oblivion of sleep to carry her away.

She spent over an hour trying to get comfortable and drift off. Neither happened, so she decided to read. As she pulled her Bible out of her tote bag, the outlines from Howard's chapel services slipped out onto her lap.

"Now that we've gotten rid of the baggage that saddles us when there's unforgiveness, we're all free to run the race God has for us." God, I'm running, but am I even in the right race?

As she read the words she'd written days before, they struck Danika with uneasiness. Her life still lacked peace. She continued down her notes. *He has plans for me—plans to give me a hope and a future. My future looks grim, Lord. What are your plans for me? Where is my hope?*

She laid that one aside and picked up another outline. *Am I straining to be all God created me to be? I don't even know who or what that is. I'm striving to live up to a twenty-year-old promise, but I have no idea what you want for me, God.*

Her mind relived the scene she hated to remember.

As a fifteen-year-old woman-child, she stood with her mother in the emergency room. They'd received the call that her father was dying, and a neighbor drove them to the hospital.

Her mother sobbed hysterically. She kept mumbling selfish, fragmented sentences about how unfair life was to her.

Danika felt angry at her mother's response. What about Daddy? He laid there, covered with blood, hooked to countless machines, struggling to draw his next breath. He spoke her name, and she moved closer.

"I want you to know how much I love you. You're my morning star and the sunshine of my life. If we could have, your mom and I would have had ten more just like you." He forced the words out between gasps of breath. She had to lean close to hear him.

"Daddy, please don't die," she whispered as tears streaked a path down her cheeks.

"If I don't make it, you be a good girl. Grow up and be a good wife and mother . . . and . . . promise . . . take care of your mother . . . She's frail. . . ."

Machines started beeping. Doctors and nurses ran into the room and chased Danika and her mother out. Her mother screamed and cried louder, and Danika had an overwhelming desire to slap her. Throughout the funeral and the weeks that followed, her mother focused only on herself, unconcerned with Danika's loss.

Somewhere along this path called life, Danika realized she'd let her mother use her father's last words to manipulate her time and time again. Every time her mother wanted to control her, she threw that promise in her face. Over and over she'd said, *You can't marry and leave me alone. You gave your word to your father.*

Danika looked back at the notes from Howard's sermon on Philippians 3. *Are you straining to please man or God?* he'd asked. She'd left the question unanswered. Suddenly, it was as if a veil had fallen from her eyes and she saw clearly for the first time: Her race had been the one her mother called her to run.

Danika had always strived to please *her mother* and keep peace.

As a fifteen-year-old child, she'd promised her dying father to always take care of her mom. She'd let that promise—along with her mother's overbearing personality—lead her on a twenty-year journey in the wrong direction. Her dad didn't expect her to stay single; otherwise, he wouldn't have told her to be a good wife and mother. Danika began to weep for the wasted years when she'd failed to run God's race.

"Are you all right, dear?" the elderly lady on her left asked, holding out a tissue.

Danika accepted the offered Kleenex and wiped her eyes. Then she remembered Katie's favorite maxim: *God takes our liabilities and makes them assets*. She'd cling to those words. With God, nothing was wasted if she allowed him to use it for good in her life.

She smiled at the kind, grandmotherly figure. "You know, I'm fine. In fact, I'm better than I've been in a long, long time."

Katie had been right all along. Honoring a parent isn't the same as being controlled by one. God never called her to this life of self-imposed exile. God never asked her to remain single forever. With a sureness she couldn't explain, she knew now that meeting Curly and falling in love with him was part of God's plan for her.

Please, don't let it be too late for us, she begged God. *How will Curly ever trust me again? God, I'm so sorry I didn't see the truth sooner. I'm so sorry I needlessly hurt him. Please comfort him until I can clear this up.*

Thank you for him and for us. Thank you I now have a hope and a future. Thank you for Howard Danby, the cruise, and my pushy friend Katie! And Lord, I know my mom fears being alone. She fears me being happy and forgetting her. Help me to be mindful of her, and help me to forgive her for the years of selfish demands.

I really do want to be free—free from the past and striving toward your plans for the future. Thanks for guiding me to the right race. May my years ahead bring glory to your name. I love you. Amen.

Danika didn't sleep a wink the entire ten-hour flight. But instead of exhaustion, she felt revived and more alive than she had in years. When the plane landed in New York City, she made her way to a pay phone. Since she had some time before catching her connecting flight to Nashville, she decided she'd call her mom.

"Mom, I'll be home before too long. Just wanted to let you know I'm safely back in the States. Are you feeling any better?"

"Oh, now that the fun's over, you suddenly care. Why worry about it now? I could have died."

Danika took a deep breath and announced, "Mom, I've fallen in love. Dad never asked me to stay single, only to care for you. That was what you wanted for me, not him."

Her mother remained quiet, so Danika continued, "Mom, even if I get married, I'll still be there for you. Maybe you can even live with us if you want."

"I'm not moving from here!"

Danika's eyes got misty. "It's OK; you don't have to. Just so you know we'll take care of you." Her voice broke with the emotion she felt for Curly. She remembered his saying he wanted to help her care for her mom. "I'm going to hang up now. I'll see you tomorrow. And, Mom—I love you."

Hanging up the phone, Danika thanked God for the loving man she had momentarily pushed away. She had nearly cost herself a blessing from God by throwing his love back at him. Thinking of her tender warrior, she smiled.

As she was beginning to make her way toward the correct gate, how she longed to see Curly face-to-face, fall into his arms, and beg his forgiveness. It would be so much harder to do over the phone.

CHAPTER ELEVEN

BY THE time Curly's flight touched down in New York City, he'd come to terms with a few things. He'd placed Danika's crumpled letter in his Bible to help him remember the lessons God had taught him on the cruise. Even if Danika wasn't part of his future, God had used her to help straighten out his past.

For the first time ever, he realized how valuable he was to God. He'd forgiven his mom and worked toward forgiving his stepdad. And for a brief season in time, he'd been in love and been loved. What was that old adage? "'Tis better to have loved and lost than never to have loved at all."

The plane finally stopped at the gate, and Curly made his way into the aisle. He didn't have a carry-on—only his Bible with Danika's note tucked safely inside. Thinking of her brought a slight smile to his lips and a sharp pain to his heart. But he no longer felt angry. It was amazing what a transatlantic flight and several hours of prayer could accomplish.

Sure, he wished with all his heart things had turned out differently, and he wouldn't stop praying for God to intervene; he'd never stop loving her. But he'd decided fifteen days with her was better than nothing. Maybe someday when she was free, she'd reconsider.

He stepped into the hectic airport after going through customs, wondering how he'd ever find the right gate for his flight to Phoenix. As he searched for the departure monitors, his gaze locked on a pair of familiar blue eyes. He stopped, and his heart forgot to beat. Time stood still.

She smiled and began to move in his direction. Somehow he knew God had heard the prayer of his lonely heart, and he smiled back. She ran the last few steps into his waiting, open arms. He enveloped her in his embrace, and she held him just as tight.

They stood there, clinging to each other. Finally, she spoke. "I can't believe I 'ran' into you. I'm so sorry. I love you, and I was wrong." Tears glistened in her eyes.

His heart exploded with hope. "Wrong?"

"About us. About my mom. About what my dad wanted. About the future. About everything."

"What are you saying?" He wasn't letting her off the hook easily. He wanted to hear the words from her mouth.

She blushed, making her even more appealing. "If you still want to see me," she stammered. "I mean . . ." She bit her bottom lip and looked away, then said in a rush, "I'd like us to have a future together."

"Why, Miss Sutherland, are you asking me to marry you?" he teased.

Her face went from pink to red. "If you still want me." A tear slid down her cheek.

"Oh, my Dani-girl, of course I still want you." He kissed the tear away. "I wasn't ready to give up on us yet."

A shocked look crossed her face. "You weren't?"

"No. I love you. I'd have waited forever."

"You don't have to."

He dropped down on one knee, and her blush was back. "Danika, I love you. Marry me?"

She quickly pulled him to his feet. "Yes," she answered, her entire countenance radiant.

Then, right there—in the middle of the congested airport—he kissed her. The people around them applauded when the kiss ended, and he felt as red as she looked.

As they both chuckled, his heart floated heavenward on the wings of love.

A NOTE FROM THE AUTHOR

DEAR Friend,

As I think back over the years to choose a favorite vacation, one that my husband, our three kids, and I took well over a decade ago comes to mind. We started our two-week trip at Knott's Berry Farm in southern California and traveled up the coast, hitting all the amusement parks and tourist attractions along the way. It was nonstop go, see, and do.

We planned to spend the last few days with my aunt and uncle at their mountain home in the Sierra Nevadas. I looked forward to seeing them but feared we might be bored after such a jam-packed week and a half. I learned such an important lesson: those were the best days of the vacation. We played games and took quiet walks. We relaxed and enjoyed time with people we loved.

So often in life, I get caught up in the *going* and *doing*. I forget the joy and peace that come from being still. God reminded me during that special vacation that people are much more important than places. Yes, I still have a burning desire to see the world, but I've also learned to be content with the simpler joys of life. I've learned to value family, friends, and tranquil mountain retreats.

My prayer is—whether your life consists of exciting destinations or mundane days filled with the repetition of life—that you will experience it all with the joy and contentment that come from knowing Christ. He takes the ordinary and makes it something beautiful.

His,
Jeri

ABOUT THE AUTHOR

JERI Odell enjoys writing, teaching, and speaking on marriage, parenting, and family issues. She is a firm believer in true love, knowing that God holds marriage and the family dear to his heart. She has been active in her church and community for the past twenty years.

Jeri is happily married to her high school sweetheart; they recently celebrated their twenty-sixth anniversary. She loves reading Christian romance, leading Bible studies, and spending time with family and friends—especially her husband, Dean, and their three kids. All three of their almost-adult children migrated to California to attend Christian colleges, so she has an empty nest, except in the summer when the two youngest come home.

Jeri's novellas appear in the anthologies *Reunited, A Bouquet of Love, A Victorian Christmas Cottage,* and *Dream Vacation*. Her articles have appeared in *Focus on the Family, New Man Magazine,* and *ParentLife* as well as in other publications. She thanks God for the privilege of writing for him.

Jeri welcomes letters written to her in care of Tyndale House Author Relations, P.O. Box 80, Wheaton, IL 60189-0080, or by E-mail at JeriOdell@juno.com.

MIRACLE ON BEALE STREET

by
Elizabeth White

CHAPTER ONE

COME on, Miranda, shake a leg, or we'll miss the duck parade!"

Laughing, Miranda Gonzales let the door slam behind her as she followed Granny's hustling Nike Airs down a plushly carpeted hallway of the historic Memphis Peabody Hotel. She was going to have a hard time keeping up with her grandmother this week. Granny's hennaed curls had already disappeared around the corner.

They'd checked into the hotel early in the afternoon, after a long drive up from southern Mississippi. Granny let Miranda drive her bus-sized white Buick but insisted on driving with the windows down and *Elvis's Greatest Hits* blaring from the CD player. Miranda had had about all the "Jailhouse Rock" she could tolerate for one day. However, she had promised her dad she'd make sure Granny had the vacation of her dreams.

The famed Peabody duck parade was next on their list of Things to Do in Memphis.

Leaning over the wrought-iron railing of the mezzanine, Miranda felt an elbow in her ribs. Granny grinned at her and said, "Look at those cute little fellas swimmin' around down there. Good thing your grandpa's not here. He used to love a good duck hunt."

Picturing Grandpa Gonzales in the elegant lobby blasting away like Elmer Fudd, Miranda smiled. But Grandpa had been firmly ensconced in the Van Cleave Baptist Church cemetery for ten years, so the ducks could swim in peace. "They're cute, but I don't see what's so amazing about a bunch of mallards in a fountain."

"It's almost five o'clock. You'll see."

Miranda found herself much more interested in watching the crowd stacking up around the ornamental marble fountain. She knew from poring over travel brochures with Granny all winter that "Memphis in May" drew people to the downtown area from far and wide. It was always possible that she'd see someone she knew from college or home.

The crowd shifted a bit, bringing the enormous flower arrangement atop the fountain into Miranda's view. Her attention was caught by a young man standing with his back to her, just behind a spray of greenery. The straight set of his big shoulders, the black baseball cap reminded her of—

Miranda shook her head. No way. Tony Mullins would never be caught dead in a place like this. His idea of a vacation ran along the lines of a deer stand in the woods.

You've been working too hard, Miranda, old girl, she told herself.

Her job in Biloxi as a public relations specialist for the largest waste management company on the Gulf Coast left her little time for goofing off. When she wasn't working, she was going to church or spending weekends helping Granny in her garden. Daddy said she and Granny both needed a vacation. Since he offered to pay for it, Miranda got up the nerve to ask her boss for a few days off.

To her astonishment, he'd agreed, and here they were.

She shuddered, watching the man with the big shoulders move behind the fountain. *Lord,* she prayed, *you gave me this vacation as a special treat, and I know you'd never play a dirty trick like sending Tony Mullins to Memphis.*

Miranda glanced at Granny and shook her head at the perpetual look of surprise on the spritelike face. Nobody could convince the dear old woman not to pluck her eyebrows so drastically. Something intent about her grandmother's expression set a warning bell jangling in Miranda's brain. Granny almost looked as if she was searching for someone in the crowd. Miranda was sure it wasn't duck hunters.

"Granny—," she began, when an earsplitting crash of snare drums suddenly replaced the Muzak coming through the lobby speakers.

"Look! The Duckmaster!" Granny exclaimed.

Miranda followed Granny's pointing finger as an elderly black gentleman in an immaculately pressed bellman's uniform made his way through the crowd, directing several other men in the placement of a roll of red carpet at the top of the steps leading up to the fountain. The carpet unrolled with great pomp and ceremony as the crowd good-humoredly shuffled back.

The drumroll gave way to the lilting strains of a John Philip Sousa march, and Miranda burst out laughing as the big blue-green mallard heaved himself out of the water and waddled with droll dignity down the steps, the four nondescript little hens dripping in his wake. Miranda and Granny cheered with the rest of the crowd as the ducks followed a roped-off path and disappeared into an elevator shaft.

Almost as quickly as it had begun, the show was over.

Miranda turned to find Granny grinning at her, crinkle-eyed. "Granny, what a hoot!" she exclaimed. "Where did they go?"

"They live in a fancy palace up on the roof. They'll come back down at eleven tomorrow morning."

"Cool! Let's make sure we're down here to see that."

Granny consulted a typed list she pulled out of the pocket of her violent purple polyester stirrup pants. For a confirmed scatterbrain, Granny was being miraculously efficient where this vacation was concerned. "Let's see," she mused, holding the list close to her face. She refused to wear her glasses because she claimed they flattened her eyelashes. "No, tomorrow morning we're going to take in the Ornamental Metal Museum."

"The Ornamental Metal Museum? Since when did you—"

Granny suddenly let out a whoop and leaned over the railing, waving wildly. Startled, Miranda grabbed the back of her grandmother's Hawaiian shirt. "Granny, be careful!"

"Geraldine! Geraldine Mullins!" Granny called, cupping her hands around her mouth. "Up here!"

Most of the crowd had by this time vacated the lobby, and Miranda's gaze easily followed Granny's to the registration desk tucked discreetly along the far wall. Leaning regally on a walking stick beside a luggage cart was Granny's neighbor and dearest friend. Geraldine looked exactly like she did every time Miranda had ever seen her: gray white hair piled elegantly on her head, charcoal pantsuit immaculately pressed, upright posture emphasizing her nearly six-foot height. The beautiful elderly woman raised a perfectly manicured hand and smiled up at them.

It was not the sight of Mrs. Geraldine, however, that caused the heat to gush into Miranda's neck and face. The man with the big shoulders stood beside Geraldine, signing a paper at the desk.

Miranda's hands, white-knuckled, gripped the slick hickory top of the railing. She squeezed her eyes shut.

If I don't look at him, he'll go away. That can't be him. Oh, dear Lord in heaven, please don't let it be him.

But she knew it was him. That was most definitely Mrs.

Geraldine that Granny had hollered at. And Geraldine had only one grandson: Tony Mullins, Miranda's brother Grant's closest friend since childhood.

Tony had spent the night at her house practically every other weekend since she was in kindergarten. He'd once dissected her Betsy Wetsy. He'd helped Grant sell her entire Smurf collection in a garage sale for fifty dollars—without her knowledge. He'd accidentally flipped her out of a tree house and broken her leg so badly it still ached when it rained.

He'd given her her first kiss.

She was going to murder Granny.

"Granny," she said, feeling strangled, "I thought you said Mrs. Geraldine wasn't well enough to travel right now."

Granny looked uncomfortable. "Actually, last week your daddy gave permission."

Miranda's father was the only doctor within a twenty-mile radius of Van Cleave. He ruled his patients with an iron fist encased in a velvet glove of compassion.

That snake.

"Besides," Granny continued, "we'd already made our plans, and I didn't want to disappoint you."

"You knew Tony was coming, didn't you? Granny, how could you do this to me?"

"I wanted it to be a surprise. The poor boy's having such a hard time right now, and Geraldine and I both thought—"

"Geraldine would never come up with anything like this!"

"Hmph," Granny sniffed. "Much you know. Come down off your high horse and let's go say hello."

"I can't!" Miranda's feelings skewed from anger to panic. There had been so many changes in her life since she'd given her heart to Jesus soon after "the incident." So many things to rectify, so many apologies to make. But Tony Mullins was a bridge she hadn't dared to cross yet.

"I must say, I've never known you to back down from a challenge before." Granny's myopic green gaze was shrewd. "Go pout in the room if you want to, but I'm going down to the lobby."

Pout? *Pout?* Miranda opened her mouth to object, but Granny had already headed for the stairs.

Hearing his grandmother halloed from the mezzanine across the lobby, Tony wheeled around and looked up from signing the hotel registration form. An elflike little woman with improbably fiery hair and a wrinkled beaming face skipped down the corner stairs and dodged the grand piano. "Nana, that looks like—"

"Roxanne!" Nana hooked her cane over her arm and clapped her hands in delight. "What a wonderful coincidence."

Within moments, Tony had the breath knocked out of him by a bear hug around the waist. "Hi, Mrs. Roxanne," he grunted, hugging her back. He hadn't seen the old lady in several years. His vacations these days were few and far between, and he seldom went home, even though it was less than a two-hour drive to Van Cleave from New Orleans, where he lived.

Roxanne Gonzales ignored her friend and looked Tony up and down, clasping his hand tightly in her plump little paw. "Great day in the mornin'! How handsome and tall you've grown," she enthused. "Geraldine, what a hunk!"

"You're looking pretty gorgeous yourself," he said to cover his embarrassment.

She preened. "Just wait 'til you see—" She suddenly looked around. "Miranda! Where are you, child?"

The hairs on the back of his neck stood up. Tony glared at his grandmother, who had the grace to look guilty.

He'd been had.

Like a marionette being pulled by the puppet master's string, Tony looked up toward the mezzanine. Sure enough, there she was. Grant's little sister. The nemesis of his childhood.

She who had once buried a whole battalion of his plastic storm troopers in her grandmother's flower bed. Fed Play-Doh to his dog, who then got sick in Technicolor on his bed. Stuck his Nolan Ryan rookie baseball card in a book as a bookmark and turned it in to the library.

And handed his heart back to him on a platter.

There she stood, looking as infuriatingly beautiful as ever. Her curly golden brown hair was caught loosely on top of her head with some kind of metal clip, and she had on an ankle-length, flowered slip-dress. Miranda had always loved pretty clothes.

Her big-eyed expression, though, was more scared than surprised. He'd only seen her look like that one other time.

Since that was a memory he had no desire to revisit, he leaned his elbows back on the counter and lifted a hand to her. Would she come down and pretend to be glad to see him? Or would she run the other way? He could see her waffling.

Miranda's gaze suddenly jerked away from his as she moved toward the stairs. She had apparently done some growing up over the past few years.

Feeling Nana's arthritic fingers gently touch his arm, Tony looked down to find both women watching him with avid interest.

His defenses rose. "Nana didn't say you'd planned to come up, too, Mrs. Roxanne."

Fluffing her thin curls, Roxanne tipped her head saucily. "Surprise is the spice of life, dear."

"I get all the surprises I need every day on the job—"

"Which is exactly why you need a vacation," Nana interrupted firmly.

Since Tony's "vacation" was the result of a suspension, pending an investigation into a certain incident in the French Quarter, he appreciated the fact that Nana chose to ignore it. He sighed and tugged on the brim of his cap. "Yes, ma'am. I sure do." Noting the drawn look on his grandmother's face, he looked at his watch. "Let's get you settled in your room so you can rest before dinner."

"Oh, I have a wonderful idea!" Roxanne literally bounced up and down. "Geraldine, why don't you move in with Miranda and me? We're in one of those darlin' little Romeo and Juliet suites, and there's plenty of room."

"Tony, do you mind being alone?" Nana's look was searching. She must know the likelihood of his running into Miranda Gonzales every five minutes would be a nuisance.

He smiled but avoided her tender gaze. Nana's happiness was more important than his own discomfort. "If you want to . . ."

Nana beamed at her friend. "All right, I will."

His fate sealed, Tony took care of correcting their registration information and continued to watch for Miranda out of the corner of his eye. When he was ready to move the luggage up to their rooms, she still hadn't appeared.

"Where did your granddaughter go?" he asked, trying to sound nonchalant as he interrupted Roxanne and Nana's conversation.

They'd been jabbering as if it had been months since they'd seen each other, rather than just yesterday.

"Which one?" Roxanne asked with a mischievous wink. "I have eight, you know."

Tony knew. Miranda was the youngest of Roxanne's sixteen grandchildren, which meant she had always been outrageously spoiled. "M-Miranda, of course." He rolled his eyes, irked that he still had trouble saying her name out loud.

Roxanne lifted her hands. "Dunno. She was headed this way. You know Miranda. Probably got sidetracked."

Tony felt a wave of totally unwarranted disappointment hit him. He did know Miranda, inside and out, and he'd hoped she might take the chance to offer some kind of apology.

He very deliberately shrugged. "No big deal. She'll turn up sooner or later. Let's get you young ladies settled in." He winked at Roxanne, who simpered and socked him on the arm.

"Geraldine," she said, "ol' Romeo could've taken lessons from this 'un."

Miranda stood in front of the rest-room mirror repairing her lipstick. She'd made it down the stairs without her knees buckling, but it was more than she could do to walk all the way across that cathedral-sized lobby, knowing that Tony waited on the other side. She'd known in the back of her mind that she'd run into him again one day, but for Granny to force it this way. . . . Every push-pull emotion she'd ever felt for him clamored for recognition. What must he think to find her here?

To give herself a little time, she'd slipped into the ladies' room to check her hair. If she had to face him, at least she wouldn't do it looking like a bag lady.

"What are you afraid of?" she asked herself aloud. "You're not the same person you were the last time you saw him."

And a good thing, too, said the snide voice that often undermined her faith. *That* was a pretty scene, wasn't it?

"'There is no condemnation for those who belong to Christ Jesus,'" she repeated, as she had done many times before. "'Those who become Christians become new persons. They are not the same anymore, for the old life is gone. A new life has begun!'"

She jammed the cap onto her lipstick with satisfaction, stuck the tube in her pocket, and smiled at herself. Good, no smears on her teeth. "Thank you, Lord!" She turned to go and gasped.

Another young woman stood with the rest-room door halfway open, staring at Miranda as if she had just escaped from Whitfield Sanitarium.

"Oh, my goodness," Miranda mumbled. "I didn't hear you come in."

The girl, who might have been anywhere between fifteen and twenty-five—it was hard to tell because of the layers of makeup caking her pretty coffee-colored face—seemed to be contemplating flight. After a strained moment she edged into the room, avoiding Miranda's embarrassed gaze. Miranda was about to leave when something about the set of the young woman's slight shoulders stopped her.

The girl stepped quickly into a stall and slammed the door.

Miranda hesitated. Her recent habit of talking out loud to God and rehearsing her memory verses had earned her many an amused look, but this one was different. There had been fright in that girl's midnight eyes, strangely mixed with—what? Hope?

"Abba," she whispered, "what do you want me to do?"

FEED MY LAMBS.

Jesus' words to Peter slipped easily into Miranda's mind. She'd read them just this morning while Granny drove from Hattiesburg to Jackson. She'd thrilled to their sweet simplicity.

FEED MY LAMBS.

But I don't know enough, she argued silently. *Besides, she'll think I'm crazy.*

She already thinks you're crazy, the enemy voice cut in. Mind your own business.

Before Miranda could move, the toilet flushed and the girl came out. She hunched over the sink, wringing her hands under the water dribbling out of the faucet. Tears poured down her cheeks in hopeless streams, leaving raccoon rings of mascara smeared around her eyes. Her purple red mouth squared in a silent wail.

Jolted, Miranda sidled toward the young woman. "Hi, I'm Miranda. Can I help you?"

The girl slammed the spigot off. "What is this, Burger King?" she said in a rusty voice. "Leave me alone."

"OK, if you're sure you want me to, but I'd feel really bad if—"

"Just shut up and go away."

FEED MY LAMBS.

Miranda winced. She propped her hip on the adjacent sink as if she badgered strangers every day. "Um . . . are you hungry?"

The girl looked at Miranda in real alarm. "Are you nuts?" She wiped her face on the sleeve of her tight black sweater and backed toward the door.

"No, I just—" Miranda fumbled for a rational explanation for her outrageous nosiness and found none. "I saw you crying, and I wanted to help. But if you won't tell me what's wrong, I can't . . ." She trailed off miserably, shut her eyes, and prayed silently, *God, help!*

After a moment of utter stillness, the rest-room door creaked. The lamb had wandered off. Defeated, Miranda looked up.

And was astonished to find the girl standing in the doorway, staring at her in wonder. "Are you an angel?"

Miranda stood bolt upright. "Goodness, no! I told you, my name is Miranda Gonzales. What's yours?"

"Bernadette." She edged back into the echoing, disinfectant-smelling room. "Bernadette McBride. I was just p-praying, probably for the first time in my life, and I find a lady in the john spouting Scripture. I'm sorry I was rude. You scared me."

"Well, I'm not used to this, either," Miranda said, joy clogging her throat. "I was probably kinda rude myself. What *is* the matter?"

"It's kind of a long story." Another flood of tears sent more mascara streaks down Bernadette's cheeks. "I was supposed to meet my boyfriend here for the weekend, but I just found out he's married."

Miranda felt herself grow cold. What in the world had she just gotten herself into?

"Geraldine, are you sure you're up to this dinner cruise?"

Struggling to squeeze her arthritically contorted feet into her best black pumps, Geraldine looked up with an indulgent smile. "A herd of wild ducks couldn't keep me from going."

Roxanne giggled. "Weren't they the cutest things?" She wiggled into her girdle and surveyed herself in the full-length mirror on the door of the antique cherry armoire. "Not bad for a sixty-something grandma, huh?"

"Roxanne, you and I are both on the scary side of seventy, and you know it." Geraldine pulled out a subtle bronze lip pencil and began to outline her lips. "I wonder what happened to Miranda. I'd hate for her to miss the cruise."

Roxanne looked uncharacteristically uncertain. "Well . . . she wasn't very happy about running into Tony."

"Roxanne . . ." Geraldine frowned, her upper lip half filled in. "I thought you were going to tell her on the way here."

"The right time just never seemed to come up." Roxanne squirmed into a pair of silky sheer pantyhose, avoiding Geraldine's minatory stare.

"Wonderful. Now we have *two* reluctant lovers, instead of just one. I thought you said Miranda's been crazy about him all these years."

"She *is!* She refuses to talk about him. Don't you think that's a good sign?"

"Oh, sure. I *love* people I never talk about. Roxanne! As your Hugh used to so succinctly put it, your cheese has done slid off your cracker! If Miranda refuses to have anything to do with Tony, we've wasted an entire week, not to mention several hundred dollars! I'm worried sick about this funk Tony's in, and I've got just about six weeks to make sure he's out of it." To her horror, Geraldine heard her own voice crack and felt the pressure of tears behind her eyes. Since learning that she had cancer, she'd not broken down once. "Oh, rats!" she said, hunting through her purse for a tissue.

Roxanne, with typical disregard for stockings and creaky knees, cast herself beside Geraldine's chair and threw her arms around her friend. "Sweetie, sweetie, don't worry, the good Lord is in control of our grandchildren. You'll see. Miranda just got shook up a little, that's all. You know how she trusts God. She'll come around and make Tony look alive." She looked up with a wobbly smile. "And if she doesn't, we'll still get to see the pink Cadillacs at Graceland."

Geraldine hid a smile. "I can hardly wait."

CHAPTER TWO

JACKET slung over one shoulder, Tony knocked briskly on the door of the Romeo and Juliet suite. He'd put on a starched oxford shirt with his Levi's, but there was no way he was going to wear a tie while he was on vacation. Dinner cruise or no dinner cruise.

He shoved his free hand into a back pocket and whistled impatiently between his teeth. Three women in the room and nobody answering the door. He wondered what had happened to Miranda. Had she bolted for home? He halfway hoped she had. But then part of him wanted to show her exactly how well he'd gotten over her.

His stomach growled as he knocked again. What were they doing in there? Mrs. Roxanne had said to give them thirty minutes to freshen up before driving down to the waterfront. He'd allowed an extra ten.

Suddenly the door was jerked open under his hand. Roxanne herself stood there, a huge pink bubble all but obliterating her face. It popped and deflated; she scraped it into her mouth with a tangerine fingernail, then tugged Tony into the room. "Tony! Thank goodness you're here."

"I told you I was—" He saw Nana's distressed face. She sat in a tapestry wing chair, clutching the phone to her chest. "Nana, what's wrong?"

"It's Miranda. I think you should talk to her."

Dread promptly sank its hooks into his stomach. He might have known she'd be in trouble already. "Where is she?" He hesitated by the door. Bourbon Street duty during Mardi Gras would be more restful than a conversation with Miranda Gonzales.

Nana shook her head and held out the phone, while Roxanne flitted around the room like a gum-chewing hummingbird. Tony reluctantly took the receiver.

"Miranda?" he said.

He heard a faint gasp. "Oh, no. I told her not to—"

"Where are you?"

Silence hummed for a moment. "Tony, would you ask Granny to bring me some money?"

Obviously Miranda wasn't going to confide in him over the phone. Under the circumstances, he supposed that was understandable. He glanced over at Roxanne, who was already slinging her purse strap over her shoulder. Anxiety was written large on her wrinkled face. "Sure," he said slowly. "Where should I tell her to bring it?"

"I'm at—" he heard her break off and mumble to someone else in the room with her—"at Precinct 1209 Station on Beale Street."

"Precinct . . . Miranda!" he shouted. "Are you in *jail?"*

"Not exactly. Can you just tell Granny to come get me—us?"

"I'll be right there. Wait! You have to tell me how to get there! Miranda!" Tony listened to the dial tone for a helpless moment, then slowly replaced the receiver.

Vacation was over.

Miranda sat, legs primly crossed at the ankles, in the chair provided by the desk sergeant. A female officer had taken Bernadette to a holding cell, leaving Miranda to explain what they'd been doing on a downtown street corner propositioning an undercover vice officer. Well, at least Bernadette had apparently been propositioning. Miranda had only been trying to bum a quarter for the phone.

"Lord," Miranda said under her breath, "is this one of those situations where I've run ahead of you unwisely?"

"Miss, I'd say where you done run is into trouble." The sergeant turned from his computer keyboard with a steely eyed frown. " 'Unwise' is the understatement of the year. What were you doin' with that hooker?"

Miranda gave him a disapproving once-over. "It's not polite to call names. Bernadette is a dancer."

"Oh really? Then maybe you can explain why she asked Officer Denton for a hundred bucks in return for a good time."

Miranda felt her face go ten shades of red. "I don't know what she said to him, but I do know she just wants to go home. Besides, I'm sure she didn't know he was a policeman."

The officer pinched the bridge of his nose, but before he could reply, the glass outer door suddenly opened and Miranda turned, startled and relieved to find Tony Mullins stalking into the room. His white shirt and black bomber jacket made his onyx eyes look even darker. His thick dark hair stood all on end as if he'd been running his hand through it, and there was a muscle jumping in his jaw.

Miranda's relief was short-lived. In the four years since she'd seen

Tony, she'd imagined all sorts of reunions. The first words out of his mouth matched none of those scenarios.

"Miranda Gonzales," Tony said through gritted teeth, "you need a keeper."

Her temper flared. "I didn't do anything!"

"Is this your husband, ma'am?" asked the long-suffering sergeant.

"No!" shouted Miranda and Tony in unison.

"I don't have a husb—"

"Miranda, for once just keep your mouth shut," Tony interrupted. He turned to the policeman. "I'm Detective Tony Mullins of the New Orleans PD. My family is on vacation here with Miss Gonzales's." He pulled a badge from his hip pocket, which the other officer scanned and returned with a nod. "Is Miss Gonzales charged with a crime?"

"Well, no—"

"Told you so!" Miranda said triumphantly.

Tony ignored her. "Then why are you holding her?"

"Just asking some questions. The girl she was with propositioned an undercover officer. She's sort of a regular customer."

Miranda shook her head, remembering clearly how Jesus had treated fallen women. *Be strong, Miranda,* she told herself, taking a calming breath. "Please, Tony, let me tell you what really happened."

He looked indecisive for a moment—a miracle in itself, with Tony—then with a resigned sigh he straddled another metal chair. "This had better be good."

"Well, I was going down to the lobby to say hello to you and Mrs. Geraldine, but I decided to stop in the ladies' room first." She shot him a nervous look, and he nodded, noncommittal. "I met this girl in the rest room. The—the Lord told me to speak to her."

"That *is* a good one," Tony interrupted, propping his arms on the back of the chair.

Miranda plowed on. "Bernadette was crying because she'd just been abandoned there in the hotel, and she couldn't afford a room on her own, so—"

"Who's Bernadette?" demanded Tony.

"The hooker," supplied the sergeant with a sly grin.

"Dancer," Miranda said doggedly. "She didn't have any money or any place to go, so I told her I'd help her buy a bus ticket." She ducked her head and mumbled, "Only I forgot my purse was in the room."

Tony gave her a bland look. "Your choice of companions hasn't changed much over the years."

Eyes stinging, Miranda jumped to her feet. "I think I'll just walk back to the hotel."

"You're not going anywhere without me. Sergeant, is she free to go?"

"Sure, Detective. I'll book the other girl, but you might want to keep a closer eye on this one." He winked at Miranda, who gasped.

"I can't leave Bernadette in jail!"

"Oh yes you can." Tony stood up and put a hand firmly under Miranda's arm. "Her—er, boyfriend will get her out tomorrow, you can count on it."

"But I promised—"

"Miranda, we're booked on a seven o'clock dinner cruise. It's almost six-fifteen now."

Four years melted away. Just like always—Tony rushing to the rescue, being logical and hardheaded and making her feel like a fool. She felt like shaking him. "Tony Mullins, can't you think of anybody besides yourself?"

"I'm thinking of your grandmother, who is beside herself worrying about you!"

The sergeant cleared his throat. Miranda dragged her gaze from Tony's angry face and realized that all activity in the station had halted, every eye in the room trained on the two of them. "Maybe you oughta continue this conversation outside?" suggested the officer.

Miranda closed her eyes. *I did what you told me to, didn't I?* she breathed to the Lord. She felt peace wash over her spirit, even though she was in the biggest mess of her life. She was not going to abandon Bernadette. She looked up at Tony, who looked back at her, tight-lipped. If she could get him to listen to reason, he might actually be a help. He had always been very good at practicalities.

As Granny often said, there was more than one way to skin a cat. Reluctantly, she shrugged. "OK, I forgot about Granny." She offered her hand to the sergeant. "Thank you for not busting me. I'll be back later to take care of my friend."

"Fine." His gruff visage cracked into a smile. "Have a nice dinner."

"Come on, Miranda, let's get out of here," growled Tony.

Miranda paused and looked up at him as he held the door for her. Though she hadn't exactly been looking forward to confronting Tony again, there was a part of her that still wanted to please him. The familiar lift of his dark brows made her heart bounce uncomfortably. She could hardly have made a worse impression on him if she'd tried.

Tony flung himself behind the wheel of his truck, aware of Miranda crowding the passenger door. He'd been more scared than angry to find her in a Beale Street police station; now that he had her out of that place, he felt limp with relief. The image of Miranda sharing a jail cell with a prostitute literally made him sick. He knew the accusations he'd tossed at her were a substitute for the urge to scoop her up in his arms and keep her safe.

It would have relieved his irritation to have laid a little rubber, but he forced himself to pull carefully out into the street. He drove silently for several blocks. Occasionally he glanced at her, wondering what she was thinking.

Hands tucked under her thighs, she looked out the window, presenting him with a cool, pixie-doll profile. A wavy swath of hair had fallen out of the pewter clip, veiling her face.

Sitting in a confined space with her now sent a huge mass of complicated feelings sloshing around in his chest. As his closest friend's little sister, she had interfered with, pestered, and annoyed him since peewee baseball days. When they were children, his policy had been to ignore her as much as possible and, when necessary, bodily pick her up and remove her from the room. Verbal exchanges never worked with Miranda, who he was convinced could talk her way out of a straitjacket.

Then, somewhere along the way, she had turned into Tony's friend. To everybody else she was Miranda the cheerleader, Miranda the homecoming queen, Miranda the class favorite. Everybody's princess. But to Tony, she was the one person who had listened to his heart without judging. Her joy had filled a lonely place inside him that nobody else could touch.

His Miranda. He'd thought she was perfect, and once upon a time he'd been on the verge of claiming her.

In college he'd discovered the bitter truth that Miranda could fall. Had fallen hard and fast. Away from Tony and from her parents and, worst of all, away from God. And Tony had not been able to keep it from happening.

A senior to her freshman, he'd tried to tell her how time- and money-consuming the sorority scene would be. Miranda took exception to his attempt to talk her out of pledging. Then when he hadn't had time to accompany her to dances and parties, she'd actually called him a prude.

His hurt had forced a distance between them that had grown until that awful night in the campus police station when he'd lost her for good.

Now, after all these years, she had crashed back into his life without warning, disturbing that empty space she'd left. No matter how she had hurt him, there was something about Miranda that drew him every time he laid eyes on her. She'd been lovely as a teenager, but now womanhood had made her alluring.

"Miranda, what possessed you?" he burst out. "You have done some idiotic things in your life, but I assumed you'd outgrown this sort of thing."

She swept the loose strand of hair behind her ear in that feminine way she had and turned to look at him. "I didn't think you'd understand." Her gray green eyes brightened with tears.

There had been a time when he understood everything about

her. Before he could stop himself, he said, "Then help me. Tell me what you were thinking."

Miranda blinked, and a couple of tears came loose to roll down her nose. "I'm just trying to follow the Lord."

There it was again, that jarring reference to God. What was that all about? That certainly didn't sound like Miranda. Unnerved, Tony reached over to fiddle with the radio. "I hardly think *God* told you to abandon your grandma and traipse off after a hooker." As he braked with a jerk in the hotel parking garage, a thought hit him. "Did you know our grandmothers were planning this little get-together?"

"Of course I didn't. Do you think I'd be here otherwise?"

Disappointment made him want to shoot back. "Miranda, you're capable of just about anything."

To his amazement, her eyes filled with a tender steadiness that looked past his question and saw the misery he'd worked so hard to control. "Tony, is there something else bothering you? Something besides . . . me?"

There was no way on earth he was going to open himself up to Miranda the Mouth. Another thing he'd learned the hard way. He shrugged. "I'm on a much deserved vacation—as I'm sure you are, too—and my Nana's tried to pull a fast one on us. I plan to put a stop to it as soon as possible."

"Put a stop to what? Tony, I sure didn't plan this, but I'm glad we met again, because I've wanted to tell you—"

"Hey, it's really water under the bridge." When hurt flashed in her eyes, he took a breath and softened his tone. "If you want to stay and play around with the old ladies, I'll go on back to New Orleans. Just make sure Nana doesn't wear herself out."

"Tony!" He felt the weight of her small hand through his jacket, and he swallowed at the sudden intimacy. "If you leave it'll break your Nana's heart. I promise to stay out of your way, just please—" her voice dropped to a whisper again—"please don't go."

He shrugged. He couldn't go back to work anyway for at least two more weeks, and Miranda was right about one thing. Nana would be unbearably hurt if he took off.

He let out the breath he'd been holding. "All right." Telling himself it was to emphasize his point, he clasped her fragile wrist. "But if you stick so much as your little toe off the straight and narrow, I'm calling in a certain favor you owe me. Is that understood?"

Not surprisingly, the tender look was wiped off her face. He could see her white teeth clenched between parted lips. "I hate you, Tony Mullins!"

"I know it," he said wearily. "Maybe that's for the best."

Later, as Tony drove Granny's tank down Riverside Drive, Miranda watched the pink rays of the sinking sun reflect off the muddy water and soften the steely glare of the Tennessee-Arkansas bridge. They hadn't spoken a single word to each other since they'd picked up Granny and Geraldine at the hotel. There wasn't time for Miranda to change clothes, so she was still in the sleeveless spring dress she'd had on all afternoon. She was going to freeze, once the sun went down, but it hadn't been worth starting another argument with Tony the Tiger.

She shivered, as if in anticipation of the cold, but it was more than physical discomfort. There was no escaping the fact that she'd told Tony Mullins she hated him, exactly as if she were a six-year-old brat instead of a grown woman who had given her life to Christ.

She sighed. She had to admit, if she were honest, that Tony's suspicions were well founded. But she wished he'd given her a chance to explain the change in her belief system, instead of provoking her to such anger.

It is his fault, isn't it, Abba? she thought, knowing in her heart it wasn't. The verses in Colossians she'd been trying all week to memorize plainly said it: "Since God chose you to be the holy people whom he loves, you must clothe yourselves with tenderhearted mercy, kindness, humility, gentleness, and patience. You must make allowance for each other's faults and forgive the person who offends you. Remember, the Lord forgave you, so you must forgive others." Then came the real kicker. "The most important piece of clothing you must wear is love. Love is what binds us all together in perfect harmony."

Miranda had left Biloxi yesterday morning determined to practice those verses this week, even if it killed her. And here she'd started off her vacation by telling someone she hated him. Not just any old someone, either. Tony Mullins, to whom she owed more than an apology.

She squeezed her eyes shut. *Abba, what should I do?*

The answer was plain: "Put on love." To a woman who enjoyed clothes as much as Miranda did, that was a clear directive. She was to dress herself up in awareness of how much God had forgiven her, and offer the same grace to Tony. She was to take the first step, no matter how humiliating that would undoubtedly be.

OK, she silently told the Lord. *I'll do it first opportunity. When we're alone. When it's quiet. You'll let me know when it's time, won't you?*

The feminine chattering behind her broke into Miranda's musings, and she put her elbow across the back of the seat, turning to listen.

"That's Cybil Shepherd's house," Granny was saying, plastering her face to the window so she could gawk at the row of mansions lining the bluff to their left.

"Really?" Geraldine leaned over and craned her neck, too.

"These entertainment people don't live like normal folks," Granny said as if she personally knew a whole gaggle of movie stars.

"I expect they have the same hurts and problems as the rest of us," Miranda murmured.

Tony glanced at her. "Since when did you get so philosophical?"

Hurt all over again, she tightened her lips without answering. Tony shrugged, while the old ladies in the back continued to speculate about famous Memphis personalities.

The *Memphis Queen* was quite a sight, Tony had to admit as he stood looking down at the pier. Inching along a silt-bottomed river in a glorified fishing boat wasn't his idea of a good time, but he was pleasantly surprised by the gleaming wedding-cake beauty of the boat, with its enormous red paddle wheels and chimneylike smokestack. Maybe this wouldn't be so bad.

He took Nana and Roxanne, one on each arm, to make sure neither slipped on the steep path down to the water. He was very much aware of Miranda following. He assumed she could take care of herself. When the Gonzales family and the Mullins family had vacationed together over the years, Grant and Tony were usually charged with keeping the younger Miranda out of trouble. No small task, that.

He grinned, and Nana asked, "What's so funny?"

"I was just thinking about the time Miranda took off on a self-guided tour of the Grand Canyon."

"Wasn't my fault that donkey went down the wrong trail!" Miranda skipped around to take Nana's other arm as she negotiated the step up to the dock.

Tony laughed. "He might have kept up with the rest of the group if you hadn't untied his lead."

"Well, I was stuck behind Carrie Ann, and she wouldn't quit singing some hokey Roy Orbison song." Miranda struck a chord on her air guitar and sang, "Anythang yuuu want—yuuu got it!"

Tony had to concede that Miranda's sister Carrie Ann, at fourteen, *had* been a bit of a pain. "You could have expressed a little gratitude when Grant and I found you and brought you back."

"You slung me across the saddle like a sack of potatoes!"

"What happened to the donkey?" interrupted Roxanne, her eyes sparkling.

"He dumped her and ran back to the barn," Tony said with relish. "We found Miranda sitting on a rock howling like a basset hound."

"I could have been badly hurt," Miranda protested.

"But you weren't."

"Was too."

"Children, children," interjected Nana mildly. "Tony, the man's waiting for you to pay him." She indicated the open window of the ticket booth, where a grizzled old fellow sat behind an open cash-register drawer. Black currant eyes twinkled from underneath a grimy sailor cap.

"Oh. Sorry." Tony pulled out his wallet.

They hurried across the gangway onto the boat, which shortly began to chug and shudder violently as its engine came to life. Tony settled Nana and Roxanne in a pair of plastic chairs on the lower deck, whose sides were open to the breeze blowing off the river. Miranda disappeared, who knew where—probably up to the highest, most dangerous level she could access.

He walked over to the railing and let the cool wind hit him full in the face. After the stifling humidity of New Orleans, it was a welcome sensation. Tony had lived there for six years and had done a few undercover drug stints along the waterfront, but never had the time for a pleasure cruise. The freedom from responsibility, the sensation of the moving boat, sent a well of unexpected emotion coursing through him. It almost felt like hope. Maybe his captain had been right. A vacation was what he needed to get his life and career back into perspective.

"Tony! Up here!"

It was Miranda's clear soprano floating over the sound of the engine. He looked up over his shoulder, and sure enough, she was practically hanging off the rail of the upper deck. "Get back before you fall overboard!" he yelled.

"Come on! We're fixin' to take off!" She gestured wildly.

By the time Tony found the ladder leading to the third deck, the boat, steam whistle screaming, was chugging lazily up the river. He climbed the stairs and stood on the upper deck, quietly observing Miranda.

Miranda had her toes hooked through the railing, arms flung wide and long hair blowing in the wind. If she'd had on a Victorian dress, she'd have looked like an old-fashioned movie poster. He shook his head. Miranda's penchant for dramatics had been one of the things he loved most about her. It had also been the one thing that never failed to drive him crazy.

The scene in the police station was a perfect example. And it would be just about par for the course if this cruise suffered the same fate as the *Titanic.*

Amused by the mental vision of violins playing as this oversized birthday cake tipped sideways and planted itself in the mud, Tony couldn't resist moving behind Miranda and placing his hands on the railing on either side of her slim hips. He spoke in her ear. "It's going to be a bad sign if the band starts to play 'Nearer My God to Thee.' "

Startled, she wobbled, and he clamped his hands at her waist to keep her right side up. With a noticeable lack of gratitude, she struggled, pushing at his hands. "Let go of me!" He did, and she backed against the railing. "What are you doing?"

He considered telling her how innocent and beautiful she'd looked, leaning like a bird into the wind, but instead he said mildly, "You used to love acting out movie scenes."

She laughed nervously. "I know, and you and Grant never cooperated. You can't have a love scene without a hero." Her eyes widened, and she clapped her hand over her mouth.

"Is that what you want, Miranda? A hero?" He studied her. "Is that why you pull stunts like this afternoon's—to get my attention?"

She stared at him wordlessly, her hair blowing in her face. Finally she placed one hand high on his chest. "I am so . . . so sorry, Tony."

His heart lurched under her hand. Off guard, he turned to look at the water slipping past in a murky rush, the sun continuing to sink toward the Arkansas horizon on the left, cotton warehouses looming on the bluff to the right. He kept quiet because he'd said too much already.

"I don't mean only what happened this afternoon. I'm sorry for—for *everything.* You know I don't really hate you."

In the past, Miranda had tended to gloss over the consequences of her impulsive behavior. Puzzled at her evident contrition, Tony glanced at her. "You were just being honest."

She sighed. "Honest isn't always good if it hurts someone else."

"You hurt me. I'm not going to let you hurt me again."

She winced.

"Look, Miranda, we can make each other miserable this week, or we can call a truce and give our grandmothers a good time. I choose the latter. How about you?"

"I want to be friends," she said slowly. "But I think we need to talk about the last time we—we saw each other."

"I don't know if I can be your friend again, Miranda." He sighed. "We said some really hurtful things to each other four years ago." Still, he searched her face without really knowing what he was looking for. He could use a friend these days.

Her fingers curled into the front of his shirt. "Oh, Tony, I know it, and I regret my part in it. But what you said that night triggered the rest of it, the way I've changed! That next Sunday I gave my life to Jesus Christ, and he's made a new creation out of me."

Tony smiled, wanting to believe her but painfully aware of how such commitments were so easily broken. "I'll believe it when I see it," he said evenly.

Noticing Miranda's teeth chattering and the goose bumps on her arms, he removed his jacket. He placed it around her shoulders, then turned away to watch the catfish jumping in the water as the sun went down.

CHAPTER THREE

CARRYING her espadrilles, Miranda turned off the bathroom light and tiptoed toward the door of the hotel suite. Granny was a light sleeper, and even though she was upstairs with Geraldine—Miranda had slept on the roll-out couch—Miranda had been careful not to make any noise as she showered and dressed in a long breezy skirt and a knit cardigan.

She was determined to take care of Bernadette and get back in time to go with Granny to the Iron Museum. It was only 7 A.M., but she'd left a note on the bathroom mirror just in case.

Last night as she watched Tony dancing a two-step with Granny to the music of a jazz band, Miranda had entertained herself by fuming with frustration that Tony was monopolizing her time with her Granny—and resenting the fact that the scent of leather and Tony that clung to the jacket around her shoulders created such a funny sensation in her stomach. Not as shocking as his big hands spanning her waist as she had leaned against the rail of the upper deck, but more of a . . . surrounding sense of his presence. Comforting and unnerving all at once.

Lord, he used to share his deepest thoughts with me when we were young. What's happened?

As she put on her shoes and slipped through the quiet hotel

lobby, mentally repeating every word he'd said to her since he stalked into the police station, she concluded that she'd done everything possible to mend her relationship with him. She couldn't *make* him cooperate, couldn't *make* him forgive her and trust her again. So she would just have to *show* him what Christ had done in her life.

That wasn't the only reason she wanted to help Bernadette, but it wouldn't hurt.

It was a long walk from the Peabody, which was on Union Avenue, to the police station on Beale. An incurable night owl, Miranda enjoyed this rare opportunity to feel the morning sun burning the dampness from the air and smell the espresso brewing in coffee shops along the street. Beale Street in the daytime exuded a campy sort of sadness, with its deadened neon signs and triple-story storefronts cracked and exposed as the fakes they were. Historic blues clubs crowded next to secondhand haberdasheries, and pawnshops competed with glaringly modern retailers of Elvis memorabilia. Miranda found it fascinating, from the patched concrete-and-brick sidewalks with their inlaid brass music notes to the tacky hand-painted signs advertising voodoo dolls, healing, and lucky mojos.

Also a bit scary. What on earth, she wondered uneasily, was a mojo?

By the time she reached the police station, her strappy, rope-soled shoes had rubbed a couple of gigantic blisters on her heel, so she limped in, her enthusiasm for her project a bit dampened. Short of presenting a Monopoly "Chance" card, she didn't have the first clue how to get a person out of jail.

It was the providence of the Lord, she was sure, that the same sergeant who had questioned her the previous day sat at his desk sipping coffee out of a black mug that said "Go Ahead—Make My Day."

Miranda read the nameplate on his desk and smiled at him brightly. "Good morning, Sergeant Coltrane! Remember me?"

He wiped coffee off his graying mustache and returned her greeting with a lugubrious frown. "Ah, the friend of the not-hooker. I see you've escaped your not-husband detective friend again."

"I don't think you're supposed to make fun of your customers." Miranda perched on the same cold metal chair she'd sat in yesterday.

Coltrane sighed and ran a hand over his balding head. "Please forgive me, Ms.—Gonzales, was it? What can I do for you at this ungodly hour of the morning?"

"I'm here to pay for Bernadette McBride."

"Pay for her?"

"Yes. Isn't that how you get people out of jail? You pay their fine and they—"

"Well, sort of. But Ms. McBride is already gone."

"Gone?"

"Her, uh, mother posted bail last night."

Miranda stared at him, stumped. Bernadette hadn't mentioned a mother. "Isn't that . . . interesting?" Now what should she do? Maybe she'd better make sure Bernadette was all right. "Actually, that's wonderful. But Bernadette forgot to give me her address. Could you—?"

"No, I could not," said Coltrane firmly. "A nice girl like you better stay away from sleaze like that."

If Miranda had been wavering before, the word *sleaze* cemented her determination to find and rescue Bernadette. She opened her mouth to excoriate the policeman, but her attention was caught by a fish-shaped metal magnet on the file cabinet behind him. If

Miranda blasted him, she'd be setting no better example of Christlikeness than he was. What kind of witness would that be?

Put on love, she reminded herself.

"Sergeant Coltrane, are you a religious man?" she asked quietly.

He ran a finger around the tight collar of his uniform. "Well, sure."

She smiled. "I know you'll understand, then, that when the good Lord tells you to do something, you'd better do it. And he told me to do everything I can to be a friend to Bernadette McBride. If you don't tell me where she went, I'll have to look all over Beale Street—" she paused—"by myself."

Sergeant Coltrane tugged the side of his mustache and regarded Miranda shrewdly. "If I tell you, will you promise not to go there without your boyfriend?"

"My boyfriend?"

"The detective from New Orleans."

Miranda blushed. "He's not—oh, all right. But he's not going to like it."

She thought the sergeant muttered, "That's what I'm counting on," as he hunted through a pile of paperwork in his Out box. He stuck a pair of reading glasses on his nose and perused a computer printout. "Here it is. The woman who posted bail was a Mrs. Zena Boudreaux. Residence 128 Beale."

"That must be close! I'll just go right—"

"Uh-uh-uh!" Coltrane admonished. "You promised. Besides, it's all the way at the other end of the street, where the seamier joints are." He pulled the glasses to the end of his nose and peered at her over them. "Go—get—your—"

"OK, you win," Miranda sighed. Tony was going to have a stroke.

Tony came out of the weight room looping a hotel towel around his neck. He'd risen at the crack of dawn, as was his habit, no matter how much or little sleep he got during the night. A police detective's lifestyle allowed little regard for proper rest and nutrition, but every day without fail he found time to work out at least an hour.

This morning he'd spent two hours working off the uncomfortable knowledge that last night he had cut Miranda's apology short. Had she actually said she listened to what he'd said to her four years ago and changed her behavior? It hardly seemed possible. But as he had danced with Roxanne, he couldn't help watching Miranda as she sat at a table chatting with Nana. She'd glanced at him once or twice, then seemed to decide to ignore him.

The mental image of Miranda wrapped in his jacket, her curly hair spilling over the collar, had sent him running on the treadmill this morning as if demons were after him. His shorts and T-shirt were soaked with sweat, so the blast of air-conditioning that hit him in the lobby came as a welcome shock.

Most *unwelcome* was the sight of Miranda Gonzales disappearing through the front door of the hotel, alone and dressed to kill. He looked at his watch. Five after seven. He knew from personal experience that when Miranda was on vacation, one could unload an entire can of shaving cream on her head and she'd never wake up until sometime around noon.

Unless she was up to trouble.

Tony tried to tell himself she was probably only going out for stockings or toothpaste or maybe even a magazine. Except all that would be available in the hotel.

It really was none of his business. She wouldn't appreciate his interfering. He had no *desire* to interfere.

But an innate and utterly unwanted protector gene kicked into gear. Tony got the most irritating feeling that he would be sorry if he went after her, and sorrier if he didn't.

He tossed the towel onto a chair and resigned himself to being sorry.

It didn't take Tony long to catch sight of her. He was dressed for running, but she had on a pair of frivolous shoes that seemed to hamper her stride. He decided to keep an eye on her, staying far enough back that she wouldn't know he was following.

Miranda had always had the sense of direction of a hearing-impaired bat, but this morning she seemed to know exactly where she was going. She headed straight for Beale Street, dodging downtown work traffic with the blithe confidence of the very young and the mentally incompetent. She had jaywalking down to a fine art.

Muttering to himself, Tony managed to keep up by force of sheer determination. Once he barely avoided a collision with a bus, which honked loud and long at the idiot dodging across one of the busiest intersections in Memphis without benefit of a Walk sign. When he caught her he was going to—

Then he saw her stop in front of the Beale Street police station. After bending to pull at her shoes, she straightened her shoulders and went in.

"Oh, no, not again," he groaned. Breathless, he clung to the pole of an antique streetlamp on the corner. *Well, Mullins,* he told himself, *you better make up your mind if you're in or out this time.*

Yesterday he had told her to stay out of trouble, basically threatened to rat on her. If he caught her at something now, he'd be forced to confront what had happened during Miranda's sophomore year in college, when he had been interning with the University of Southern Mississippi campus security force. He still had occasional nightmares about Miranda standing on a second-story window ledge of an old dorm building, drunk as a wheelbarrow, preparing to jump into a bedsheet held by fellow carousers below.

She had assured him yesterday that she'd changed. "A new creature," she'd called herself. Some rusty gate to former habits screeched open in Tony's mind. That was a phrase from the Bible. He used to read the Bible a lot himself, back when he was in high school and college. It wasn't easy, because his parents were nominal Christians at best. It was Nana who had made sure he went to church and had money for youth-choir tours and retreats.

That thought made him cup his hand over a plain gold band he wore on a silver chain under his T-shirt. He never took it off, had almost forgotten why it was there. Leaning against the lamp pole, he pulled the ring loose, remembering a summer night at a bonfire on the beach, when he was sixteen years old. That night he'd accepted the ring from his youth pastor with a promise that, with God's help, he would remain sexually pure until he could give the ring to his bride. He hadn't been thinking of Miranda at the time, of course, but as she grew into a lovely young woman, he had begun to look forward to offering it to her.

Tony shook his head. The hard realities of police work, all the sights and sounds and smells of human corruption, had gradually constructed a wall between him and God. He never had time for reading the Bible anymore, and he only went to church for funerals and weddings.

In the past, he recalled, Miranda herself had talked a pretty good religious game, though Sunday morning never made much difference in the way she behaved on Friday nights.

Tony shoved the little ring back under his shirt. The way things looked this morning, it still didn't make much difference. Was she still trying to make friends with that prostitute?

Suddenly, the door to the police station opened. Miranda came out, smiling up at the sergeant who had interviewed her yesterday afternoon. Poor sucker must be pulling double shifts.

Tony waited until the officer went back inside and Miranda limped down the sidewalk away from him before he sauntered up behind her.

"Excuse me, miss," he tapped her on the shoulder, "I wonder if you could give me directions to the Iron Museum."

Shrieking, Miranda elbowed him in the gut and scurried away as fast as those ridiculous shoes would let her.

He gave a startled grunt, then shouted, "Wait, Miranda! It's me," and took off after her.

At the sound of her name, Miranda slowed and looked over her shoulder. "Oh, ma-a-an . . ." she groaned. Her heart literally throbbed in her throat as she stopped and waited for Tony to reach her in two long strides. "Would you please quit sneaking up on me? You're going to give me heart failure."

"If you'll quit trying to pump my stomach the hard way," he retorted, putting a hand to his flat abdomen. "Where do you think you're going?"

It was on the tip of her tongue to tell him it was none of his business, but then she remembered how comforting his solid presence could be in unfamiliar surroundings. Miranda moved his hand and gently investigated his ribs. "I took a self-defense course last fall."

"You must have graduated top of the class," he growled, dodging her fingers. "Never mind, I've had worse. What are you up to?"

Miranda gave up trying to be sympathetic. "Don't take that tone with me, Tony."

"I told you you'd better stay out of trouble—"

"What are you going to do, arrest me for walking down the street?"

"You're not looking for that prostitute, are you?"

"As a matter of fact, I am, and I could really use your help, Detective Mullins."

"If you think I'm going to spend my vacation chasing some streetwalker, you're fair and far off."

Oh, Jesus, Miranda prayed silently. *Where is the Tony I used to know? Help me see him like you do.* She waited, searching his face. His eyes were flint black, opaque. Still, he had followed her, so that must mean he cared about her in some weird fashion.

She sighed. "Fine. I'll be back by ten to go with y'all to the museum." She turned and walked away. It was painful, because her feet hurt.

But not as much as her heart.

Then she felt more than saw him stalking beside her, his shoulder topping hers by at least six inches. He'd always made her feel small. "Why are you so dead set on this?" he asked quietly. "I don't understand. You never used to care about anybody who wasn't 'fun.'"

"I told you I'm not the same person I was in college." She shrugged. "Jesus changed me."

Tony snorted. "So you're going to adopt this girl like a stray kitten? You know she'll be back on the street by tonight. Look what she did yesterday."

"All I know is the Lord has told me to do what I can for her, and what happens after that is up to his grace and her faith."

"You people are so naive," Tony muttered. He took Miranda's elbow when she would have crossed a street without looking, making her wait for the light.

She snatched her arm away, feeling burned by his touch. *"You people?* Tony, you're a believer, aren't you?"

"A believer?" He stared at her. "I used to think so. But it feels like somebody quit believing in me."

A deep shiver quaked through Miranda. He was going to tell her what had hurt him so much, right out here in the middle of the street. *Lord, please let him tell me. Use me to bless him.* She wanted badly to touch him, to hold his hands or hug him, but she knew he was likely to build a stronger wall between them if she did. She waited quietly, her eyes filling.

The light changed, and Tony put his palm to the small of her back. "Let's go," he said abruptly. "I'll go with you, but don't be surprised if ol' Bernadette isn't very glad to see you."

After a couple blocks' walk that took them into increasingly squalid surroundings, Tony stood with Miranda outside a dilapidated building near the river end of Beale Street. A big gap in the crumbling brick front revealed a decayed rooftop, like an old lady with periodontal disease, and the wooden door showed signs of a recent violent entry.

128 Beale Street. He shook his head.

"Sister Zena," he said, reading the hand-painted sign propped on an easel next to the door. "Lucky Mojos and Healing. Voodoo Dolls, Palm Reading, Etc." He'd seen similar signs in the New Orleans French Quarter and was well aware of what went on in such establishments. His skin crawled in spite of himself.

Tony felt Miranda move closer to him, and he grimly met her eyes. She lifted her chin, as though daring him to comment. "Are you coming in with me?" she asked quietly.

Miranda, he thought, contemplating her sweet mouth, *if only I could make us ten years old again and erase the complications of our relationship.* But there was no going back, so he might as well show her what a fool's errand this was.

He shrugged, then slammed his palm against the door twice. Miranda jumped. "Do you have to make so much noise?" she asked nervously.

"They're all asleep in there, I can guarantee you."

"How do you—"

The sound of a sliding dead bolt interrupted Miranda's question. A black-ringed silver eye appeared in the crack crossed by a heavy chain. "What do you want?" It was a heavy, bass-pitched female voice, raspy from years of inhaling cigarette smoke. A phosphorescent glow emanated from the interior of the room, along with a strong sulfurous odor.

Tony felt Miranda's small, cold hand slip into his. She had to be scared out of her mind, but she spoke firmly. "We're looking for Bernadette McBride."

The pale eye narrowed. "Ain't nobody here by that name." The door shut.

Tony moved quickly, shoving his hand against the door.

"Bernadette sent us here for a reading. She said you're the best in town."

He heard Miranda gasp, as the pressure against the door eased and the gravelly voice snarled, "I don't work before noon."

For Tony, it was as natural as breathing to gain access to criminal haunts with a covering of subterfuge. Miranda, however, had no way of knowing the danger of blurting out the truth. He squeezed her hand to still her mutterings. "We're leaving this morning," he said. "Come on, we'll pay well."

There was a moment's silence. Tony felt Miranda shift against him, grip his hand tighter. Finally the chain slid and clanked against the door, which jerked open.

In his two years as a homicide detective, Tony had developed a wide acquaintance among the Bourbon Street mystics, but this one beat anything he'd ever seen. She was a heavyset white woman with a face so ravaged by piercing, so cloaked in makeup, that it was impossible to tell her age. Her hair, which had been peroxided to a greenish yellow, projected from her head in a mass of beaded braids, and she wore a floor-length, African-print caftan.

The woman ignored Miranda, but gave Tony a leisurely head-to-toe scan. She smiled, revealing big yellow teeth with one gold cap in the upper row. "What's a pretty white boy like you doin' down here on this end o' Beale?"

"I'm in town for the Festival, and everybody says don't leave without visiting Sister Zena."

Tony could tell the woman was pleased at her notoriety, but just as she stood aside for them to enter, Miranda snatched her hand away. "I'm afraid Detective Mullins has misled you, Mrs. Boudreaux," she said sweetly. "I'm not here to get my palm read—"

"I ain't lettin' no cops in here."

Fury and fear suffused Sister Zena's face, and the heavy green door hit Tony hard on the shoulder. He thought he saw the flash of a small, businesslike knife, so he stepped in front of Miranda, ignoring her squeal of protest.

Quickly he snagged the mystic's wrist and stood firm. Her grunt of frustration was followed by a soft metallic clink.

He kept his tone courteous, just short of sarcastic. "You tell us where Bernadette is, and we'll forget you just threatened a police officer, ma'am."

"You get lost right now, and I'll forget you just tried to enter my home without a warrant, Detective." Her pale venomous gaze remained fixed on his.

"Tony, this is not helping!" Miranda said, trying to squeeze herself between him and the door. "Mrs. Boudreaux, we don't want any trouble. We just want to know where we can find—"

"Miranda, be quiet." Tony could see the evil in this woman's face, and there was no telling what other tricks she had up her voluminous sleeves. He backed away, easing his grip on the thick wrist. "We're leaving, but we'll come back with a warrant."

"Where's Bernadette?" Miranda insisted as Tony grabbed her arm and tried to pull her away from the doorway.

Sister Zena uttered a short bark of laughter. "She's working—hasn't come home yet."

"Then she *does* live here?"

"Miranda, *shut up!*" Sick with fear for his intrepid and mulish companion, Tony suddenly bent and placed his shoulder in her midriff. Ignoring her startled exclamation, he hoisted her up and called loudly, "Bernadette, if you're here, and you decide you want out of this hellhole, you can find us at the Peabody Hotel. Ask for Tony Mullins."

With one arm clamped across the back of Miranda's knees, he turned and stalked down Beale Street. He covered a full block before he deposited his squirming burden on a bus-stop bench. Before she could open her mouth, he propped one foot beside her on the bench and leaned over so that he was so close he could have kissed her if he hadn't been in the mood to strangle her instead. "Miranda Gonzales, if you ever pull another stunt like that—"

"You say that to me one more time, and I'll—I'll scream! And if you ever again pick me up and carry me anywhere I don't want to go, I'll take your bottom lip and pull it up over your head!"

It was an old line from a comedy record they used to listen to when they were children. He hadn't heard it in years. Startled into laughter, Tony watched Miranda smooth her tangled hair, her eyes stormy and her hands shaking. He sank down beside her on the bench, resting his elbows on his knees. He looked at her sideways.

One side of her mouth quirked up. "I'm serious," she said.

"I don't doubt it," he said, chuckling. "But what possessed you to contradict everything I said to that woman? I nearly had her going."

"You were telling lies."

"Lies? The woman is a criminal!"

"Palm reading is of the devil, but as far as I know it's legal."

"Miranda, she pulled a knife on me! You could have gotten us badly hurt, if not killed."

"If you would have let me tell her the truth straight-out, she never would have done that."

He sat up with a heavy sigh and flung his arm across the back of the bench, observing her with sudden curiosity. Miranda was obviously still perturbed with him but exhibited not one iota of concern over their brush with danger. Her eyes were bright and clear, with mossy flecks glinting in the brilliant May sunshine. Strength and determination radiated in her expression, drawing him to seek to understand her.

"How do you know she'd have let you in?" he probed.

"I didn't, but I was praying like crazy, and I knew the Lord would protect us."

"You were praying," he echoed, experiencing that twinge of discomfort. Unconsciously his arm moved around her shoulders. "I guess I messed up, huh?"

"Well, I don't know." Miranda looked up at him gravely, and he suddenly wanted to see her smile again. "We'll keep praying and see what God will do. Maybe Bernadette heard you yelling at her."

"I don't imagine she was there. Sister Zena said she was working."

His diversionary tactic didn't work. "Tony," she persisted, "do you ever pray anymore?"

"Sometimes."

"Would you pray with me now?"

His throat absolutely closed with shame. "We'd better get back to the hotel," he said, getting up and holding a hand to out to her. "Please, Miss Gonzales, could you find it in your heart to accompany me back to the Peabody?"

His teasing did nothing to erase the disappointment and hurt in her eyes. She swallowed and looked down.

He tried again. "Please, Your Worship?"

After a moment, she gave him a faint smile, Miranda-fashion, and shook off her pensive mood, allowing him to pull her to her feet. "Since I'm feeling magnanimous, I'll let you buy me a big plate of grits and eggs and sausage, with bacon and gravy on the side." Sticking her nose in the air, she sashayed ahead of him with a distinct limp. "Remind me," she said over her shoulder, "to pitch these shoes in the garbage when we get back!"

CHAPTER FOUR

OK, LORD, I know he's in there somewhere," Miranda muttered to herself. She sipped a cup of coffee with Granny and Geraldine at a table in a 1950s-era diner, while Tony stood in line at the counter to purchase tickets for a tour of Sun Studio next door. She'd have to give him credit for being tolerant of Granny's Elvis mania. His expression was patient, if not exactly thrilled.

Geraldine, seated across from her, laid a bony, elegantly manicured finger on Miranda's wrist, stopping the swirl of coffee in her thick white cup. "You've been mighty quiet all morning," Geraldine observed. Her fine eyes, deep-set and black like Tony's, were soft with concern. "Aren't you having a good time?"

Miranda smiled. "Of course I am. I guess I'm . . . tired, a little."

"I would think so," said Granny, "since you got up with the chickens this morning."

Miranda grimaced. "Oops, I was hoping I hadn't woken you two up."

"I rarely sleep past five anymore," said Geraldine. "I was just lying in bed being lazy for a change."

Granny's eyes twinkled with avid curiosity behind a rooster feather dangling from her gray felt cloche. "What were you up to, anyway? You and Tony?"

Oh, dear, the Inquisition begins. Miranda began to slosh her coffee again. Granny had not been happy about the first Bernadette episode, even though it was exactly the sort of thing she would have done herself. "We had breakfast together."

Granny blinked. "For two and a half hours?"

"Well, first we had an errand to run."

"Roxanne, this is apparently none of our business," Geraldine said, giving her friend a look. "Just be glad that Tony and Miranda are renewing their friendship."

Miranda frowned. "Is that what you two intended with this vacation? A little matchmaking on the side?"

The older women exchanged glances again, and Granny deferred to Geraldine, who nodded serenely. "We prayed about it, and the Lord gave us the go-ahead."

Miranda goggled. "Mrs. Geraldine, you are certainly aware that telling Tony what to do is the fastest way to make him run in the opposite direction. Even if *I* were inclined to go along with you—which I'm not," she amended hastily.

"Goodness, girl," Granny tsked, "nobody's trying to force anybody to do anything. We just wanted to give nature a chance to take its course."

Miranda laid her forehead in her palm and groaned. "I guess I'd better explain something to you, Granny." She looked at her grandmother, praying that she wasn't about to lose practically her best friend in the world. "I don't want you to tell Daddy and Mom, because it would only hurt them. OK?"

Granny hesitated. "OK."

"Good." She looked around to make sure Tony was still occupied. There were still two people ahead of him in line. "I'm sure you know Tony and I dated some in college—when I was a freshman and he was a senior."

"We were naming grandbabies, weren't we, Ger?" Granny elbowed her friend with a wink.

Miranda sighed. "I don't remember ever loving anybody but him," she said quietly, "but then he graduated and went to work for campus security. He got to be such a killjoy all of a sudden, and I just wanted to have a good time. I went to all the sorority parties . . . you know what goes on at those things . . ." She swallowed against the shame. "Tony and a couple of other officers were called in one night when I was involved in something very stupid and dangerous. He got me out of trouble, but he—he told me if I didn't straighten up he would tell Mom and Dad, so I told him to take a flyin' leap, and . . ." She petered out miserably. "That was the end of Tony and Miranda. He hasn't spoken to me since then. Until yesterday."

"Oh, darlin'." Granny grabbed Miranda's hand.

Geraldine's dark eyes burned with tears. "Have you and Tony talked about what happened back then?"

Miranda shook her head, thinking of Tony's withdrawal when she suggested praying with him. "He won't even let me apologize. It would take a miracle to break through to him. I just can't see it happening."

"Well, Jesus said, 'Blessed are those who haven't seen me and believe anyway.'" Geraldine's expression lightened. "Roxanne and I believe, and we're going to pray for the Lord to increase your faith. Do you still love Tony?"

Miranda was saved from answering when Tony approached triumphantly with four tickets in his hand, but the question ping-ponged around in her head all during the tour.

The four of them trooped next door to the studio, along with a dozen other tourists armed with cameras, baby strollers, and notepads. They all crowded into a tiny outer office, which reminded Miranda of the set of a World War II movie. The guide, obviously a frustrated stage actress, gestured dramatically. "Here we stand—" the young woman emotionally pushed her bangs away from eyebrows that had been shaved off and penciled back on—"in the birthplace of Rock and Roll." Miranda could hear the capital letters beginning those last words and listened with amusement as the guide began a detailed account of Elvis Presley's single-minded and rather naive pursuit of his first recording contract.

She glanced at Granny, who eagerly soaked the story in as if she'd never heard it before. Geraldine leaned on her cane, eyebrows politely raised, though Miranda knew opera was more her forte. Tony cupped his hand under his grandmother's elbow, gently supporting her. He watched the guide's face, his firm mouth slightly curled on one side.

Do I love him?

She certainly had at one time. She'd been ready to trust her life to him. Miranda knew, from several heart-to-hearts with a married Christian friend, that sentimental emotions could change with the winds of circumstances—as hers for Tony had. But it was a truth she'd learned from Scripture that the kind of love God intended between a man and a woman should be built on a commitment of faith. A commitment to trust the Creator in every part of the relationship. A commitment to seek the best in and for the other person. A commitment to never give up hope.

It was a frightening thing for Miranda to recognize that she had never really given up the hope of mending her friendship with

Tony. And now Granny and Geraldine had given them the opportunity to do exactly that.

She looked up at his face. There was still a strength, combined with a new maturity, in Tony that made Miranda long to lean on him. His tenderness toward his grandmother proved that he still had elements of the quiet sweetness she'd found in him when he was younger. But his brittle refusal to discuss spiritual things more than gave her pause. She could not, indeed must not, give herself to a man who was spiritually empty.

Father, she prayed, watching Tony's strongly defined profile, *only you can change his heart. Let your Holy Spirit soften him and bring him back to you. Help me see him with your eyes, and show me how to reach him. Amen.*

Even as Tony suddenly looked down to meet her eyes, peace flooded her heart, helping her accept the reality of her attraction to him. She made herself smile at him, then focused her attention on a life-sized poster of Elvis looming on the wall to her left. Dead rock stars were a lot easier to deal with than real-life heroes.

"I have to say, Sun Studio was not what I'd imagined it would be," Roxanne said, taking a huge bite from a cheeseburger that according to the laws of physics should not have fit into her mouth.

Tony grinned behind his hand, hoping the old lady's dentures could handle the strain. Byrdie and Alice's was a Beale Street restaurant recommended by his police buddies as an experience not to be missed. He supposed by civilian standards it would be considered a joint: the lighting was dim, the blues memorabilia on the walls dusty and untended, the rattle and thunk of pool balls a constant counterpoint to conversation. He sopped a few greasy French fries in ketchup and savored the hot, vinegary crunch. This was a meal after his own heart.

"It's hard to imagine Elvis and Jerry Lee Lewis and Johnny Cash recording in that dinky little cinder-block room," Miranda said in response to her grandmother's comment. She picked up a fry, looked it over carefully, and finally laid it down again. She shoved away her burger, of which she'd only taken a couple of bites.

Tony frowned. Miranda had always had a healthy appetite. He hoped she wasn't sick. "What's the matter?" She was seated next to him in the booth, and he wanted to touch her, but instead took a swig of his root beer.

She looked at him for a moment as if surprised he'd noticed her preoccupation. "Nothing," she finally said and dropped her gaze.

"Come on, Squirt, if you don't like this place we can go somewhere else." The old nickname slipped out, but it was too late to call it back. Hopefully the old ladies wouldn't notice. Hastily he added, "I just thought we needed some authentic Beale Street atmosphere."

"Great cheeseburger," mumbled Roxanne around a mouthful, giving them a thumbs-up sign.

Nana, who had chosen a salad, dabbed at her lips with a paper napkin. "Atmosphere we got."

Miranda's shoulders lifted and dropped. "You know what I read about that room upstairs?"

Tony glanced at the stairs, where a bluish haze of smoke filtered down, along with the wail of a saxophone and the heavy rhythm of bass and drums and piano. "No, what?"

Miranda tipped her head so that a string of old-fashioned Christmas lights above their booth threw a multicolored prism across her troubled face. "They say back when the trains ran through here regularly, that was a . . . well, you know, a place where men came to meet women."

Tony shrugged. "I guess that's not so surprising."

"I just can't help thinking about those poor girls living in a dump like this, with no place else to go, no way to get out."

So that was it. She was thinking about Bernadette again. Miranda hadn't mentioned the girl all day, but he should have known she wouldn't forget.

"I'm sure they must have felt helpless and hopeless."

Astonished, Tony looked at his grandmother. Her expression was flat and calm, but her words had been filled with a very personal sort of compassion.

"But there is always hope in the good Lord," chimed in Roxanne. She met Nana's gaze, winked, and lifted the jelly jar that served as a tea glass. "Here's to hope!"

Nana solemnly clinked her jar against her friend's, while Tony looked in confusion from the older women to Miranda. A tiny smile lit her eyes. There was something very odd going on here, some sorority of secrets they were not letting him in on.

Fairly sure he was better off not knowing, he finished his hamburger and tossed his napkin on the table. "Anybody want to take me on in a game of snooker?"

The fine points of snooker eluded Miranda. She had grown up playing pool with her brothers and sisters in the family's basement rec room and in her college days had even been capable of occasionally beating the sharks at the local pool hall.

Maybe it was the smaller size of the table; maybe it was the distraction of the music emanating from the upper floor; maybe it was lack of practice.

But more likely it was the sheer fact of Tony's presence that made her scratch over and over. His relaxed grin sent a jolt of something straight to her stomach that had nothing to do with its emptiness.

She racked the balls, propped her cue on her thumb and leaned over to shoot. And fizzled the break. She glanced over at Tony, who stood with his shoulders propped against the paneled wall, twirling his own long cue in one hand.

He rolled his eyes and pushed away from the wall. "Come on, Miranda, you never used to do that. Let me show you."

"No, I can—" But he'd already reracked the balls, then reached around her to place his hands over hers on the cue.

His arms were right around her. "OK, now sight down the middle," he said in her ear. She could hardly breathe, much less think about billiards. "Now pull back real easy, and . . . here we go!" The cue shot forward, and with a burst of sound and color the triangle of balls shattered wildly.

Miranda felt her heart do the same thing. The noise in the room contracted into a buzz in her ears as she waited for Tony to move away from her. Squeezing her eyes shut, she thought, *Oh Lord, it's so wrong for me to long for him when we're not even on the same spiritual planet. Oh, God, help me do your will!*

She felt his hands on her shoulders. Quietly he said, "OK, now try it by yourself." When she didn't move, he sighed, his breath ruffling across the top of her head. "You're still thinking about her, aren't you?"

"Is that so bad?"

"It's not bad, it's just—a waste of time." He turned her so that the top button of his pullover was in her line of vision. "Listen, Miranda, I arrest people like Bernadette and Sister Zena every day. They never change."

"Of course they won't, if no one cares!"

Tony shook his head. "But there *are* people who care. I see street preachers down in the Quarter all the time. There are social workers and the Salvation Army and mission groups—you name it!" His voice hardened. "Evil and crime go on and on, and it's like God just shrugs and turns his back!"

"I'll never believe that, Tony. God has changed me, and if he can do that, he can do anything! I'm not perfect, but I belong to him, and he'll never let me out of his hand. And because he loves me, I've got to love, too." She stood trapped under his big hands, laying herself open to his searching gaze. Wanting to melt away, praying, *Lord, I'm so unworthy to be your instrument,* she let Tony look through the window of her eyes. What if he saw her love for him? Would he pity her, or mock her?

His lips tightened, and she could see him struggling with what to say. Tony had rarely been free in sharing his feelings. She'd heard his father drum into him the "big boys don't cry" mantra. "Did you really look at that woman this morning?" he said abruptly.

"Well, I . . . not exactly." Miranda had had an impression of bizarre cosmetics, the smell of decay, and had deliberately avoided looking the woman in the face.

"I did. Every bead in her hair was a symbol of a curse or blessing she's been paid to incant on someone else. You know what she had around her neck?" Miranda mutely shook her head. Tony's face was grim, implacable. "It's called a mojo. A little flannel bag, and it contains all her personal charms. Voodoo, Miranda. If she's got your Bernadette under her thumb, there's no way in God's earth we're getting her loose."

Miranda shivered and pressed her hands to her face. The murky atmosphere of the pool room added to her sense of horror. If Tony hadn't had hold of her shoulders she'd have run looking for her grandmother, who was sipping coffee with Geraldine in the front of the restaurant. *Dear God, what have you gotten me into?*

No way in God's earth.

Miranda drew a breath. It *was* God's earth. God was stronger than any voodoo hex ever cooked up. The Holy Spirit whispered Scripture into her mind: "He rescued us from the domain of darkness, and transferred us to the kingdom of his beloved Son, in whom we have redemption, the forgiveness of sins." And again, "Greater is he who is in you than he who is in the world."

She dropped her hands and looked at them, amazed that they no longer trembled with fear. She wasn't afraid of what Tony might see, either. "Listen to me," she said, leaning close to him, palms flat against his chest. "The awful fact is that my sins of evading truth, my selfishness and worldliness, separated me just as far from God as anything Bernadette or even Sister Zena has done. I needed redemption just as badly as they do. You made me see that, Tony, that night I nearly jumped out of that window. If I'd fallen, I'd have ended up in hell. I'll never get over being grateful that you were there."

She watched him swallow hard, and an odd sheen glossed his eyes. His jaw shifted as he looked away. "I'm glad I was there, too," he said gruffly. "But do you understand why I don't want to see you get involved with these people?"

Miranda couldn't tell if he'd really heard a word she said. She sighed and dropped back on her heels. "I suppose." An odd bump under the front of his knit shirt caught her attention. She poked at it. "What's this?"

Tony pushed her hand away. "Nothing." He stepped back and moved to put away the pool cues. "We'd better get back to our grandmas. They'll be picking up men if we don't watch 'em."

Miranda pressed the heels of her hands to her eyes. *Lord Jesus, we've still got a long way to go.*

Tony slouched in the wing chair in his hotel room, one booted foot propped on the coffee table, thumb on the television remote. If he turned it on it would drown out the silence broken only by cars whizzing down Union Avenue. Maybe it would cover the clamor of his own heart and mind.

He tossed the remote onto the table and laid his head back against the chair. "What's the matter with me?" he asked the empty room.

As soon as they had entered the Peabody lobby, Nana and Roxanne announced that they were tired, even though it was only 10 P.M. Tony wanted, with an inexplicable urgency, to keep Miranda with him. He wanted to take her out for coffee or just sit in the lobby and talk, like they used to when she was a high school senior and he came home for college breaks.

But the bruised look in her eyes had stopped him. He got off the elevator on the fifth floor, while the women went on up to the twelfth, where the suites were located. Then he stood in the hall popping the key with his thumbnail, thinking he might follow them up after all. He and Miranda could talk in the parlor while the older women went to bed.

He wanted to ask her what made her so sure that girl was worth saving. He wanted to follow the trail of Miranda's life from a near fall out a dorm window to the security that now seemed to guide her every step. He wanted to explain why he couldn't talk about God. He wanted to tell her why he still wore the ring.

For a young man living in the city whose motto was Let the Good Times Roll, the temptations had been great. At first he'd resisted because he wanted to please the Lord. Even in his bitterness toward Miranda, he knew that God wanted him to remain pure for his future bride. Then cynicism had built, as daily he saw the violent results of self-pleasure. Pride in his own moral uprightness began to replace his dependence on the Father.

Now as he drew the little golden ring from under his shirt and slid it onto the end of his little finger, he knew that for him it was more than a symbol of purity. It represented faith in God and hope for the future. At this moment it represented God's faithfulness. God had rescued Miranda, not because of him but in spite of him.

It was time to stop making excuses for his own falling away from his Savior. He could no longer blame Miranda.

Maybe he should call her after all.

He moved to sit on the bed, and as he reached for the phone, the blinking message light caught his attention. He frowned. His family and his captain knew where he was, but his parents were in Europe, buying antiques for their Internet business. They wouldn't call unless it was an emergency.

He picked up the receiver, pressed the button, and heard a gruff familiar voice. "Mullins. Warrington here. Thought you might want to know that the hooker who agreed to testify against Delacroix wound up in the morgue last night. She OD'd on crack, best we could tell from the preliminary autopsy. We're back at ground zero. Hang in there, kid. We're working on it." *Click.*

Tony stared at the receiver in his hand, nauseated to the core. *God, I could go to jail, and I didn't do anything but my job. I didn't take any bribe, and I didn't beat anybody up. Why are you doing this to me?*

He slammed the phone back into its cradle and wearily rested his head in his hands. This just proved his point to Miranda about the realities of redeeming prostitutes. A dog would always go back to its vomit. Wasn't that in Scripture somewhere, too?

Roxanne stood on the balcony landing above the parlor and looked down on Miranda, who slept crossways on the roll-out bed, face down and arms flung wide. Her legs were tangled in the sheets and her pillow scrunched under her stomach. Roxanne shook her head. It was going to take a strong man to hold his own against that one. Even in sleep she made her presence known.

The bedroom door opened behind her, emitting the chemical smell of hairspray and Geraldine's delicate cologne. Roxanne looked around and smiled. "Mornin', Ger. Feeling better after a good sleep?"

"Yes, thanks." Geraldine smoothed the jacket of her plum-colored, raw silk pantsuit over her narrow hips and opened her handbag to catalog her belongings. "How about a cup of coffee while we wait for Miranda to wake up?"

The two women quietly left the suite and took the elevator down to the lobby, where a small coffee shop and bakery nestled in a side room. A gospel standard drifted from the grand player piano in the lobby, underscoring the clink of dishes and quiet conversation.

Roxanne dumped a quarter cup of half-and-half into her coffee, not bothering to offer the pitcher to Geraldine, who drank hers black and stout. After shoveling in some sugar, she took a sip and sat back with a blissful sigh. "So. How are we doing?"

"We?"

"Us—you and me and our mule-headed progeny."

Geraldine cracked a smile. "I didn't know you knew that word."

"There are a lot of things you don't know I know. Like how worn out you are. You don't have to come with us to Graceland this afternoon. Why don't you stay in and nap, then we'll go to the opera tonight."

"I'm not spending three hundred dollars a night to take a nap. Besides, I've got to keep an eye on you."

"What are you talking about?" Roxanne bristled.

"You have that look in your eye."

"What look?"

"The one that says if God's not moving fast enough to suit me, I'll give him a little boost."

"Geraldine Mullins, you take that back!"

Geraldine just looked at her. Roxanne was relieved to see, however, that the sparkle had returned to her friend's eyes. Maybe there was something to be said for being a pain in the neck.

"OK," Roxanne sighed. "Maybe I did have a little plan—which I will abandon, I promise." She grinned at Geraldine's doubtful look. "But I'm still keeping my options open!"

CHAPTER FIVE

AS SHE hovered in the doorway of the coffee shop, Miranda found herself filled with a strange sense of foreboding engendered by the sight of her grandmother's red head bent with intense concentration over a strawberry bagel loaded with fig preserves. Determined to ask Geraldine to keep a tight rope on Granny today, Miranda prepared herself to stand firm against manipulation.

She was relieved to see that Tony was nowhere in sight. To fortify her jumpy nerves, Miranda ordered a large orange juice at the counter, then approached Granny and Geraldine with a tray containing the frosty glass and a huge blueberry muffin.

"May I join you ladies?" she said brightly and pulled out a chair.

"Mornin', sunshine." Granny had a guilty glint in her eyes, but quickly shoved away the coffee cups and crumpled napkins cluttering Miranda's place at the table. "You look like you been rode hard and put up wet, girl. Didn't you sleep good last night?"

That was a diversionary tactic if Miranda had ever heard one, but she was too tired to quibble. "As a matter of fact, I have a little headache," she said. "I had weird dreams all night."

"That's too bad." Geraldine patted her hand sympathetically. "Want to talk about it?"

Miranda's stomach lurched at the thought. She shook her head. "What's on the agenda for today?"

"The Hunt-Phelan Home this morning—" Granny ticked the items off on her fingers—"Graceland after lunch, and the opera tonight."

"Boy, Tony's gonna love that." Miranda managed a grin. "Has he put in an appearance this morning?"

"Not yet." Geraldine carefully blotted her lips. "I called a few minutes ago to see if he wanted breakfast, but there wasn't any answer, so I left a message."

"I think he likes to work out—oh, there he is!" To her chagrin, Miranda felt her cheeks heat as she waved, trying to catch Tony's eye. He stood in the doorway of the cafe, both hands stuffed into the back pockets of his well-worn Levi's, looking nearly as bleary-eyed as the apparition that had greeted her in the bathroom mirror this morning. Apparently he hadn't slept well either.

One corner of his mouth lifted as he dodged tables to get to them. "Nana, I must have been in the shower when you called," he said, but his gaze was on Miranda. His hair was still damp, and she noticed he'd cut his upper lip shaving, just above the scar left from a college baseball injury. She'd gone with him to the emergency room to get it stitched up.

Remembering the pastiness of his face, the way he'd crushed her hand as the doctor sewed his lip back together, Miranda's stomach gave an odd flip. She scrambled for a conversational topic. "Did anybody check the weather station this morning?"

"Yeah, it was on in the weight room. Thunderstorms predicted most of the day." Tony made a face and glanced at his grandmother. "Nana, I really don't think you ought to go out in such bad weather."

"I assure you I won't melt, dear." Geraldine gave him an amused look. "You're not getting out of the tour that easily."

He sighed. "Can't blame a guy for trying. What's a Hunt Feelin', anyway?"

"For your information," Granny informed him loftily, "the Hunt-Phelan Home is one of the few antebellum homes in the nation preserved in its entirety."

"Well, slap me with a bread-and-butter pickle," he drawled, winking at Miranda. "We certainly wouldn't want to miss that."

A huge clap of thunder suddenly shook the entire building. "I sure hope my umbrella's in the car," Miranda said morosely.

"If I were one of those Peabody ducks, I'd be in heaven."

Tony glanced at Miranda, who stood with her nose pressed against the plate-glass window of Elvis Presley's Graceland Gift Shop. The rain was coming down in sheets, blowing against the window with gale-force determination. He figured the weather just about matched the condition of his life.

He picked up a coffee mug molded in the shape of Elvis's head and considered buying it for Captain Warrington as a joke. "Spend a few days in New Orleans and this little drizzle wouldn't bother you."

"Yeah, well, it could be a hurricane out there and Granny would still insist on touring Graceland." She peeled her nose off the window and peered at her watch. "How long before the shuttle comes to take us over to the estate?"

"Ten minutes, I think." He set down the mug and grabbed her wrist. "I can't believe you still have that thing."

"I'll have you know Barbie keeps very good time." Miranda looked around at Nana and Roxanne, who were examining velvet-backed portraits of the King. "Hope Granny doesn't buy one of those things. She drools over them every time we pass the gas station back home." She snatched her hand away and backed up a step.

Tony followed her. "What's the matter with you today?"

"She's got enough tacky Elvis stuff already—"

"No, not that." He examined the shadows under her eyes. "You're jumpy as a squirrel on a doghouse."

They stood there looking at one another, years folding back on one another, and Tony wished they were someplace quiet. Unpredictable Miranda might be, but she knew how to listen. He wanted to tell her his worries about Nana and about his job, maybe even ask her to pray.

When the intercom in the gift shop thumped and squawked, Miranda looked away. "The shuttle for the one o'clock tour is now boarding," announced a syrupy female voice. "Ticket holders please report to the front loading area."

"We'd better get our blue suede shoes out there before they leave us," Miranda muttered uneasily. "Come on."

Tony shook his head and followed her and their two grandmothers outside the building, where a covered concrete drive-through gave them some protection from the blowing rain. A bored college student handed each of them a cassette player and headphones, with instructions to turn it on once the shuttle got under way.

Tony soon found himself squeezed onto a bench seat between Miranda and a hefty matron wearing a straw hat, tiger-framed sunglasses, and an electric blue jogging suit. He put his arm behind Miranda's shoulders—to give the tiger-woman more room, he told himself—and settled back to endure.

The inclement weather seemed not to have dimmed most of the tourists' enthusiasm for the pilgrimage to the mecca of American pop culture. Tony couldn't quite comprehend the fanatical hero worship of the almost exclusively female tour group. How could a man who'd been dead for more than twenty years inspire such loyalty? As the bus entered the famous iron gates of the fourteen-acre estate situated on one of the busiest highways in the South, Tony listened to Priscilla Presley's honeyed tones in his ear, explaining how her ex-husband got his start from humble beginnings in Tupelo, Mississippi.

Women, he decided, had a unique way of coloring the past. He glanced down at Miranda, who seemed to be in her own private world that had nothing to do with Vernon and Gladys Presley or their twin sons, Jesse and Elvis. She sat stiffly in the hollow of Tony's shoulder, watching her own slender fingers pleating the damp leg of her jeans. One of her sneakers was turned sideways, the other propped on top of it, and its soggy laces had come untied. Typical Miranda. He had a sudden and inexplicable urge to get down on his knees, take off her shoes and socks, and warm her feet in his hands.

Mullins, you are out of your mind, he told himself and gave his attention back to Priscilla. You pay ten bucks for a tour, you might as well listen.

Tarzan would have been right at home in this Jungle Room, Miranda thought, peering into the dimness of Elvis's basement retreat. Shag carpet covered nearly every surface, and the brown-and-green 70s-style color scheme created a cavelike atmosphere, which was unmitigated by dark wood paneling and the undulating light of a lava lamp on a monster-sized end table. The tour cassette explained that Elvis's daughter, Lisa Marie, used to love curling up in the grotesque corner chair; its fuzzy upholstery and gnarled arms and legs reminded Miranda of the throne of an African king.

She shuddered and lost interest, choosing instead to study the people around her. The lady in the tiger-frame glasses was just to her left, arm in arm with a man in a matching blue jogging suit. Expressions glazed, they appeared spellbound at the thought of Elvis and his "Memphis Mafia" entertaining and recording in this very room.

"You reckon they thought this was cozy?" Tony moved aside Miranda's earphone to mutter in her ear.

"I suppose." Miranda shifted to look up at him and felt the rain on his jacket soak through her thermal knit shirt. He'd made sure Granny and Geraldine stayed dry, but the umbrella had failed to cover his broad shoulders. She shivered at the look in his eyes—sort of hungry and anxious, all at once, focused right on *her.* She knew he wasn't thinking about Elvis.

"Let's go outside to the Trophy Room," he said with a grimace. "This place is depressing."

"OK." Miranda told Granny where they were going. Granny nodded absently, evidencing an alarming desire to jump over the rope keeping tourists out of the Jungle Room. "We'll meet you at the Meditation Garden in an hour or so."

"Meditation Garden?" Tony grumbled as they squeezed through the clumps of tourists in the narrow hallways, following the tour signs. He took off his headphones and hooked them around his neck. "We're supposed to meditate on Elvis? In the rain?"

Miranda shot him an amused look over her shoulder. "Actually, Elvis claimed to be a Christian. I think you're supposed to meditate on God's love. That's why he called the place Graceland."

Tony rolled his eyes and took Miranda's hand when a family of four blocked the exit. "Excuse me," he said politely but firmly, and tugged Miranda out the back door, where a covered sidewalk led to a series of outbuildings. The lawn was blindingly green, obviously well tended, and the buildings gleamed white against the heavy gray sky. A magnificent stable beyond a white-railed paddock attested to the Presley family's love of horses.

Miranda didn't object when Tony kept her hand as they wandered into Elvis's original office, a freestanding building with a couple of curtainless windows and a creaky wooden door that stood open to tourists. At the moment, Tony and Miranda were the only ones there to disturb the quietness of the room. Its furnishings were perfectly neat, the office machines and calendars arranged in orderly fashion, but their datedness gave the room a sad, abandoned air. Lightning flashed, followed by a grumble of thunder in the distance, and Miranda edged a little closer to Tony. He didn't seem to notice that his long fingers curled around hers with casual intimacy.

Miranda noticed. Oh, yes, she noticed. She could even feel the calluses on the pads of the fingers of his left hand. "You still play your guitar?" she asked, breaking the silence.

Tony paused in his examination of the heavy green metal desk, with its typewriter and black phone, and the oscillating fan perched on a file cabinet. He nodded absently, brushing his fingers over a desk calendar dated May 1959. "Sometimes. We do a little jamming at the precinct once in a while."

She grinned. "What about your trumpet? In high school you were so gung ho about marching band . . ."

"Oh, man, don't remind me." To Miranda's delight, Tony actually blushed. "I was the definitive band geek."

"You were not!" Miranda protested, squeezing his hand. "The first time I saw you in one of those cavalier hats and that white shirt with the satin sash, I thought—" She stopped, nearly swallowing her tongue in confusion. *I'm gushing.*

Tony stared at her, and it seemed to Miranda that all the air suddenly got sucked out of the room by some giant vacuum cleaner. Awkwardly he said, "You thought what?"

"Nothing."

"I could never figure it out." He cocked his head, eyes intent. "You remember that night—your first football game as a cheerleader. They all wanted you to go for pizza afterward, but you got on the band bus instead, with Grant and me." He paused, but Miranda couldn't speak, couldn't admit how she'd yearned for his attention, even then. "And you sat with me," he finished.

"You didn't act too happy about it," she said wryly, trying for a lighter tone.

"I—I didn't know how to act." He looked away. "I was only seventeen years old, and you'd been my best friend's little sister nearly all my life."

"So why did you kiss me?"

There, the question was out. She'd never had the nerve to ask him, because he'd seemed almost angry with her after it happened. It was another three years before he'd even asked her out. Well, to be technically correct she'd asked *him* out first.

"Never mind, forget I asked." Miranda yanked her hand out of his and turned toward the door, which got caught by a gust of wind and suddenly blew shut in her face. A flare of lightning lit up the room, simultaneous with a deafening crack of thunder that made the floor vibrate beneath her feet. Miranda gave a little shriek of surprise as the lights went out and the hum of the air conditioner quit.

"Oh, man," Tony said from directly behind her. "Let's get back to the bus quick." He reached around her to shove on the door, but it refused to budge. "Hey, what's going on?" he muttered. "Miranda, move a second so I can see."

Miranda moved out of the way and went to the window. It looked out on the empty lawn, on the opposite side from the sidewalk. She could hear people running and exclaiming through the blast of wind and rain that whistled around the little outbuilding and slashed viciously under the awnings.

She went back to stand beside Tony, who was still fiddling with the doorknob. There was enough light coming through the window that she could see the frown of concentration and worry hooking his eyebrows together.

"It seems to be locked," he said without glancing at her.

"Locked? How could that be?"

"I don't know. Maybe it's an automatic security system."

"Well, for pete's sake, bang on the door so somebody will let us out!" Miranda hugged herself, trying not to sound panicky.

They both began to shout, pounding on the door, but the wind made so much noise they could barely hear themselves, and it quickly became apparent that nobody suspected the darkened office building was occupied.

Miranda leaned back against the door, shivering a little. She looked up at Tony, who stood with his forearm braced just above her head. "You reckon it's a tornado?" she asked.

She could see just a white glimmer of a smile. "We sure ain't in Kansas, Dorothy."

Miranda gave a sputter of laughter. "No, but we're in Memphis, and they call the area tornado alley. Shouldn't we get down and cover our heads or something?"

"Remember those tornado drills we had in grade school? Where you sit out in the hall and put your head between your knees?"

Miranda groaned. "For hours on end. No talking."

"The ultimate torture for you, I'm sure."

She heard the teasing in his voice and felt a measure of comfort. "Surely the power will come back on before the shuttle leaves."

"Nana and Roxanne wouldn't let them leave us. They'll come looking for us soon."

"You think?" Miranda considered. An uneasy feeling slipped through her midsection. "Granny wouldn't—no, of course she wouldn't . . ."

"What?" Tony straightened and caught Miranda's shoulder. "Do you know something I don't know?"

"Well, it's just—Granny had a mighty conniving look on her face this morning."

"Of all the—" Tony's hands lifted, and he turned a full circle of frustration. "We could be stuck in here all night!"

"No way!"

"OK, let's be logical." Tony closed his eyes and rubbed his temples. "Nana will make sure somebody finds us."

"Unless Granny convinces her we've already gone back to the hotel."

Tony's expression was a study in horrified disbelief. "Nobody's that much of a noodle-head."

Miranda bristled. "Whose grandmother are you insulting? Yours or mine?"

"Neither. Never mind." Tony released a pent-up breath and yanked Elvis's Naugahyde chair away from the desk. He plopped into it and swung his feet up on the desk with a thud. "We might as well make ourselves comfortable. No telling how long we'll be here." He folded his arms and glowered at Miranda, as if the situation were her fault.

She made a face at him and slid down the door to sit on the linoleum floor. "Well, look at the bright side. At least you won't have to dress up and go to the opera."

Standing in the pouring rain without the benefit of an umbrella, Roxanne twirled Geraldine's cane like a drum major's mace, while her friend laboriously climbed the shallow steps up into the shuttle. She helped Geraldine settle into a front seat, then sat down beside her with a sodden plop. "Whew! What a frog-strangler!" She bent to wring the water out of one pants leg.

Geraldine removed her plastic rain bonnet, folded it into a precise one-inch cube, and slipped it into a pocket of her handbag. "Where did you say the children went?"

"Oh, I dunno," Roxanne mumbled, blinking her wet eyelashes so that spikes of mascara radiated around her eyes. "Tony said they were going on ahead."

"What does that mean? Ahead to the hotel?"

"I'm not sure. But they looked like they wanted to be alone." Roxanne winked broadly.

"Roxanne, they're not on the bus. We can't leave them here."

"Why not? Tony's a police officer, for goodness' sake. He can take care of himself—and Miranda, too, for that matter."

"This isn't any ordinary storm. It looks like a tornado to me." Geraldine glanced out the window. "I have a very bad feeling about this."

"What time does Barbie have?" Tony asked.

"I don't know; it's too dark to see," Miranda answered with an irritated little snort. "My stomach says past dinnertime."

There was a moment's silence while Tony listened to water dripping off the eaves of the building and to Miranda drumming her nails against the floor. The wind and rain had stopped, but apparently tour hours were over, and not a soul had come looking for them. The power was still off.

"Miranda, I'm sorry I was such a grouch."

He heard her suck in a breath of surprise. "It's—OK. I was a little shook-up, too."

"You're not scared, are you?"

"Well, to be honest, I'm not really looking forward to staying here much longer in the dark. This is a really old building . . ."

Tony was suddenly aware of the chilly, damp air that had seeped in through the concrete under the linoleum. He was in the only chair in the room, and Miranda was still on the floor. "Hey, I'm sorry." He jumped to his feet. "Come sit here, and I'll sit on the desk."

"No, it's OK, I'm comfortable—"

"Or better yet, you can sit in my lap. I know you must be cold."

"Tony!" Miranda sounded scandalized. "This is not Ice Station Zebra."

"Well—," he gulped, suddenly feeling like a fool. "You've been wet from the knees down most of the day. I'd hate for you to get sick." Concern was evident in his voice.

He heard her sigh. "That's very sweet. Really. But you're confusing me."

"I'm confusing myself," he muttered. "Why in the world did you wear tennis shoes on a day like today?"

"I'm going to scream. Yes, I really think I will. You'd better cover your ears; it's going to be a loud one."

"Miranda."

"What?"

"I've never stopped loving you." The words were out before he could call them back.

Miranda gasped. He heard her head clonk back against the door. "Your timing is so wonderful."

He crouched beside her. He could see the dim outline of her hair curling wildly around her face, caught a subtle hint of raspberry mixed with the harsher smell of wet denim. "I know I've acted like a jerk, sort of, the last couple of days, but I was just so mad because you hurt me so bad. In a lot of ways you haven't changed a bit, but there's something different about you, too—" He stopped when he saw her head drop to her knees. Was she praying? He shifted to sit beside her with his back against the door, afraid to touch her.

There was a short silence, then finally Miranda said, "That's the problem, Tony, I *am* a different person. I've been trying to explain that to you." She turned her head so that her voice was no longer muffled by her jeans. "You don't seem to be comfortable with either who I *was* or who I *am* now. What do you want from me?"

"I want to know who you are now," he said eagerly, suddenly aware how true that was. "You asked me why I kissed you that night on the bus. Miranda, I've never been able to tell you how you light up a room just being in it. But you were so much younger, and I knew Grant would either razz me to death or take me apart piece by piece. So I kissed you because I wanted to, then acted like it was your fault."

"Oh, Tony."

"I know. Then I went off to USM and tried to keep busy until you grew up a little, and then you asked me to your senior prom." He stopped, remembering Miranda in a sapphire-colored, floor-length beaded gown, her curly hair tamed into a chignon at the back of her slender neck.

"I would never have done that if Gavin Willis hadn't dumped me when it was too late to ask anyone else."

"I know that. But I was honored you felt like you could depend on me."

"I thought Grant was going to hurt himself laughing."

"He's a pain," Tony agreed with a grin. "But we love him anyway."

"So are you."

"But you love me anyway, right?" He held his breath.

She finally said slowly, "It's . . . complicated."

"Do you—you don't have a boyfriend, do you?"

"No, I've been too busy to date much."

"Then—"

His surge of elation was flattened by her tense tone. "Tony, we can't just skip over everything that happened between my senior prom and now. You're coming back to me, but there's a big hole in you that really worries me."

"What do you mean?"

"You say you love me, but I don't think you understand the most important thing in my life." She uttered a bitter little laugh. "And the ironic thing is, it used to be the other way around."

"Do you have to bring God into every conversation? I'm trying to tell you I've forgiven you for getting drunk at that frat party and hurting me so deeply. Obviously you wouldn't do anything like that anymore. I'm ready to go on from here, but quit poking around in my spiritual life, OK?"

"Oh, God, I can't do this!" Miranda choked out and hunched into her knees again. He thought she whispered, "It hurts, it hurts," so he put both arms around her taut body and pulled her against him.

He could feel her shivering. "What is it? What's the matter?"

"I had a dream this morning, right before I woke up." Her voice was high and thin, as if she held back tears. "I used to dream all the time about being up on that window ledge again, with the sheet wobbling below, and being so scared. But this time I was down on the ground, and I looked up and *you* were up there about to fall. Only the window was about four stories higher, and I knew you'd be killed, and I kept screaming for you to go back inside where it was safe. I watched you fall and fall . . ." She shuddered violently, suddenly threw her arms around his waist, and burrowed her head into his chest. "Oh, Tony!"

"And you think that means something?" He held onto her, but shook his head skeptically.

"Don't you see? If you keep going on this road away from God, I don't know what will happen! He loves you so much, he'll do whatever it takes to get you back."

CHAPTER SIX

"LET me get this straight," Tony's voice rumbled under Miranda's cheek. "God's gonna push me out a window if I keep following you around?"

She shoved away from him, straining against his arms. "This is not funny! You know that's not what I meant!"

"Come on, Miranda. I never thought I'd say this to you, but lighten up. If anybody's falling, it's that hooker that got you arrested the other day."

"Tony, listen to yourself! You're labeling people like soup cans. Yes, Bernadette is a sinner and needs Christ, but so am I. I was self-centered and proud, determined to be my own boss until I realized what a stinking mess I was. The Bible says we're *all* like sheep who have gone away from the Shepherd." She struggled to her knees and placed a hand on either side of Tony's rigid face. "Oh, please, beloved, tell me what's taken you away from him."

"What—what did you call me?" His arms nearly crushed her, and she collapsed against him again.

"Tony, I love you so much, but something's not right, and I don't know how to pray for you. I have this awful feeling it's my fault—"

"*Your* fault?" He laughed, but Miranda could feel tension in every line of his powerful body. "No, I've managed to mess things up really well all on my own, with a little help from people like your new friend."

"What do you mean?"

"I'm on suspension from the New Orleans PD right now. They're investigating charges that I took a bribe in return for looking the other way on a drug and prostitution ring. Me—the eternal soul of rectitude! There was a woman who had agreed to testify for me, but she managed to get herself planted six feet under before she could be deposed."

"But how could anybody think that about you?" Miranda whispered in horror.

"Listen, what I do every day is turn over rocks, and you'd be amazed at who comes slithering out. Nobody's above suspicion, and I happened to be in the wrong place at the wrong time."

"But that's not fair! Surely there's somebody else who could tell them—"

"I'm sure there is," he interrupted. "But they're not coming forward, and there's nothing I can do about it."

"See, this is exactly why we need to pray." Miranda spoke against Tony's chest. "You have an advocate with the Father—"

"Miranda." He loosened his hold, his hands sliding up to cup her shoulders. "I've prayed until I'm blue in the face, and God's just not listening. I guess I ignored him long enough that he gave up on me."

"No, no, you've got it backwards! You've got to trust him *in spite* of this awful circumstance. It's just like this dark room. I'd be really scared if I were by myself, but you're here, and God's here, so there's nothing to be afraid of. Don't you see? He loves us enough to give us another chance to make our relationship right, but our part is to show our faith by obedience."

"All I want to do right now is kiss you."

"No, I'm talking about spiritual things now!" She tugged at his shirt.

"Is that an ultimatum, Miranda? You'll kiss me when I make some kind of verbal acknowledgment of God?" He pulled her hands away from his shirt. "Well, find somebody else to take you to the prom this time. I'm outta here."

As he stood up, the lights suddenly came on. Miranda crouched on the floor, blinking away hot tears.

It wasn't long before a security guard pounded on the door. "Hey, who's in there?" There was a rattle of keys, and the door swung outward. A dark moon face under a flat law-enforcement cap peered in, and the guard's eyes widened at the sight of the two captive tourists. "Y'all been in here all this time? I saw you on the monitor when the power came back on."

Miranda looked up and for the first time noticed a security camera mounted in a corner near the ceiling.

Tony reached a hand to Miranda to haul her to her feet, then let her go like a hot potato. "We've enjoyed about all we can stand," was his clipped reply. "Can you call us a cab?"

"Sure enough," the man replied genially, leading the way back to his tiny office in the mansion proper. "I'm sorry you folks got stuck out there. It got kinda crazy gettin' all those people out of here with no electricity."

Miranda followed the two men quietly with her arms folded across her stomach. *Dear God in heaven, I know you're working, but I just can't see it,* she prayed. *Help me know what to do now.*

In an attic "bedroom" above Sister Zena's, Bernadette McBride sat cross-legged on her lumpy futon under a naked thirty-watt bulb dangling from the low ceiling. She was taking inventory of her Bible collection. There was the *Children's Picture Bible* she'd "borrowed" the first time the bus from the Waterfront Mission took her to Sunday school. On the floor was a beat-up King James Version that had belonged to the woman at her last foster home. It was all marked up, and Bernadette often touched the crooked ink lines, wondering what they'd meant to Mrs. Coker at the time.

There were more stuffed behind the bed, but in her lap was the most recent prize: a compact Gideon's Bible she'd sneaked into the waistband of her pants the last time she'd had a "date" at the Peabody. Bernadette brushed a hand over its hard burgundy cover. It was clean and unmarked, and it made her think of Miranda and the guy who'd been with her when she came banging on the door loud enough to wake the dead.

Bernadette had stood at the top of the stairs listening to Zena deal with them; she was blown away that they'd managed to find her, scratching her head that they'd cared enough to do so. Zena hadn't been happy that Bernadette was making acquaintances outside the riverside slums. Dangerous, she had said. That guy—Tony Mullins, he said his name was—was a *cop*.

Bernadette touched the bruise on her cheek. Zena didn't want her to leave, because her income helped pay the rent on this dump. In fact, it was already dark outside, about time to go out and start hitting the bars. Lots of potential customers slumming during these blues festivals.

She opened the Bible at random and lay back on the futon with the book spread across her chest. She watched a spider crawl across the ceiling and fantasized about waltzing into the Peabody, dressed like Miranda in a swirly skirt and feminine shoes. She'd go up to the desk clerk, smile shyly and say, "I'm here to meet Detective Tony Mullins. He's expecting me." And there would be no shame, no fear, just the promise of protection and unconditional love.

"That's all I want, God," she whispered. "Just somebody to love me."

The light on the phone was flashing again when Tony entered his room. His already tense shoulders braced as if for a blow as he sat on the bed and punched the numbers to receive his messages.

"Tony, this is Mrs. Roxanne," he heard, and relaxed momentarily. Her next words had him on his feet. "I'm at Methodist Hospital with Geraldine—now, don't get all excited, she's fine. Just had a bit of pain, and they wanted to watch her overnight, so of course I thought you should know. Don't rush over here; there's nothing you can do. I'll stay with Gerrie tonight, and you can come see her in the morning. Tell Miranda to pray."

Tony gulped and sank back onto the bed, the phone buzzing in his ear. Nana in the hospital? He knew she'd been tired and ill a lot lately, suspected there was more going on than the flu. But not living right there in town with her, he could only take her word that she was just showing her age.

He wondered if he should try to call his dad. But Roxanne said it wasn't serious, so maybe he should wait until he saw Nana in the morning before he got his parents all upset.

Man, the *hospital.* He slowly replaced the receiver. Tony had a healthy man's aversion to hospitals. He was responsible for Nana this weekend, though, so maybe he'd better go check on her for himself.

Tell Miranda to pray. That was a good idea. Besides, she needed to know where her own grandmother was. She was probably in the room, worried sick by now. *She won't call me to find out, that's for sure. I made sure she'll never ask me for anything else. Oh, Father, I am so stupid. How could I think I can handle anything on my own? I can't even talk to the woman I love without hurting her.*

For the first time in a long time, Tony began to understand his own arrogance, and a tide of remorse built up until it finally forced him off the bed and down on his knees. That didn't seem low enough, so he lay facedown on the floor, groaning with an almost physical pain.

"Oh, God, Miranda says you want me. I'm not anything, but here I am. I've looked at the scum of New Orleans and considered myself superior, but you know better. That bribery charge is the least of my problems. Miranda's right—there's a hole in my heart where I've held myself away from you. I want you to come in and fill it and make me new like Miranda. I want to love like she does, and if it's too late for her to love me back, then you can help me stand it. I'm asking you to care for my Nana, because she's a woman after your heart; at least give me a chance to tell her how much she means to me. Oh, God . . ." he repeated over and over, gradually quieting until he lay limp and spent with his cheek pressed to the hotel-room carpet.

Finally he got up, feeling whole and light and a bit disoriented, and went into the bathroom to splash water on his face. He stared at himself in the mirror, amazed to find no difference in his appearance.

Miranda. He had to call Miranda and then go see Nana.

Better yet, he'd go up to the suite and tell her in person.

Five minutes later he was standing outside the door of the Romeo and Juliet suite, shifting impatiently from one foot to the other. There had been no answer to his repeated knocking. Possibly she was in the shower. Or maybe Roxanne had called her after all, and Miranda had gone to the hospital without him. He wouldn't have thought she'd do that.

Hunching his shoulders, he headed for the elevator.

He went out to the parking lot for his truck and quickly drove to Methodist Hospital a few blocks up on Union Avenue. Inside, nobody paid any attention to him as he walked down the brightly lit antiseptic-smelling hallways, his stomach getting jumpier with every step. He hoped Miranda would be there. On the sixth floor, he stopped in front of the room number given him at the reception desk and knocked softly. It just then occurred to him that Nana might be sleeping.

Roxanne's gamine face appeared in the crack in the doorway. "Tony! I told you there was no need to come tonight."

"I know. Is Nana asleep?"

"Well, no, but I don't think—just a minute." She turned her head. Tony heard a murmur from inside the room. "Are you sure, Ger? You need to rest."

Tony waited until Roxanne reluctantly let him in. "I'll only stay a minute," he said. "I just want to make sure she's OK."

"All right, five minutes." Roxanne patted Tony's cheek and moved out into the hall. "I'll go get a cup of coffee."

He quickly noted that there was no sign of Miranda, but the sight of his grandmother hooked to an IV, her face devoid of makeup and looking grotesquely pale, her hair a bird's nest against the white pillow, shocked him to the core. Gently taking her free hand, he studiously ignored a parade of Band-Aid strips along her left arm just above the drip needle.

"I can't leave you alone for five minutes without you getting in trouble." He tried for a weak joke and was pleased to see her smile.

"Me? Where have *you* been, young man?"

"Miranda and I got caught in an office building in the storm when the power went off. They just let us out a little bit ago."

"Ah." Nana's eyes twinkled. "That sounds promising."

"It was a disaster," Tony said shortly. "I take it y'all didn't make it to the opera?"

"We were getting dressed, when Roxanne insisted on taking me to the emergency room. I—well, I passed out in the shower."

"Nana, are you going to tell me what's going on? Was it a heart attack?"

Nana sighed. "No. Pull up a chair. I need to tell you something."

Tony complied, dread fisting in his midsection. He took his grandmother's fragile fingers again.

"OK, I've got a tumor close to my brain." Her voice was perfectly calm, tender as always. Tony stared at her, wanting to throw something across the room. He couldn't speak. "I wasn't going to tell you all, because at my age I didn't want to go through the trauma of surgery. I was hoping I could get to the end without scaring anybody." Tony mutely shook his head, and Nana squeezed his hand. "Didn't work out that way, did it? Listen, sweetheart, I'm ready to go anytime. But I have to know if you are."

"Wh-what?" he croaked.

"One reason I wanted you to come with me this weekend was to make sure your relationship with the Lord gets back on track." She looked away. "It would have been nice if you'd patched things up with Miranda, but I realize we can't force your heart to go where you don't want it to go."

Tony put his forehead against the cold metal bed rail and wept. He felt Nana's hand rest on his head, stroking his hair as if he were eight instead of twenty-eight. He knew better than to argue with Nana over the surgery. He just wished he'd known how important this vacation with her was. He wept for love of his grandmother. He wept for the time he'd wasted resenting and avoiding the Savior who would have steered him back toward his family and his church and his love.

Miranda. Maybe it wasn't too late to patch things up with her. He sat up and swiped the heels of his hands over his face, torn between the humiliation of his tears and determination to straighten out his life. "Nana, you know how much I love you," he said simply.

"I know, son."

"And I want you to know that just before I came over here, I made things right with the Lord."

A beautiful smile lit his grandmother's face. "Oh, I'm so glad!"

"I'm just going to miss you so much . . ." His voice splintered.

"Oh, dear, that's just what I wanted to avoid." Nana grabbed his ear and tugged.

"Ow!"

"No regrets, now. Plenty of things to look forward to."

He gave her a dubious look but was distracted by Roxanne bouncing into the room like an ADHD Chihuahua. "OK, everybody out! No, not you, Geraldine. Why didn't you bring Miranda with you?" She regarded Tony with bright, inquisitive eyes.

He frowned, remembering. "I assumed she was be here. She didn't come to the door when I knocked."

"But you were together . . ."

"We were, but we went our separate ways after Graceland." He didn't see any point in explaining the whole thing.

"Where could she be?" Roxanne muttered. "It's after ten o'clock." She picked up the phone on the bedside table, where she'd scribbled the hotel number on a scrap of grocery list. "Let's try her again."

When there was no answer, Roxanne frowned and dialed the hotel concierge. "Yes, this is Roxanne Gonzales, and I wonder if my granddaughter left a message for me. Miranda Gonzales. She did?" Roxanne met Tony's eyes, and the dismay in her face told him exactly where Miranda had gone.

Before she had even hung up the phone, he said, "She's gone after that Bernadette girl, hasn't she?"

Roxanne nodded reluctantly. "I'm afraid so. She said not to worry, that she'd be right back."

"Unbelievable," Tony muttered, heading immediately for the door. "She knows how dangerous that part of town is, even in the daytime. Besides, she's wasting her time trying to convert a woman like that."

"Wait just a minute, Tony." Nana's firm voice stopped him with his hand on the door latch.

He turned. "Oh, sorry, Nana, I'll be back to check on you in the morning."

"I'm happy to hear it," she replied, "but before you leave, I'd be interested to know if you think the good Lord has retired from the business of redeeming prostitutes?"

Tony shifted, impatient to be gone. "Well, no, but this is just Miranda being Miranda. She doesn't know what she's doing."

"Oh, is that right?"

"Geraldine, be careful," warned Roxanne.

"It's time to tell," Nana replied, meeting her look.

Puzzled by this odd interplay, Tony waited in the doorway. "You already told me—"

"There are truths I've never told *any* of my family. Where I came from before I met your grandfather, how I survived during the Depression." Nana paused, her voice softening. "How I met Roxanne."

Tony stared at her. "I don't understand."

"I was very much like Miranda's Bernadette," Nana said, not proud but starkly honest. "Lost, full of despair, and yearning for a way out. One day I sat smoking on the back step of a club in New Orleans, when a happy-faced, red-haired girl walked by with her daddy. He was a street preacher there for Mardi Gras week. Roxanne, being Roxanne, made him stop and give me a tract. They invited me for a meal, shared the hope of Christ with me, and my life has never been the same since."

Tony hung his head, tears stinging his eyes. "Nana, you couldn't have been—"

"Oh, yes, I was. Look at me," Nana commanded.

When he made himself meet her eyes, she held her hand palm out, as if in blessing. "Make no mistake, Tony: The love of the Father and his power to reach his lost lambs are great beyond your comprehension."

He could only swallow in shame at the difficulty of practical love. *Lord, I want to change,* he inwardly shouted, and looked at Roxanne. "I don't know what to say," he confessed.

She grinned at him and sank into a rocking chair in the corner, setting it wildly in motion. "How about, 'Can I have your granddaughter's hand in marriage?'" she said, rendering him even more speechless.

"Now go after Miranda," his grandmother said with a smile. "And try to remember that what's on the surface is very often not all there is."

He backed out of the room, his head spinning.

Lord, this is not working out like I thought it would, Miranda silently complained, shifting uncomfortably on her bar-stool perch. In the note, Bernadette had asked Miranda to meet her upstairs in the lounge at Byrdie and Alice's, which had seemed like a good idea at the time, since she had eaten there with Tony and their grandmothers and knew exactly where it was.

However, a place that had seemed perfectly safe in daylight in the company of others now made her feel miserably conspicuous. She tugged at the hem of her skirt, wishing she'd worn slacks instead of this short jumper and tights. . . .

Everybody's looking at me. They know I don't belong here. Thank God I don't belong here.

Why didn't I call Tony and ask him to come with me? He'd make me feel like a fool for even asking, that's why. A fresh wave of embarrassment washed over her as she remembered his crack about the prom. *I'll never ask him to bail me out again,* she decided for the tenth time. *Never.*

Unhappily fanning herself with a paper napkin in a vain attempt to hold at bay the suffocating fog of cigarette smoke that permeated the lounge, she looked up when a side door to her left opened and Bernadette sidled into the bar with a furtive look over her shoulder. She wore a short leather skirt with stack heels, and her hair looked like it had been freshly permed. It floated around her head in loose black curls. Immeasurably relieved to see her, Miranda slid off her stool and stretched out her hands. "I was afraid you weren't coming!"

"Come on, let's get out of here," Bernadette said, ignoring Miranda's welcoming gesture. "It ain't safe."

Miranda clattered behind her down the dark stairwell. "Then why did we meet here? You could have just waited in the lobby of the hotel until I came back—"

"I had to work this last job," Bernadette tossed over her shoulder. "If I didn't show up, Sister Z would've been after me. Even as it is, she might—"

"Job?" Miranda grabbed Bernadette's shoulder, halting her just as they got to the bottom of the stairs. "You mean you were—"

"Shut up. Just shut up." Bernadette closed her kohl-lined eyes and jerked out from under Miranda's hand. "You can preach at me later. We gotta hurry."

As Bernadette opened the door at the foot of the stairs, the clatter of pool balls and conversation from the restaurant collided with the music from upstairs. It took Miranda a moment to realize that Bernadette was frantically shouting at her. "Go back!" she finally screamed in Miranda's ear, shoving past her to pound back up the stairs.

"What?" Miranda hesitated, peering into the patches of bizarre light in the pool room. Then she saw what had spooked Bernadette. A caftan-clad Sister Zena loomed in the opposite doorway, the only other exit from the room.

For a second, Miranda considered confronting the woman, demanding passage for herself and Bernadette, but the sight of the little mojo bag dangling on the massive bosom—and the memory of a small, vicious knife—gave her pause. If Bernadette was afraid of her, it was probably for a very good reason.

Heart knocking against her ribs, Miranda turned to scramble up the stairs after Bernadette. *Oh, Father, let there be another way out of this building.*

Panting, Miranda burst into the lounge and searched for Bernadette. There she was, motioning frantically at the doorway of the same room she'd come out of earlier, one finger against her lips. Trying not to call attention to herself, Miranda smoothed her hair and crossed the room. Bernadette yanked her inside and shut the door, and Miranda found herself in a dark, airless closet. No, it was apparently another stairwell, for she could hear Bernadette's heels clattering away just above her head. Miranda followed, stumbling, reaching blindly for a handrail and finding none. Frightened, she stopped.

Bernadette hissed, "Come on!" The blackness suddenly lightened to gray as another door opened above Miranda. Miranda staggered up the final three steps. Bernadette pulled her into the attic room, then hauled her by the wrist toward a window covered by a tatty flocked velvet drape.

Miranda tried not to look around, but she couldn't help noticing the king-sized iron bed jammed into a corner under the eaves. There was a claw-footed tub and open toilet, of all things, in the raised opposite end of the room. An ugly glass lamp squatted on a rickety table beside the door. The ceiling was low, so they must be directly under the roof.

"Where are we going?" Miranda asked as Bernadette shoved aside the curtain and tugged at the window frame.

"Out," was the brief answer.

"But we must be on the third floor," Miranda protested. The window showed only her own wide-eyed reflection floating in a pool of blackness.

"Fire escape." Bernadette succeeded in wrenching open the window and flung one leg over the sill, heedless of modesty.

"Oh, Bernadette, this is silly. We'll just tell the woman—wait a minute! You'll fall in those shoes!"

Bernadette laughed, yanked off her shoes, and tossed them into the alley below, then clambered barefoot down the iron stairs. "Come on," her urgent voice floated upward out of the darkness.

Miranda leaned out the window and heard the shoes land with a distant clunk on a Dumpster. The smell of garbage rose with sickening strength. She thought she might vomit. She couldn't see anything past the first landing of the fire escape, had no idea how high they were. If the condition of the building was any indication, the fire escape was likely to be just as dangerous as facing Sister Zena.

"Lord Jesus," she whispered. "Help me."

She was gingerly sliding her foot across the windowsill when a big shadow covered her, just as a heavy hand clamped around her upper arm.

"Where you think you're goin' with my girl, hmmm?"

Miranda looked up into the menacing face of Sister Zena.

CHAPTER SEVEN

TONY parked his truck in a loading zone next to a warehouse at the river end of Bealse Street, assuming God and the Memphis police would make allowances for an emergency situation. He bolted from the truck without bothering to lock it and hurried across the street, praying with every step.

If Sister Zena's place had looked unprepossessing in the daylight, it was downright creepy at night. Sagging strings of multicolored Christmas bulbs outlined the windows and door with garish inconsistency, and behind the flimsy curtains the interior pulsed with a greenish glow.

He pounded on the door with the flat of his hand.

God, here I am. Let me find her, OK? Please keep her safe. I'm sorry about my attitude toward that hooker. If my own Nana can come out of that lifestyle, then I guess anybody can.

He jerked violently at the doorknob, caught himself on the point of cursing, then remembered who he was talking to.

Lord, wash my mouth and my brain. Please help me. Where is she?

"Miranda!" he shouted, using both fists on the door. "Sister Zena! Open this door!"

Dead silence greeted the echo of his own voice. A couple of dark figures down the street scuttled into an alley like cockroaches, as if he'd scared them away. Wild with frustration and anxiety, Tony stepped back and raised his foot to kick in the door.

Wham! His heel connected with the warped wood, and he could hear it splinter slightly. "Miranda!" he shouted again.

Poised to kick once more, he heard a feminine voice call his name from somewhere close by. He turned, regained his balance, then nearly lost it again as a girl with long, curly dark hair barreled into him. "Are you Tony?" she panted, then without waiting for an answer, "Miranda's not here. Sister Z's got her, I think."

"What are you talking about?" He grabbed her arms and shook her hard.

"She was right behind me at Byrdie and Alice's, but I got to the bottom of the fire escape and she never came down, so I ran."

"What were you doing at—never mind, come on, let's go."

He ran across the street toward the truck without looking to make sure Bernadette followed. At least he assumed it was Bernadette. Unless Miranda had picked up another street urchin.

After scrambling into the truck and screeching into the street, he glanced at her. She was very pretty and young, maybe only fifteen or sixteen. And barefoot as a yard dog.

"Where are your shoes?"

"Lost 'em coming down the fire escape."

"And you were coming down the fire escape because . . ."

"Sister Zena was blocking the front. Miranda said she'd take me back to the hotel with her and buy me a bus ticket home."

"I see." A light turned yellow, then red, but Tony zoomed under it. They were almost there. "Where's home?"

Bernadette looked out the window. "The Baptist Children's Home in Collierville."

God Almighty, Tony thought. *Forgive my hardness.* "How old are you, Bernadette?"

"Almost fifteen."

Freshly fueled by anger, he stopped outside the restaurant. "Wait here so the police won't tow the truck. I'll be back quick as I can." He opened the door and turned. "If you know how to pray, now's the time to do it."

This section of Beale on a Friday night was hopping with pedestrian traffic. Tourists and locals streamed in and out of every bar and blues club on the block. Music poured from open doorways, neon glowed in every window with incandescent ferocity, and strips of dark alley cut into the activity like black lines in a coloring book.

With fear for Miranda tightening his chest, Tony circled the three-story building, looking for the fire escape. The side? The back? Noise from the front of the restaurant faded as he entered the alley. The stench of old garbage hit him in the face, and he slowed, automatically reaching under his armpit for a gun that wasn't there. What was he going to do if the palm reader had a backup crew? What if they were armed with more than a stiletto?

It occurred to Tony that he had no physical defense at all. All he had was the Lord, and that, in the end, was all he needed. A passage from the Bible that he had memorized as a teenager, who had thrilled to the warriorlike language, burst into his mind. He repeated it silently, mouthing the words as he crept forward, muffling his steps on the broken pavement as much as possible.

Take up the full armor of God . . . gird your loins with truth . . . put on the breastplate of righteousness . . . shoes of the gospel of peace . . . shield of faith . . . helmet of salvation . . . sword of the Spirit. . . . He had always had those things; because he was in Christ, he had never been lost from the Father's hand, despite his own unfaithfulness.

Fear fell away as Tony rounded the back corner of the building. A streetlight illuminated the back alley, and he could see a warehouse looming to his right. An elephant-sized Dumpster, the source of that wretched smell, blocked his view of the restaurant building, but as he skirted it he could see the bottom section of the fire escape dangling three feet above the ground.

He heard scuffling above his head, looked up and up, and felt his heart bound into his throat. There was Miranda, teetering on the top landing, as if she were about to jump off into the Dumpster. A horrible flash of the drunken college incident superimposed on the present, so that Tony had to shake his head to find reality.

Then he realized that someone had *pushed* her out the window onto the fire escape. Miranda clung to the narrow railing, uttering unintelligible cries of distress, resisting the force of the powerful arms trying to shove her off. Despite the murky light of the streetlamp, Tony was sure the arms belonged to Sister Zena, who was enraged that Miranda had dared to invade her territory and remove a major source of her income.

"Miranda!" he called.

"Tony!" he heard in a strangled scream. "She's pushing me off—"

"Hang on, I'm coming after you!" He swung onto the fire escape and started to climb, afraid to look up again. If Miranda lost her grip and fell from the third story, she'd be dead. *Be strong in the strength of the Lord,* he reminded himself as he reached the second-floor landing.

"Hurry, I can't hold on much longer!"

Taking three steps at a time, Tony lunged to the top and grabbed Miranda's arm just as she pitched over the side of the rail. She hung, struggling to regain her hold on the rail, all but pulling Tony over, too. But a supernatural strength filled his arms, enabling him to reach down and grab her around the waist and haul her back up.

Together they sank onto the rusty iron grid of the landing, Tony enfolding her in a crushing embrace, pressing her head into his chest. "Oh, God!" he panted. "Oh, thank you, Jesus!"

They sat there a minute or so, Miranda dousing his shirt with tears of relief, Tony simply glad to hold her and feel the adrenaline seep out of his body.

Finally Miranda looked up and sniffled. "Where'd she go?"

"Who?"

"Sister Zena."

"Anybody's guess," he said, wiping a smear of tears off her cheek with his thumb. "Back to the dragon's lair she came from, I suppose. I'd love to see her put in the slammer where she belongs, but I'll leave that to somebody else."

"How'd you know where I was?"

"Well, you certainly didn't make it easy," he complained, but without much heat. "You could have left a note or something. I went to Sister Zena's first, ran into Bernadette, and she told me where to look."

"Is she OK?"

"That one will always land on her feet. She's out in my truck—I hope."

"Maybe we'd better go see."

"I'd rather sit here with you." His arms tightened again. "I was so scared, Miranda."

"I know, I'm sorry." She sighed and gave a little wiggle. "Tony, I want to be sure Bernadette's safe."

"All right," he agreed, "but we've got to talk soon."

He stood up and pulled her to her feet. He jerked both thumbs. "Inside or outside?"

Miranda shuddered. "I never want to go in that place again. Let's go down the fire escape."

Tony went down first and at the bottom jumped lightly to the ground, then grabbed Miranda by the waist to soften her landing. He took her hand.

"Peee-ew!" Miranda complained as they walked around the Dumpster. "This belongs to my company, and Mr. Greenlee would have a duck if he knew how bad the service is up here."

Tony laughed. "Tell him you've been doing personal inspections and ask him for a raise."

They rounded the front corner of the building to a burst of flashing blue lights. A Memphis police car was parked behind Tony's truck.

His empty truck.

"Oh, man, I knew she'd take off!" He tugged Miranda toward the cruiser. "Maybe I can talk them out of a ticket."

But the police car was empty, too. Puzzled, Tony leaned over to peer in the window, until he heard Miranda suddenly shout with laughter. She dropped Tony's hand and started clapping.

"Look, it's Sergeant Coltrane!"

Tony looked. Sure enough, coming out the front door of Byrdie and Alice's was the dour-faced policeman, his mustache twitching with irritation, escorting a rigidly unconcerned Sister Zena. Her hands were cuffed in front of her, but she strode one step ahead of the officer as if *she* were the one in charge. Two steps behind skipped Bernadette, looking more like the adolescent she was with every step.

She waved at Tony. "I hope you don't mind—I used your cell phone to call 9-1-1!"

Miranda struggled out of sleep and for a minute couldn't figure out where she was. The pillow smelled like coconuts, and the ceiling was low, not the twenty-foot ceiling of the parlor where she'd been sleeping for the last two nights. She bounced a bit and stretched. This was a king-sized bed!

She sat up abruptly. She was in the upstairs bedroom of the Romeo and Juliet suite. Mrs. Geraldine was in the hospital, and Granny had stayed overnight with her. Bernadette was asleep on the couch downstairs.

After Miranda had fallen asleep in the truck on the way home last night, Tony had said good night to her at the door, refusing to talk until they'd both had a good night's sleep. He'd kissed her lightly on the forehead, brushed her cheek tenderly with his finger, and walked off whistling softly. Miranda had scrubbed her face and fallen into bed, too tired to even think about the night's events.

Now a series of faint thuds coming from downstairs penetrated her musings. Must be what had woken her up. She yawned and crawled out of the big bed, pulling Granny's white terry robe over her Larry-Boy T-shirt. Barefoot, she padded over to open the bedroom door.

The thuds got louder. She went out onto the landing and leaned over the rail to watch Bernadette roll off the sofa bed and stumble to the door, muttering under her breath. Shoving a tangle of dark curls out of her face, Bernadette yanked open the door. Her scowl turned into a feline smile. "Tony . . . Hi!"

Miranda squeaked in dismay and ducked back behind the bedroom door. Peeking through the crack, she saw Tony stride into the parlor wearing jeans and a silver gray polo shirt that emphasized his dark hair and eyes. Her heart began to thud. He had come to her rescue again last night, but he'd said nothing to indicate a change in his spiritual condition, except that heartfelt prayer of relief when he'd pulled her back onto the fire-escape landing. He'd driven her to the police station so she could give her statement, where he sat beside her with his arm draped protectively around the back of her chair.

He'd kept glancing at her, his eyes dark with some emotion she couldn't read, but she was too occupied with filling in Sergeant Coltrane on the details of that awful fifteen minutes before Sister Zena tried to throw her off the fire escape.

Miranda shuddered. *Lord, you kept me safe, and you helped Bernadette find Tony. I'm so grateful.*

"Miranda, Miranda, wherefore art thou, Miranda?" Tony called from underneath the balcony.

Miranda tried to squint down over the railing from behind the door, but Tony had moved out of sight.

Bernadette stood in the center of the room, one hip cocked, her eyes alight. "I think I'm gonna be sick," she said and climbed back under the covers, pulling a pillow over her head.

"Come on, Miranda," she heard Tony mutter. "It's nearly ten o'clock. You can sleep later."

"Come back in ten minutes," Miranda said loudly.

"No way," he said, backing up and craning his neck. "I've worked out and had my breakfast and been to see Nana. I even called the children's home in Collierville to see about getting Bernadette back in there. I'm tired of waiting."

Miranda debated, glancing at her eclectic getup. *This is the man who's seen your tubby little body in your Tinker Bell costume,* she reminded herself.

Yes, but he's also the man I love.

Tightening the belt of Granny's robe, she opened the door a little wider and looked at him. There was something clean and open about his expression that she hadn't seen in years. He looked a bit anxious, too. Interesting.

She stepped out on the landing and moved to the railing.

He grinned. "Ah, it's the sun and Miranda is the East."

"You are pathetic," she said sorrowfully. "You're getting this all mixed up."

"What?"

"Well, first of all, you stole my line, and you got the next one backwards."

"So I got a C in ninth-grade English. Are you coming down?"

"I told you I have to get—"

"OK, then I'm coming up there." He took the narrow spiral stairs two at a time and stopped three steps below her before she could either protest or hide. "Please, Miranda, I have to talk to you now."

She inched along the railing toward him. "I can't go anywhere looking like this."

He affectionately eyed her tousled hair. "You look like an angel," he said, "though I have to admit you smell kind of like a—"

"—a coconut," Miranda finished with a giggle. "This is Granny's robe."

He smiled. "We can just sit here." He sat on the carpeted steps and looked up at her hopefully.

She walked down to join him. The intimacy of the narrow stairwell took her breath away. His denim-clad knee brushed hers, and her bare foot looked tiny next to his hiking boots. *Oh, Lord, please direct this conversation,* she prayed desperately.

Tony picked up her hand and laced his fingers through hers. "I'm ready to pray with you now," he said, looking at her steadily.

"Y-you are?"

He nodded. "God has sort of brained me over the head in the last couple of days with how much I have to be grateful to him for." His eyes were tender and looked as soft as drops of dark chocolate. "Not the least of all, the fact that you're willing to keep giving me chance after chance. Just like he did."

Miranda could hardly breathe. Had he come all the way back to her? She clutched Tony's hand.

"The other day you said there was a hole in me," he continued, his thumb drawing agitated circles against hers. "That made me so angry because you were right. I thought I could run my life very well by myself, but I've found out it's all out of control without leaning on the Lord."

"Oh, Tony—"

"Wait, that's not all," he gulped, eyes bright with emotion. "I've got to face this charge against me when I get back home, but I can't do it without God's strength and without you. Miranda, will you forgive me for being so hardheaded and arrogant? I love you so much. . . ."

Miranda launched herself at him, throwing her arms wildly around his neck.

Finally he gave a strangled little laugh. "I guess this means yes."

"Yes, yes, yes!" Miranda exclaimed, planting hard kisses under his ear. "Oh, Tony, I've never loved anybody but you, and I was so afraid I was going to have to let you go back to New Orleans without me!"

She felt his hands on either side of her face, so she reluctantly left off nuzzling his throat. "Listen." He kissed her nose. "Miranda, we can talk about this later, but I'm not going to be one of these guys that just assumes his wife will follow wherever I go—"

"Are you crazy?" she interrupted. "I'm not letting you out of my sight. There's a perfectly good Greenlee Systems office in New Orleans."

"Then you will marry me?"

"Not unless you kiss me first."

Miranda felt him chuckle against her mouth, then lost all interest in waste management. Several minutes later she gasped, "You kiss by th' book, Romeo."

"I've learned a thing or two since high school," he smiled, brushing his thumb across her tingling lips. "Which reminds me . . ." He drew back a little and reached inside the neck of his shirt.

Miranda's eyes widened. In his palm lay a small solid-gold band suspended from a silver chain. That was the bump she'd noticed under his shirt yesterday. "Oh, my," she breathed.

"You know what this is?"

"It's your True Love Waits ring, isn't it?"

He nodded. "I want to give it to you on our wedding night."

"Oh, my," she said again, feeling tears spring to her eyes.

"I'm so thankful the Lord somehow kept me pure for you, even in my rebellion. Miranda, I love you." He kissed her again, then said, "Now can we pray together?"

Smiling through happy tears, Miranda leaned into Tony and bowed her head. *Lord, you sure do love to work miracles,* she thought as Tony began their engagement with a conversation with their Savior and Lord.

A NOTE FROM THE AUTHOR

DEAR Friend,

Because Scott and I got married during spring break of his first semester of seminary, we didn't have time or money for a real honeymoon. Then our two children came along. We had a busy ministry and lots of bills to pay.

On the eve of our tenth anniversary I was bathing the children when the doorbell rang. It was my mother-in-law! "Hi. I'm so glad to see you," I said, thinking, *I'm going to murder Scott for not telling me she was coming!* Of course, I felt much more charitable when I learned she was going to stay with the kids while Scott and I "took a little trip."

No amount of cajoling could get my dear hubby to tell me where we were going. He'd packed my suitcase—thankfully he let me check to make sure I had everything I'd need for "someplace warm"—and cancelled all my piano students. The next morning we flew to Dallas.

In the Dallas airport we held hands and walked down the concourse, passing gate after gate. "Houston?" No. "Albuquerque?" No. "San Francisco?" No. I became even more incredulous. *"Hawaii?"*

Scott tugged me past the Honolulu gate, then grinned and turned back. "No way!" I whispered. I finally believed him when he showed me the tickets, and I nearly strangled him with a hug.

That night we stood on the deck of a cruise ship under the Aloha Tower, watching the sun go down. Dream vacation, indeed. And what a dream hero God has given me!

In Christ,
Beth

ABOUT THE AUTHOR

ELIZABETH WHITE grew up in northern Mississippi, barely a mile from Graceland. A "real-life" music teacher, Beth always dreamed of following in the footsteps of Louisa May Alcott, her all-time favorite writer. She kept very busy studying classical voice, flute, and piano; singing in contemporary Christian bands; playing in Mississippi State University's famous Maroon Band; and participating in church missions trips. Nevertheless, Beth could often be found with her nose firmly planted in a book.

After a five-year stint in Fort Worth as a bank teller, Beth moved to the beautiful Gulf Coast of Mobile, Alabama, with her minister husband. After the birth of their two children, she decided to beef up her music education degree with some English courses. One fiction-writing course was all it took to get her hooked.

A love of romance, combined with a strong desire to tell stories illustrating Christ's incomparable love for his children, draws Beth to writing inspirational romance. "Miracle on Beale Street," set in her own stomping grounds, is her first published work but hopefully not her last!

Beth welcomes letters written to her in care of Tyndale House Author Relations, P.O. Box 80, Wheaton, IL 60189-0080, or you can E-mail her at scott2beth@aol.com.

Current HeartQuest Releases

- *A Bouquet of Love,* Ginny Aiken, Ranee McCollum, Jeri Odell, and Debra White Smith
- *Dream Vacation,* Ginny Aiken, Jeri Odell, and Elizabeth White
- *Faith,* Lori Copeland
- *Finders Keepers,* Catherine Palmer
- *Hope,* Lori Copeland
- *June,* Lori Copeland
- *Prairie Fire,* Catherine Palmer
- *Prairie Rose,* Catherine Palmer
- *Prairie Storm,* Catherine Palmer
- *Reunited,* Judy Baer, Jeri Odell, Jan Duffy, and Peggy Stoks
- *The Treasure of Timbuktu,* Catherine Palmer
- *The Treasure of Zanzibar,* Catherine Palmer
- *A Victorian Christmas Cottage,* Catherine Palmer, Debra White Smith, Jeri Odell, and Peggy Stoks
- *A Victorian Christmas Quilt,* Catherine Palmer, Debra White Smith, Ginny Aiken, and Peggy Stoks
- *A Victorian Christmas Tea,* Catherine Palmer, Dianna Crawford, Peggy Stoks, and Katherine Chute
- *With This Ring,* Lori Copeland, Dianna Crawford, Ginny Aiken, and Catherine Palmer

- *Freedom's Promise,* Dianna Crawford—coming soon (February 2000)
- *Magnolia,* Ginny Aiken—coming soon (April 2000)
- *Olivia's Touch,* Peggy Stoks—coming soon (May 2000)

Other Great Tyndale House Fiction

- *As Sure As the Dawn*, Francine Rivers
- *Ashes and Lace*, B. J. Hoff
- *The Atonement Child*, Francine Rivers
- *The Captive Voice*, B. J. Hoff
- *Cloth of Heaven*, B. J. Hoff
- *Dark River Legacy*, B. J. Hoff
- *An Echo in the Darkness*, Francine Rivers
- *The Embers of Hope*, Sally Laity & Dianna Crawford
- *The Fires of Freedom*, Sally Laity & Dianna Crawford
- *The Gathering Dawn*, Sally Laity & Dianna Crawford
- *Home Fires Burning*, Penelope J. Stokes
- *Jewels for a Crown*, Lawana Blackwell
- *Journey to the Crimson Sea*, Jim & Terri Kraus
- *The Last Sin Eater*, Francine Rivers
- *Leota's Garden*, Francine Rivers
- *Like a River Glorious*, Lawana Blackwell
- *Measures of Grace*, Lawana Blackwell
- *Passages of Gold*, Jim & Terri Kraus
- *Pirates of the Heart*, Jim & Terri Kraus
- *Remembering You*, Penelope J. Stokes
- *Song of a Soul*, Lawana Blackwell
- *Storm at Daybreak*, B. J. Hoff
- *The Scarlet Thread*, Francine Rivers
- *The Tangled Web*, B. J. Hoff
- *The Tempering Blaze*, Sally Laity & Dianna Crawford
- *Till We Meet Again*, Penelope J. Stokes
- *The Torch of Triumph*, Sally Laity & Dianna Crawford
- *A Voice in the Wind*, Francine Rivers
- *Vow of Silence*, B. J. Hoff

Heartwarming Anthologies from HeartQuest

Dream Vacation—Sometimes the unexpected can be the best thing for your heart. Novellas by Ginny Aiken, Jeri Odell, and Elizabeth White.

A Bouquet of Love—An arrangement of four beautiful novellas about friendship and love. Stories by Ginny Aiken, Ranee McCollum, Jeri Odell, and Debra White Smith.

A Victorian Christmas Cottage—Four novellas centering around hearth and home at Christmastime. Stories by Catherine Palmer, Jeri Odell, Debra White Smith, and Peggy Stoks.

A Victorian Christmas Tea—Four novellas about life and love at Christmastime. Stories by Catherine Palmer, Dianna Crawford, Peggy Stoks, and Katherine Chute.

A Victorian Christmas Quilt—A patchwork of four novellas about love and joy at Christmastime. Stories by Catherine Palmer, Ginny Aiken, Peggy Stoks, and Debra White Smith.

Reunited—Four stories about reuniting friends, old memories, and new romance. Includes favorite recipes from the authors. Stories by Judy Baer, Jan Duffy, Jeri Odell, and Peggy Stoks.

With This Ring—A quartet of charming stories about four very special weddings. Stories by Lori Copeland, Dianna Crawford, Ginny Aiken, and Catherine Palmer.

HeartQuest Books by Ginny Aiken

The Wrong Man—A feisty young woman makes one last-ditch effort to meet the right man—and it backfires in hilarious fashion. But as she seeks God's will, she learns that the "wrong man" may be just right for her. This novella by Ginny Aiken appears in the anthology *A Bouquet of Love.*

Log Cabin Patch—In a logging camp in turn-of-the-century Washington State, a Log Cabin patch quilt symbolizes the new hope awaiting a lonely young woman. This novella by Ginny Aiken appears in the anthology *A Victorian Christmas Quilt.*

Something Borrowed—Emma's prayers are answered when she inherits a ranch. More than land is at stake, however, when a former bounty hunter disputes her claim. This novella by Ginny Aiken appears in the anthology *With This Ring.*

Magnolia—Magnolia Bellamy can't believe she's just hired a carpetbagger to restore a treasure of the Confederacy, the fabulous Ashworth Mansion. Against her better judgment, Maggie hires the Yankee contractor, Clay Marlowe, whose credentials are impeccable. As the officer in charge of Louella Ashworth's construction loan at Bellamy Fiduciary Trust, Maggie's job is to keep an eye on him during the renovation.

Clay Marlowe loves a challenge. When he first saw photos of the Ashworth place in Bellamy, Virginia, he groaned at the mess. He knows he's the man to restore the structure to its original glory. But he hadn't reckoned on the delicately beautiful Magnolia Bellamy, the project's self-appointed overseer—nor on the meddlesome but lovable ladies of the Bellamy Garden Club!

A rollicking, delightful novel from award-winning author Ginny Aiken. Coming in April 2000.

HeartQuest Books by Jeri Odell

A Christmas Hope—In fashionable San Francisco, a society beauty's bravery following the loss of her family's fortune captivates her ruggedly handsome new neighbor. This novella by Jeri Odell appears in the anthology *A Victorian Christmas Cottage*.

Come to My Love—A young widower, tormented by his broken past, struggles to open himself to God's forgiveness and grace—and then to love again. This novella by Jeri Odell appears in the anthology *A Bouquet of Love*.

Scarlett Dreamer—Years after a best-forgotten summer together as teens, Katie and Rick meet at a Christian conference center in northern New Mexico. Can they deal with the mistakes and hurts of the past, or are some secrets better left untold? This novella by Jeri Odell appears in the anthology *Reunited*.